REBECCA

Volume II

A WAY BACK

A NOVEL BY STEPHEN M DAVIS

The name Rebecca comes from the Hebrew name Rebekah

The first scriptures relating to the name Rebekah referred to her as the wife of Isaac. She originated from Padan Aram, among pagan families. She was a woman of strength and beauty. The bible suggests she embraced those around her with her wisdom, tenacity, and splendour. The name Rebekah is mentioned in Genesis 22:23 within the Old Testament and dates back to the beginning of Christianity.

1

Stephen M Davis was born in East London in 1957. He was educated at Woodbridge High School, Woodford, Essex, and St John Cass Royal School of Art, East London. He started writing in 2009 once retired from Royal Mail.

First Published 2018

Typeset Stephen M Davis

Cover Design Stephen M Davis

Published by DMS Literary Publications

Author's website stevedauthor.wordpress.com

Setting – Modern Day

Rebecca is a little older now and after her first year at University, common sense rears its head a little too often for her liking. She finds herself applying rational thinking to all that life offers, and this includes her previous meetings with Meredith and the information within the three boxes.

What university could not teach her is how to prepare herself for what is about to happen. Again, all balanced thinking is going to tumble into a world beyond common sense.

Many believe we just get one go at life. Some think otherwise.

Just suppose we inherited memory and could see the world through the eyes of our forefathers.

Rebecca can...

PROLOGUE

Here is an insight into Rebecca's world. This is a synopsis of Volume I, *Rebecca & the Spiral Staircase*.

Rebecca's relationship with her 11-year-old brother, Tommy – who was forever kicking his football in her direction - was typical of a young brother and older sister. Rebecca shared a delightfully close bond with her mother, Elizabeth. Often though, she felt troubled by her mother's passive relationship with Rebecca's father, James. In particular, Elizabeth's inert response to James's Victorian marital attitude maddened Rebecca. On occasions, she would escape her frustration, and find solace in an imaginary world beside the whispering pond, which nestled in the grounds of the family home in Cheshire.

Just before Christmas, James announced he had bought a big old gothic mansion up by the lakes for a bargain price. Seemingly oblivious to sentiments and feelings, he informed everyone that they should be ready to move soon.

Although Rebecca missed her old house, she quickly delighted in her new surroundings and set about exploring the vast grounds. Her imagination really kicked in when she found an ancient key and discovered it unlocked the door to a derelict summerhouse down by a lake. One day, when alone inside the summerhouse, a previously locked door opened, leading her to a spiral staircase.

Taking to these stairs, she embarked on a series of journeys into the history of their old family house. Her first encounter was with a woman named Meredith in the 1853. She was a troubled woman whose husband had a lover named Millicent. Millicent was an unsavoury character, with a chequered past.

She challenged Millicent's unpleasant behaviour. She then set about showing Meredith an alternative approach to her marital situation. Ultimately, she helped Meredith resolve her issues. Back in her own time, Rebecca later discovered by way of an old newspaper article, found in a tallboy in the summerhouse that Millicent had been shot to death. The article went on to say that Meredith had been indicted for Millicent's murder.

Reading this article left Rebecca both troubled and frustrated, feeling powerless to do anything about Meredith's predicament. She had established an instant mother-daughter relationship and strong connection with this woman, and felt certain she was incapable of a murderous act.

The next time the door opened, it took her to 1943. Here she found the mansion was being used as an orphanage for children evacuated from war-torn London. She soon learnt that Judith, the lady of the house, was an outcast in her own home. Instantly, aware of the bizarre similarities between Judith's life and Meredith's, she set about untangling this relationship. Observing this woman's complex plight, she drew upon her experiences from the previous trip, and helped Judith towards an amiable resolution.

Back in her time and with school finished for the summer holidays, Rebecca sat on her balcony sketching. For a couple of days, she felt an overwhelming pull towards the summerhouse. Having not been able to get Meredith's predicament from her consciousness, she wondered if this was the reason for this almost tangible sensation. Today, unable to resist the call, she headed down to the derelict building, and once again took to the stairs. This time, she found herself in 1911, where the family relationship was the complete opposite of her previous experiences. This time, the woman was a passive aggressive who controlled all. With little to do here other than observe, she headed back to the summerhouse, wondering why she'd ended up in this era. On entering the summerhouse, she uncovered a sixty-year-old suicide note written by Millicent. Armed with this note, she now knew why she'd arrived in this time, and that her next mission was to find her way back to Meredith.

Although her next journey was complex and fraught with difficulties, she drew solace, now convinced that Meredith's troubled spirit was leading her way. Assured by this belief, she followed her instinct, and found her way back to 1853. Armed with the suicide note, she proved Meredith's innocence.

Attempting to return home, Rebecca inadvertently travelled three months ahead of her own time. Here, she witnessed the aftermath of a tragic accident involving her mother. This time, unlike her previous adventures, she found herself invisible to all. Only able to stand and listen, she heard her sobbing father wishing he had taken notice of Elizabeth and fixed the heating boiler. Before returning home, she concocted a plan that would convince her father to take action, and in so doing, prevent her mother's death.

The plan worked and unwittingly she'd opened the door for her parents to re-establish their forgotten love, something Rebecca had always known was there. Reflecting on all that had happened over the last year, Rebecca believed that Meredith had exposed this impending disaster as recompense for the suicide note. She was now certain that Meredith had been her guardian angel throughout her journeys. She believed her mission in all of this was ultimately to help Meredith's tormented spirit, which in turn led to her parent's rediscovered love. She again sat on her balcony, considering everything, and believing Meredith's spirit had finally found a resting place, reckoned her jaunts into the past were now over.

That indeed seemed to be the last of her journeys, as she suspected. Now entering her eighteenth year, Rebecca left home to take up residence at Warwick University. Returning home for the winter break, she learnt that her father had commissioned the rebuilding of the summerhouse. If there were any doubts before, with the old spiral staircase gone, replaced with a new shiny one, she was certain her journeys were over for good.

During supper, her mother told her that they had found four boxes in the loft of the summerhouse during its restoration. With an element of apprehension, she set about the boxes. The first box contained sepia photos of Rebecca with Meredith in the 1850s. With the nagging dream notion dismissed, she opened the next box with eagerness, only to find little other than some history relating to the house and its occupants. This third box contained a letter from Meredith addressed to Rebecca. It stated that Rebecca's soul and spirit had always been present in this house. It also proposed that Rebecca could manifest herself into her previous existences, where she would see that world through her eyes. Not only had this turned rational thinking on its head, it had forever opened the door back.

Next is box four, and time to read on if you are ready.

CHAPTER 1 - UNI OR BOX 4

Having spent her first few months at university, Rebecca arrived home for an autumn break. Sitting in her bedroom alone, she was considering all the information she'd unearthed in three of the four boxes found in the summerhouse loft during its renovation. Although she wanted to look in the fourth box at the time, for some reason, she hadn't been ready and reckoned this was because she still hadn't come to terms with what she'd already discovered.

While at university, although she'd focussed her attention on her studies, the letter from Meredith found in the third box was never far from her thoughts. As she sat there, thinking about how she felt, she decided to re-read the letter.

Dear Rebecca, I hope that when you find this letter, in the future, you are well. By future, I refer to a life beyond the 1800s. The first time I met you in 1853, I knew immediately you were from another time. Although you were my daughter, in essence, I was aware I had two of you in my time. I must add that we were fortunate that my daughter was staying with an aunt, which kept you separate. I need to explain further, as I am certain that the coming words will bamboozle your conscious mind. Although the subconscious, I suspect, will be more open.

Your soul, spirit, and being have always lived in this house as Rebecca. Your first journey started in 1635, soon after the house was built. As hard as that is for you to understand, you must remain unprejudiced and flexible in your thinking. Something I know you are capable of with ease. I recall how I felt the first time I learnt the truth of your immortal existence.

You will find two photos in this envelope, of which one is my beloved Rebecca and I in a boat. It is the same boat, which you saw me in when I was trying to establish contact with you. I suspect the

Rebecca from the twenty-first century is reading this, as you were the only one who found your way back to me. I am sure you concluded the boat lady in the mist, was my tormented spirit, hanging in limbo awaiting your intervention. You were correct. The other photo is of you with me by the oak tree, before it fell in that horrid storm. Under that tree, you found the key, the key that brought you back to me. You have already uncovered - I suspect - the third photo that I placed for you in the bureau. That photo was my Rebecca - the one from my time - wearing the cardigan you left behind. I hoped you would see its relevance and the message would be sufficient for you to continue your quest. In my other unmarked box, I hope the mothers from the future have been as objective as I have and have added to my papers. You will find evidence showing a trail of your existence and lives in this house. Some of the older papers are sketchy and lack proof. I hope you find some answers to your many questions. I also hope that your journey to me was one of many your life brings you. Either way, you have in your deepest mind, evidence that you have been here before, and I hope and believe, will continue to remain happy in this house for always.

You will see at the top of the fourth box, Millicent's suicide letter, and a newspaper stating such. You brought this letter to me. I cannot find words deep enough to express my gratitude.

Of incident, my own spirit engaged me to write this letter to you, long before your first visit. This is my understanding of this bizarre and beautiful series of events. I am unable to find any other reasoning.

Finally, I have your marriage certificate from 1858 to a gentleman named Joshua Elm. You may recall the house was once named Elm Manor. You had a happy life with 3 beloved children. Your children loved your drawings and writings of fairies. I suspect you, my dear Rebecca still have that within you. I would love to have met you when you knew of all this. However, I am certain the powers-at-be would deem that too consequential. Be safe, be well, be happy, and continue to remain true to your farsightedness.

My love,

Meredith

Rebecca sat around thinking about Meredith's letter, still trying to comprehend everything therein. Over the next couple of hours, she re-read the letter repeatedly, drawing her closer to opening the fourth box. Each time, she thought she was ready to look inside something held her back. She considered her feelings over and again, uncertain if her trepidations and apprehension were created by the information within Meredith's letter. Eventually, she reckoned when the time was right, Meredith - someone she now considered a kind of guardian angel - would let her know.

The following morning, while her mum and Tommy were out shopping, she chatted to her father about the boxes they'd opened. They sat there for an age, going through all the photos and papers, both agreeing it was a little more than bizarre.

'I must say, Rebecca, it is all rather perplexing, if that's the right word.'

'Hmm, I really don't know what to think, Dad. Rational thinking suggests it can't be real, but...' She glanced again at one of the photos of her with Meredith in 1853, and handed it to her father. 'How can this be? On one hand, the evidence is staring us in the face, but common sense says it's ridiculous.' She looked down. 'Mind you, I know what I know, and this reincarnation thing is no more irrational than the time travel I experienced.'

Her dad laughed, 'common sense, since when have you applied common sense to this type of thing. Going full on, is what makes you so special. If you had applied common sense, you would never have gone anywhere near the summerhouse, let alone up the spiral stairs.'

'That's University for you, I guess. Okay, so let's skip the rational thinking. With it or without it, this is far more than bizarre, and

12

certainly perplexing. To be honest, I am not altogether sure how I feel about it all. It would seem there is more for me, but what is my role in all of this if there is one. With the other trips, I helped all the women I met, and in return, they helped me. However, I feel I may have a bigger part to play.'

'You seem to be avoiding looking in the last box, any reason?'

'I really don't know, and can't give you an explanation. I wouldn't say I was spooked, or anything, just not ready yet.' She paused for a moment considering her inner thoughts. 'For sure, intrigue has a good grip, but something is telling me to wait. Gut instinct, if you like. Maybe, and I mean maybe, Meredith is telling me to wait.' She then laughed aloud.

'Is she indeed, this muse of yours?'

'Muse is an interesting choice of words, Dad. I guess she is my muse, or maybe just a guardian angel.'

'I like knowing my girl has a guardian angel.' He then thought for a moment. 'Perhaps we need to talk to someone about it.'

'The way I see that, we would just be talking to someone who is guessing.'

'Well, maybe you could do some research on your computer?'

Over the next couple of days, Rebecca did a lot of research on reincarnation and anything else she could think of that was remotely associated with this type of thing. Everything though seemed to be an opinion, and frustratingly, she discarded everything, reckoning it all added up to very little. She again chatted to her father about it, and they both agreed some thinking time might help. Over the next few days, as much as she'd had enough, she kept going back to the computer. *Surely I am not alone* she kept thinking. She read page after page, hoping she might find something to suggest someone else had been down a similar route. Having read some clap-trap about being reincarnated back as a goat, she mumbled, 'enough of the drivel,' and slammed her laptop closed.

Although Meredith's letter was permanently at the back of her thoughts, she tried to focus on enjoying the next few days with her family. Joining her mother and father outside for breakfast after another night of tossing and turning, she slumped down at the table.

'Morning, Rebecca, how are you this fine morning?'

'Fine, Mum, just a little tired. I had a bit of a rough night.'

'Seconds later, Tommy's face appeared through the kitchen window, grinning like a Cheshire cat.'

Still beaming, he joined them at the table, and much to Rebecca's surprise greeted everyone individually.

'What you looking so pleased about?' Rebecca asked, 'and what's with being so polite?' she giggled and gave his finger a little twist. 'As much as it pains me to say, I might have missed you. A bit'

Still grinning, he replied, 'whatever. 'Didn't miss you.'

'So, young Thomas, any news?'

'Yep.'

'Well tell us then.'

'Got another year at the club, in fact two.'

'Wow, how brilliant, still a twit, but well done.'

'Rebecca,' her mum frowned. 'Great news, Tommy.' She said and smiled, 'in fact, fantastically well done the pair of you. Great news about Tommy's football combined with Rebecca getting brilliant results is more than we could have hoped for.'

'Both you, Rebecca, and Tommy have made us proud parents, and we thank you both. Your commitment to your individual avenues has been more than any parent could hope for, and we are looking forward to seeing where it takes you,' James said and smiled. 'Liz and I were only talking yesterday about this very subject, and we've decided another Disney trip this Christmas would be a good plan. Unless you're both too old,' he said and chuckled.

'Dad, no one is ever too old, as you and Mum proved last time we were there. We had to drag you two away just to eat.'

'Hmm, well I just thought I would check, he said and grinned. 'Tommy, no reaction?'

'Yeah, I was just thinking exactly that,' Rebecca said, and gave him a gentle nudge.

'I'm fifteen you know,' he grumbled from the side of his mouth. He seemed to think for a moment, then nudged Rebecca back, and said, 'well as long as no one tells my team mates.'

'Yippee, no cooking for me,' Elizabeth said, grinning. She then waved an imaginary football scarf over her head, and blurted, 'way to go, Mickey.'

The next few days passed in the blink of an eye, and before she knew it, Rebecca was packing to head back to university. It was 10:30am, and her friend Roxy, wasn't due to pick her up until the afternoon. Sitting in her room staring at the fourth box, she decided to wander down to the Summerhouse. When she arrived, her emotions were in an odd place. Mixed with memories of Meredith and her trips, was this tangle of thoughts surrounding the letter. Since she'd first read it, she had tried to give it some rationale, without much success. With the rebuilding of the summerhouse, she'd avoided coming anywhere near it. However, for some reason, today, it had popped into her head and there was this all too familiar pulling sensation. Now here and staring at the new front door, she decided to have a look inside. She took hold of the handle and gently eased it open. *Well, that makes a change*, she thought, as the door moved silently.

As she opened the door fully, she was both surprised and delighted to see a brand new spiral staircase. 'Bless, that has to be Dad's idea,' she mumbled. Walking up to the stairs, even though they were well lit, brought memories flooding back of the first time she opened the third door and found the stairs. For a moment, it was as if she'd never been away, and with a shiver creeping up her spine, she peered up. With a tingle of anticipation kissing the back of her neck, she wondered if, just if, these stairs would work in the same way.

She stood there for ages, trying to decide if she should go back and look in the fourth box, or climb the stairs and see where she ends up. Eventually, common sense took hold and told her these were not her stairs, and besides Roxy will be here soon.

As she ambled up to the house, she felt a little disappointed she hadn't at least had a look upstairs, and mumbled, 'so gotta do something about this blinking common sense taking over.' Just as she was considering going back, she noticed her mum standing by the front door.

'Hello, Mother, kiss kiss. I'm famished.'

'Have you been down to the Summerhouse, Rebecca? Snooping around,' she said, and chuckled. 'Well, Roxy has arrived early, and she out back chatting to your Father. I was just preparing lunch and thought I would come to find you.'

'Oh good, I'm looking forward to catching up with her.'

She joined her father and Roxy outside, moments later Elizabeth joined them, having prepared Rebecca's favourite lunch, a spicy chicken salad.

'My word, Rebecca, you're eating that with gusto. Anyone would think I hadn't fed you since you've been home.'

'It is delicious, Mum, my fav, thanks.'

The four sat around chatting mostly about University, until Tommy joined them. The subject then immediately changed to football, and Rebecca could see Roxy was grimacing.

'Fancy helping me to pack my last bits, Roxy? Mum, Dad, that okay?'

'Yeah, for sure,' her mum said, smiling to Roxy.

'Sounds like a plan, Bex,' Roxy said, clearing the lunch plates and cutlery away.

'We will clear up,' Rebecca said, staring at Tommy.

After tidying up, they headed up to Rebecca's room, chatting about Tommy's football on the way.

'Brilliant about Tom, Roxy said, 'Although, I do find it all a tad boring when he keeps going over everything in such detail.'

'At least you don't have to live with it every day,' she said, and giggled. 'I don't mind to be honest, and am actually proud of the little twit.'

As they entered Rebecca's bedroom, Roxy asked, 'what are all these boxes, Rebecca?'

Having not told Roxy any real details about her trips, Rebecca chose her words carefully, just keeping it very basic. Then unexpectedly, Roxy opened one of the boxes, and picked up a photo.

'Bex, what's this?' she asked, waving the photo. 'It looks like you, but it can't be. I reckon this needs an explanation of sorts,' she frowned, 'and not the crumbs of a story you've offered up so far.

Rebecca took a deep breath, and then started to explain everything in more detail. She went over the first time she found the key, and how it opened the door to the summerhouse. Then she explained about the spiral stairs, and that those stairs led her to Meredith.

'In eighteen-fifty-three, you went to eighteen-fifty-three, and met some bird named Meredith.' She frowned. 'I thought you weren't giving me the full picture earlier,' she said, again waving the photo.

They chatted for ages, while packing, stopping every now and then to look at another photo. Roxy seemed to take it in her stride, which pleased Rebecca no end. Other than probing for more details, not once did Roxy question its validity.

'Well, sounds like you need someone professional to get involved.'

'What do you mean by professional? Because my Dad suggested a psychic, and I told him, I wasn't at all comfortable with that. Besides, their opinion would be exactly that, an opinion.'

'Oh, I didn't mean a psychic, shrink, or anything like that. I meant a hypnotist. As you know, my Father is a hypnotist. Although he works helping people will addictions and such like, he also has some strong views about re-embodiment.'

'I am not sure I know what you mean, or how that would help.'

'Well, he believes, along with inheriting eye colour and such, that people inherit memory from the parents, grandparents and so on.'

Looking again at one of the photos, she paused for a moment. 'Maybe he could help you regress back, and that might answer some questions. Because whichever way you look at it, it's either you in these photos or someone who looks exactly like you. Perhaps you've inherited their genes to the point where you actually look similar too.'

'I would have to give that some thinking time. I still don't understand any of this myself, and until I do, I don't want an outsider's opinion. Obviously, I believe that I went back in time, met Meredith and all. That is bizarre enough on its own, but the idea that I have lived in this house forever, is beyond logic and makes me a tad edgy.'

'Well, the offer is there, as I am certain that my Dad would love to be involved. He often goes on about this type of thing, so I am sure he would love to help in some way. All that said, I understand how you must feel, and I know you will find a resolution because you always do.'

They finished packing and headed downstairs. After a brief chat with Elizabeth and James, the girls said their good-byes and headed back to Warwick University. Once there, they occasionally chatted about Rebecca's story. With their focus on work, they spent most of their time talking about any upcoming projects. This was broken up by a few nights out on the town, when the subject turned to boys. Although Rebecca engaged in the conversation, it was more Roxy's thing, especially since she was dating the *best-looking* guy on campus, so she said, often. Before she knew it, Rebecca was heading home for Christmas and another visit with Mickey.

Chapter 2 - Mickey and

Rebecca arrived home three days before the planned family trip to Florida. Feeling a little tired, after a very late end of term party, she wasn't in the mood for Tommy acting like an 11-year-old. However, when he appeared in the kitchen with a Mickey mask on, she couldn't fail to see the funny side.

'I thought you didn't want to go to Disney,' she said, giving him a gentle poke.

'Yeah, well two of my team-mates are going too.'

'So, that makes it ok,' she said a laughed.

Her mum appeared in the kitchen pointing her finger, 'don't you two start bickering.'

'Mum, we are only messing, Tommy and I are far too grown up for that,' she said, sneering at him, and then smiling.

That evening, while having a long supper, they chatted about University and Tommy's football, when suddenly Elizabeth piped in.

'Oh, Rebecca, I had an odd phone call the other day. A woman – I think her name was Mary – anyways, she said she was the daughter of a woman called Tabitha. She asked to speak to you.' She narrowed her eyes, 'does the name ring any bells?'

'Bells, Mum, more like Big Ben,' she said and shook her head. 'Tabitha, oh my goodness, could be the young girl from the orphanage who was adopted by the people who lived here.'

Her mother looked blank, which although it irritated Rebecca a little, she understood why. Just as she was about to say something, her father started speaking.

'I remember you telling us all about Tabitha,' he said, and nodded very slightly in the direction of Elizabeth.

'So, Mum, did this Mary say anything?'

Still appearing vague, her mum said, 'no, not really, just something about Tabitha being poorly, and wanting to re-visit this house.'

The word re-visit sent Rebecca's thoughts spiralling. 'Well, there you have it. It must be the same Tabitha that lived here in the orphanage.'

'Yeah, I guess so. Anyways, she has left her phone number if you want to give her a call.

After supper, Rebecca chatted to her father about Tabitha. They both agreed it had to be the girl from the orphanage. They also recognised why mum was so uncomfortable with the whole scenario, and agreed it would be best if she were only tentatively involved.

The following morning, Rebecca rang Mary's number. Frustratingly, it went through to voice mail and she decided not to leave a message, and instead try to call again. After breakfast, she started getting her stuff ready for the holiday, when her mum walked in.

'Glad to see you still don't need any encouragement to pack, unlike your brother. I think he has packed a pair of socks, football ones at that,' she said and laughed. 'Sorry, I was a bit vague last night. I do remember you talking about Tabitha. I find it a little - I want to say confusing, but it's more complex than that.' She hesitated briefly and then continued, 'I guess in the past your stories of fairies and such like, were just that, stories, and well, since the boxes turned up, it's all become a little too real for me.'

'I know, Mum, and it is okay, just take your time and when you're ready, we can talk about it as much or as little as you want.'

'I will get there; I promise you.' She gave Rebecca one of those smiles that would warm any heart. 'So, did you ring Tabitha's daughter?'

'I did actually, but it went through to voice mail.' Just as she finished speaking, her phone started ringing. Wide eyed, she looked at her mum, then glanced at her phone, and nodded. 'Hello, Rebecca here.' She raised her eyebrows towards her mum who was now standing by the door.

Elizabeth nodded and mouthed, 'I will leave you to it Rebecca.'

'Hello Mary, how can I help?' She then listened for a moment then answered, 'crumbs, well I do know of a Tabitha, but it is a very long story, and I am not so sure I am comfortable chatting on the phone about it. My Mum, who you spoke to originally, said you wanted to visit with Tabitha. That may be the best way forward, if nothing else Tabitha can see where she grew up,' Rebecca said, barely able to contain her emotions.

'Tabitha also said she was hoping to meet up with a young lady named Rebecca, and I am guessing that is you,' the woman said, with a distinct element of uncertainty in her voice.

'That's interesting. I think it really would be good all-round if you both came to visit. I will be delighted to show you around the house and grounds. The thing is we are going to Florida for two weeks.'

Rebecca chatted for a little while longer and agreed to call Mary as soon as she returned from holiday. She headed downstairs not sure what to think or say. On one hand, her emotions were overwhelmed at

22

the idea of meeting Tabitha, who she last saw as a five-year-old girl, while her newfound rationality was saying it was just a name coincidence. As she walked into the kitchen, her mum was sitting drinking her coffee.

Appearing as if the cat had hold of her curiosity, her mum lifted her palm, and asked, 'well, what did she say?'

'Well, indeed,' Rebecca said, still battling with the two sides of her head. 'It was the daughter of a lady called Tabitha. Evidently, she grew up here during WW2 when this house was an orphanage.' She hesitated, knowing her mum would struggle with the concept that Tabitha wanted to meet someone called Rebecca and so decided to give that bit a miss. 'I said I would ring her when we are back from Florida.'

Her mum smiled in a way that Rebecca recognised, and knew to change the subject.

The next two days flew by, and before she knew it, Rebecca was checking in her suitcase at the airport.

Once again, the whole family had a fabulous time. Watching Tommy hide every time he saw one of the Disney characters, Rebecca realised he was getting older, and it might be time to drop the twit tag. It was unusually hot and humid, to the point where James suggested a beach holiday next year. When he offered up the Caribbean, it went down well with everyone.

The holiday seemed to fly by and while Rebecca was packing to go home, she thought about the change in her father. She particularly loved how he was now engaging with every part of family life. This led her on to think about his acceptance, and the amount of understanding that he'd shown for every aspect surrounding Meredith. With his support, it had helped her deal with everything that had come her way, including her mum's understandable indifference. That morning, she'd mentioned Tabitha to her father. Without hesitation, he said it had to be the same woman, and even recalled Judith's name. This had stirred up vivid memories for Rebecca, to the point where her dad's words were still ringing in her ears as she boarded the plane. Every time she tried to focus on something else, her thoughts jumped to Tabitha, which led back to Meredith and all her experiences. Although she had been aware for some time – especially with the summerhouse being re-built – that her trips were over, she found herself wondering again. Thinking about Meredith's letter, the photos, and the unopened fourth box, she mumbled, 'I wonder if...'

Her father leant over and said, 'you wonder what, if there's a way back to Meredith?'

'Dad, are you a mind reader now?' she said, and chuckled.

'Rebecca, your brain works exactly the same as mine did when I was your age. In fact, you have brought all those hidden thoughts back to life. I actually can't wait to see what the next chapter brings for you. I was doing some research on the house and didn't find much more than you did. I did find out that there has been a dwelling exactly where our house is ever since the fourteenth century. Prior to that there is tentative evidence of some kind of Roman encampment.'

'How did you find that information, because I found very little and searched the Internet to within an inch of its life?'

'Haha, it was more by luck than judgment. Have you ever watched a TV program called Time-Team? I know you don't watch TV, but...'

'Yeah, I do actually, and I enjoy it very much. So go on, spill the beans.'

'Well, I had a phone call from one of the team, and they want to do an investigation of our land. They have modest evidence that there could have been a Roman camp within our grounds.'

'Wow, how exciting.'

'Oh right, I thought you would be – 'don't let them dig up our garden' – or a similar reaction.'

'Well, they can dig all they want, because it's not going to change anything to do with Meredith. Or me always living...' She paused for a moment. 'You know what I mean Dad.'

The chat with her father, refocused Rebecca's attention, and she actually enjoyed the remainder of the journey home. Especially now she had something else to think about other than her impending phone conversation.

CHAPTER 3 - TABITHA AND

They eventually arrived home around ten in the evening and after some cocoa with her mum and dad, Rebecca headed up to bed. Although she woke up while it was still dark, she managed to get back off quickly. Next thing she knew, her mum was gently waking her with a light breakfast just after ten.

'Oh joy, Mum, a properly proportioned breakfast. As much as I love Denny's, in the end...'

After her orange juice and toast, she pottered about in her bedroom, unsure if she was ready to phone Mary. Still struggling with the contents of the previous three boxes, she sat staring at the fourth box. She asked herself several times what was stopping her opening it, and what she was waiting for. In the end, she reckoned, as with Mary, something would tell her when the time was right.

On the way downstairs, she stopped to look at the paintings of Meredith and Millicent. In a flash, memories of her journeys filled her thoughts. For some reason, ever since Mary called, Meredith had seemed closer than she had for some time. After her last time with Meredith, she'd felt her time with this woman was over, and as such her time jumping was over too. Just as she had in the past, she was once again feeling strange urges to visit the summerhouse. Although, she'd popped down previously to have a look, it had just felt like a building by the lake. For sure, the new spiral staircase had stimulated her emotions, but it wasn't anything like the feelings she'd had in the past.

She glanced at the floor, then back at Meredith, and thought, *right, let's ring Mary.* Seconds later, she felt her phone vibrate in her pocket and just knew it would be Mary. As she took her phone out and answered, she smiled to Meredith and nodded. After a brief conversation, she made tentative arrangements for Mary and Tabitha to visit tomorrow.

After smiling again to Meredith, convinced this woman had played a part in the phone call, she headed to the kitchen. 'Morning, Mother. Nice breakfast, thanks. I have just come off the phone to Mary and have arranged for them to visit tomorrow. I said I needed to check with you first. Tabitha is rather poorly, and her daughter is desperate to get over here sooner rather than later.

'That will be nice. It is just you and me tomorrow. Your Father and Tommy are going to football training. Did they say a time; maybe I could sort some lunch.'

'I will call her back now and suggest lunch.'

'Around one this afternoon they will be here, Mum,' she said after coming off the phone.

The remainder of the afternoon, Rebecca helped her mum in the kitchen with the holiday washing. Her mum held up her pink dress and said, 'looks likes this has had it.'

'Mum, it was so brilliant seeing you run from the car and jump straight in Typhoon Lagoon still wearing your dress. The look on Dad's face was worth ten new dresses.'

'I was so damn hot, and uncomfortable. To think, I thought having a soft-top Mustang, would mean no need for air-con, hmm.'

Later that afternoon, James rang and suggested eating out, which went down well with Elizabeth and Rebecca, having subtly mentioned the idea the day before.

The following morning, Rebecca tried to distract herself by again helping her mum, but her curiosity was almost at bursting point by lunchtime. She was with her mum laying out lunch, when she heard a car pull in the drive. Taking a deep breath, she smiled at her mum.

'Are you okay, Rebecca?'

'Just a little apprehensive, I guess, not knowing what to expect.'

'It will be just fine.'

As Rebecca headed for the front door, she glanced at Meredith and wondered if she was again playing some part in today's visit. 'I thought you'd gone Madam,' she mumbled.

She opened the door, and although she said hello to Mary, couldn't take her eyes from Tabitha. Even though this woman's face was frail and weathered, she could see the 5-year-old in her. The way this woman was looking at her, she realised she was having similar emotions.

Tabitha stepped forward, touched Rebecca's cheek, while looking directly at her, almost as if she was peering into her soul. 'It is not the house that I have come to see my dear Rebecca. Somewhere in my deepest thoughts, I had this wild dream that I would see you, and it would seem I was right.'

Meanwhile, Mary was staring at the two of them, clearly confused by her mother's reaction and words.

Tabitha turned to Mary, 'do you recall me telling you of a young girl who visited me during the war? This is her.' She then lifted the palm of her hand, and said, 'I don't know why or how this can be the same girl, but it is. Perhaps Rebecca may help us to understand.' She then paused for a moment, 'of course this could be her daughter. Although, old as I am, I recall the way Rebecca looked at me all those years ago, and this young lady looks at me in exactly the same way.

With her mouth open, Mary - with a look of disbelief on her face - went to speak, but no words came out.

'It is okay, my dear Mary. I am certain it will all become clear and there will be a rational explanation.'

Although Rebecca's feelings should have been all over the place, she was oddly calm. Some time ago, she'd worked out that Tabitha might have still been alive, and had considered trying to contact her. 'My Mother has prepared some lunch, would you like to join us?' She then thought for a moment, and continued, 'Tabitha, may I ask that we don't talk about this in front of my Mum. She struggles with the concept that I might have been here all those years ago.'

'I knew it was you my dear Rebecca,' she said, and turned to Mary. 'I am as confused as you are, however…'

Mary narrowed her eyes, and asked, 'so you are saying that you were here with my Mother in the nineteen-forties? How can that be?'

Rebecca shook her head slightly. 'I don't know myself and am still trying to understand. What I do know is that I was here with your Mother in nineteen-forty-three. When I opened the door, I instantly recognised the young girl in your Mother. I have in my room, some very interesting photos. Perhaps after lunch we can have a look together, and I will try to explain.'

'Are we having bread and cheese again, Rebecca?' Tabitha asked with a delightful grin on her face.

'Haha, I thought about that yesterday, I am surprised you remember.'

Tabitha touched Rebecca on the arm, 'how could I forget. We were all starving, and you arranged food for us. We never went short again, thanks to you.' She then lowered her head briefly, looked up and asked, 'So where did you go? Although a Rebecca – who looked like you – came back the next day, for some weird reason, I felt it wasn't you.'

'After lunch I will try to explain, although, I am still unravelling it all in my head. Maybe talking to you will help me put some of the pieces together.'

During lunch, they sat around chatting about Tabitha's life as a child in this house, and her time with Judith.

'So when did you leave this house, Tabitha, because we have struggled to find any history after the war. In fact, we have struggled to find any history full-stop.'

'As soon as the war was over, the family moved to Liverpool for work. Sadly, we fell on difficult times and were unable to sustain the upkeep of the property. We could not find anyone to take it on, and I guess that was because of post-war austerity. I have often thought about this house, even while I was living in Canada, it was always within my deepest thoughts. It was a special time, and place for me.'

They continued to chat about the house, when unexpectedly, Rebecca's mum suggested Tabitha and Mary may want to see the boxes and photos in Rebecca's room.

During lunch, they didn't mention Tabitha recognising Rebecca or any aspect of this bizarre situation. So Rebecca was a little startled by her mother's suggestion, but not surprised when she followed it up by saying she would clear away lunch while they went for a look.

They sat in Rebecca's room going through the opened boxes while she tried to explain the story, including why she hadn't opened the fourth box. Tabitha seemed to take it in her stride, although Mary was clearly perplexed.

'It is okay to be confused, Mary. It is confusing. When we are young, our minds and thoughts remain open to anything. However, as we grow older, we lose our ability to see what is in front of us, and instead allow common sense to rationalise everything. That said I have found - as I enter my last chapters – that I am again able to see, and importantly accept things for what they are. Rather than what society says it should be.' She shook her head, 'I wish I had always known this. Life is a rainbow, but peer pressure, culture, and sneering opinions order everything to be just so, colourless. We tell our children fairy stories, and then as they grow older, those fairies become unreasonable.'

Rebecca beamed a smile, 'I am always saying to my Mum that adults lose their ability to see what's in front of them. Since I have been at University, I have found common sense annoying the hell out of me.' She paused for a moment, 'I am still able to find my way back, but it is becoming increasing tricky. I guess my reincarnation story is so complex that it is understandably difficult to comprehend. It is for me, and how others would react or accept it, is beyond me. And I am open, after all, I met you all those years ago, and to do that, I had to travel through blinking time.' She again paused for a moment. 'I had a conversation with one of the students in my short stories group at uni. I was writing - as fiction – about the spiral staircase in the summerhouse, and going up to a third floor. Michael - a guy in the class – said that it would be impossible because there are only two floors. I didn't know what to say, and then my tutor said, and I suppose a police box can't travel through time.'

Mary, as if she had suddenly got it, smiled, and said, 'I get that, what a great way to see things. I don't know that I will ever understand or acknowledge that you met my Mum all those years ago. However, I can't ignore the bond that the two of you so clearly have. Perhaps, Rebecca, I will take your Mother's stand point, and accept it for what it is, at a distance.'

After some tea and cakes, Mary and Tabitha said it was time to head on home. At the door, Rebecca struggled to say good-bye to Tabitha, realising she might not see her again. Once they'd left, she considered her day with this lady, carefully going over every step. After some considerable reflection, although tearful, found comfort knowing she had another piece of her jigsaw firmly in place. Importantly for her, she finally had hard evidence that she'd actually travelled back in time.

CHAPTER 4 - THE GREEN DRESS

Although Rebecca enjoyed her first few months at University, today for some reason, she couldn't motivate herself to pack in readiness for another term. She sat next to her empty case, with her thoughts jumping between Tabitha and the unopened metal box that was staring back at her. As Roxy wasn't picking her up until tomorrow, she decided to go and chat to her mum. At the bottom of the stairs, she glanced at Meredith's painting. Although this woman was never far from her thoughts, she suddenly seemed closer than she had for some time. Recognising this feeling all too well, she looked at the painting, narrowed her eyes, and mumbled, 'where are we going?'

As if Meredith had answered her, an idea stirred in her head. 'Mum,' she called out, 'where did you say you put that green dress?'

Coming to the kitchen doorway, her mum answered, 'Oh, I think it is in the spare room next to Tommy's bedroom. I believe your Father had it vacuum packed or something. You know what he is like with detail, and such like. Need, I ask why? Be careful, although I know you will be.'

'I am always careful, and it's nothing important Mum, just another hunch.'

Before heading back upstairs, she again glanced at Meredith's painting. This time though, she spotted something she hadn't seen before. In the bottom right corner of the painting, she spotted a metal box, identical to the one sitting in her room.

She headed back to the kitchen, 'Mum, where's the magnifying glass?'

'In the draw next to the cutlery. Why, how closely do you need to look at the green dress?' her mum asked, and chuckled.

On her way back to the painting, she thought about how much she'd missed her mum's chuckle and how good it made her feel.

She smiled, then refocused her thoughts and peered through the magnifier. She wasn't sure what she was looking for, that was until she spotted an odd-shaped key lying on top of the metal box. Her instant reaction was to swear, a little too loud.

'Rebecca, nineteen-years-old or not, never too old for carbolic soap,' came her mum's words from the kitchen.

'Sorry, Mum.'

Having made a sketch of the key, she trawled the Internet looking for something similar. After an unsuccessful search, she decided to go back to her initial idea and look at the green dress.

On her way past Tommy's room, she noticed a pad-lock, tied with string on the outside, and a sign saying "Go-Away." She giggled, and mumbled, 'Seems he is still a twit after all.'

She opened the door to a pitch-black spare room and immediately memories of the bedroom in the summerhouse flooded her thoughts. She headed over to open the curtains, wondering if she would ever find her way back to Meredith.

As she opened the curtains, her attention was immediately drawn by the green dress, which was lying neatly on the spare bed. She looked at it and thought, *vacuum packed indeed.* She carefully lifted away the loose plastic cover. The second she handled the dress, her thoughts, senses, and emotions were all over the place. So strong was this vibe, she even looked around the room to check she was still at home.

Having not felt like this since the last time she climbed the spiral staircase, she breathed deeply trying to apply some rationale thinking. That idea dissipated instantly as she lifted the green dress, and could

33

feel something in the pocket. She hesitated for a moment, wondering where this would take her, and then lifted out a small metal box.

She couldn't make out why it looked so familiar, and then recalled her Gran had one similar that she used for her mints. Staring at the tiny box, she could feel Meredith beckoning her. Twiddling the box in her fingers, she stared at it wondering if it contained something that might offer her a way back. *Well, no point in wondering* she thought.

With her fingernail, she gently eased open the lid, revealing a small carefully folded piece of paper. Her emotions were now tangled between anticipation and uncertainty. Slowly, she opened the paper, and started reading…

Rebecca, you require a key. Follow your instinct to me. I will be eleven-years-old.

My love, Meredith

Breathing deeply, Rebecca read the note again. 'Follow my instinct,' she mumbled.

Right, better go and see mum, she thought.

On her way back down stairs, she momentarily considered going to finish off her packing, but something was telling her to go to the summerhouse. Common sense was saying it's a brand-new building and couldn't possibly offer her any answers. Her gut though, was telling her to go and have a look. She'd had enough of being sensible at university, and besides this kind of sensation hadn't taken hold since first discovering the spiral stairs.

'Mum, I'm just going for a look down at the summerhouse. I want to have a good look at Dad's new stairs.'

'Okay, sweetie. That was nice yesterday with Mary and Tabitha. What a coincidence.'

A little shocked by her mum's choice of words, Rebecca asked, 'coincidence, what do you mean?'

'Oh, nothing really, just that she lived here during the war and I don't know, maybe...' She glanced at the clock, 'don't be too long Dad's taking us out for supper tonight.' She then chuckled, 'don't be late, or he'll get huffy.'

Grinning, she said, 'now I see where Tommy gets the twit from, Mum. I do have all afternoon,' she said and smiled. 'I do love you so much, and I love to see you laugh and joke so often.' On her way down the hallway, she called out, 'what time are we out tonight, Mum?'

'7pm, and I love you too.'

'Kiss, kiss,' she called, and pulled the door closed. It was so long since she'd headed towards the summerhouse with these kinds of emotions, and it was making her feel a little strange. It wasn't that she felt uneasy, or spooked, just peculiar. As she walked up to the front, she tried to free her mind and stay as open as possible. Although she felt certain Meredith would lead her, she now had this nagging thought in the back of her head that Meredith may no longer be around to guide her way. Her concerns were short lived because as she eased the door open that smell of almonds that she had learnt to associate with Meredith filled the air, stimulating her emotions.

Oddly, she felt a tinge of uncertainty, but reckoned this was only because the building had been renovated and just didn't have the same edge to its appearance. Casting that feeling to one side, and focussing on her intuitive, spontaneous side, she headed towards the spiral staircase.

She stood at the base of the stairs, and in spite of their new shiny appearance, her memories were still strangely stimulated. With Meredith now enveloping her senses, she peered up not knowing what to expect. Feeling a tad uneasy, but nonetheless, animated, she took a deep breath and started climbing. Arriving at the top, she looked around the open-plan area, complete with new furniture, and pristine curtains. Although it should have felt soulless, there was a glint of something creating an attention-grabbing mood.

She went over and sat on one of the sofas, not knowing what to do or think. As memories of the little boy and the apple tree unexpectedly took hold of her consciousness, something was telling her to look out of the rear window. She headed over and pulled back the curtains. Shaking her head, she rubbed her eyes, unable to believe that she was looking at an apple tree, in all its glory. The last time she saw an apple tree in that spot was during one of her trips when she picked some fruit for a rag-tag boy from the village. This one was much smaller and looked so perfect it had an almost surreal appearance. Racking her brains, she tried to recall when she had last seen the apple tree, and realised it was with young Chris, in 1911.

With the hairs on her arm standing up, and at a loss what to think, she tried to steady her thoughts. Not only was the apple tree there, to compound her emotions further, the stool she fell from was just to one side.

Taking a deep breath, she turned to look around the room, but everything was in the same pristine condition. She decided to check the stairs, but they were still the new ones. Shaking her head, and a tad confused, she was certain she hadn't gone back in time, but there was an overriding sensation that although strange, was somehow familiar. Then an idea came to her that the apple tree was also a recent addition and was actually artificial. *Besides it is January*, she thought. Then laughed for thinking it might be real.

That's it, she thought, *dad being thoughtful again.* With her nerves back in place, she headed down the stairs and to the front door. Then as she opened the front door a warm, a sweet-smelling air caressed her consciousness, again sending her wits spiralling. Inhaling deeply and holding her breath, she tried to focus her senses.

Although it was clearly far too warm for January, she was trying to hold steady and was still thinking the apple tree would be artificial. She breathed out slowly through her pursed lips, and turned back to the front door.

'What,' she muttered, standing looking at the old summerhouse, just as she remembered it. Realising she was somewhere other than home, she heard a child's voice, sending shivers up her already befuddled senses.

'Mummy, where are you?'

Following the voice, Rebecca headed around the back of the summerhouse. Sitting on the stool, with her back to Rebecca, she could see a young girl, aged around ten or eleven she reckoned. She didn't know why, but she instantly knew who this was. Without hesitation, she called, 'Meredith, are you looking for your Mother.'

The girl turned and appearing a little surprised, said, 'Yes, Miss, have you seen her?' Squinting as if unsure, she paused briefly and shaking her head, asked, 'Are you Rebecca, my mother's sister?'

Unable to believe what was happening, and what this girl just asked, she uttered, 'umm, yes, I guess so.'

'My Mother said you were a funny person. Are you guessing if you are Rebecca?'

'Sorry, I was in a tiz-waz. I am Rebecca,' she said, at a total loss what to say next. She knew the moment she saw this girl that she was a young Meredith, but her quizzical, almost adult manner had thrown her a little.

'What is a tiz-wiz, may I enquire?'

'Oh, I am just in a muddle,' she said, as memories of her conversations with Meredith flooded her head. She thought she should try to pick her words a little more carefully. 'Shall we see if we can find your Mother?'

'Let us do that,' the girl said and smiled. 'You are different.'

'What do you mean by I am different?' She asked, sensing from the way the girl had spoken, that something unexpected might be coming.

'You seem different, unless you are the other Rebecca.'

Taken aback, Rebecca shook her head. 'Other Rebecca, what do you mean?'

'My Mother's sister, Rebecca, told me that a young woman named Rebecca may visit one day. She said she will look somehow different, and will talk with strange words.' The girl smiled, clearly unperturbed. 'And are you that Rebecca?'

She somehow knew what the girl was going to say, but she wasn't prepared for that. With her eyes wide and her mouth open, Rebecca shook her head, trying to gain some composure. 'Err, yes I am, I think so.'

'You are her. You talk so silly. You are like my brother. He is silly, and he is six.' She nodded, 'I have something for you that my Rebecca gave to me.' She fumbled in her pocket and produced a small key wrapped in a silk hanky. 'She said to say that this would open your box, future girl.' She then beamed a smile, and with years beyond her age, squeezed Rebecca's hand. 'I have carried this in my pocket, since my Rebecca went away.

Before Rebecca had a chance to respond, a woman's voice called, 'Meredith, sweet-pea, where are you hiding?'

From behind the summerhouse a tall, elegant woman, in long white dress appeared and walked towards Meredith. She spoke, seemingly oblivious to Rebecca, 'hello, Meredith, there you are, 'she said, smiling.

'The little girl turned to Rebecca and whispered, 'go now; my Mother can't see you. People, who need to see you, will see you. The other Rebecca went to the America's this past year, so it is only me who can see you.' She squeezed Rebecca's hand, and indicated towards the summerhouse, 'I will see you again,' she said, and nodded.

She blew Meredith a kiss and nodded several times. As she turned away, the woman started to speak.

'Whom were you speaking with, Meredith, your fairies again?'

'Yes Mother, I was speaking with my fairies again. It is a shame that you cannot see them as I do. Rebecca can see them,' she said, and glanced towards Rebecca.'

Seeing Meredith so young left Rebecca feeling quite peculiar. As she watched her speaking with her mother, she could see the woman in her every movement and motion. Although she was desperate to stay with her longer, she sensed her time was up, for now.

Heading around to the front, her thoughts jumped between Meredith, getting back home, and box four. Shaking herself down, she knew if she remained focused, the pieces would fit together. Taking a deep breath, she approached the door, gripped the handle, and thought, *here we go again*. Hearing the lock click, tangled her senses further. As she was about to open the door, something told her to close her eyes. She hesitated, and then reassured herself, guessing it was probably a message from Meredith. 'Here goes,' she mumbled, closed her eyes and pushed at the door. The door didn't move, nor did it need to move. Just turning the handle was enough to take her back home. Although this bizarre way of moving between times should have left her feeling uneasy, she somehow knew it was perhaps the start of a completely new episode. She breathed a sigh of relief as she felt the key the young Meredith had given in the corner of her pocket.

'It's not the stairs at all that takes me back; it's the bloody summerhouse, or something that surrounds it,' she mumbled. Seconds later, she heard her father's voice calling her.

Turning, she was surprised to see him approaching her.

CHAPTER 5 - FINALLY BOX FOUR

'Dad, I am so pleased to see you.'

Her father narrowed his eyes, 'Where this time, Rebecca?' he asked with a knowing look on his face. 'I thought travelling through time was over for you, especially now the summerhouse has been rebuilt.'

'Dad, it's not the stairs that takes me back. Thank you by the way for the new ones,' she said, and smiled. 'It's actually seems to be the summerhouse that acts as a door back, even though it has been rebuilt. It is as if there is a force-field or sorts around it.'

He lifted both hand in a questioning manner.

'I only came down here to have a look.'

'Hmm, I guess that is what happens every time. So, what happened?'

Rebecca nodded. 'So, I went inside, up the stairs, and bang there I was, back with Meredith. Coming home was even more bizarre. I closed my eyes, gut feeling and all that, turned the door handle, and here I am, back.'

'And?' he said, and again lifted his hand.

Rebecca laughed, 'Oh, yeah, so I met Meredith, however, this time she was a child, maybe eleven, or so. She gave me this,' she said, and produced the odd-shaped key from her pocket. 'This, Dad, is the same key that's on top of the box in the painting.' She then took a deep breath. 'And by the way, the box in the painting is the same as the unopened box in my room.'

He held his hand out and took the key. He then narrowed his eyes, and said, 'Let me get this straight. You met Meredith, except she was a child. She then gave you a key, which I'm guessing you believe will open the other box.'

Rebecca nodded several times.

'And all this happened because you found a,' he paused, 'a little box, in the green dress, and that box had a note in it from Meredith.' He took a deep breath, 'This key has also mysteriously turned up, along with the fourth box, in the painting, having never been there before.'

'I just think we have never seen it before, the key and box in the paintings that is.'

'Rebecca, you study those paintings to within an inch of their life. If there had been a key, let alone a box, you would have known.'

'Hmm, I hadn't considered that. She has some tricks up her sleeve, our Meredith.' She then narrowed her eyes, as something occurred to her. 'When I met Meredith as an adult, she never let on that she knew I was from the future. I say this because the young Meredith called me "future girl." She also said the only people who see me are those that need to. So it is reasonable that the older Meredith knew all along.'

'Well perhaps the adult Meredith considered it wouldn't be prudent to tell you all she knew. Especially as it was the first time you travelled.'

'It's funny you know, when I look back now, I sensed she knew more than she was letting on. That said she still managed to look surprised when I told her I was from the future.'

'I know you initially believed it was her tormented spirit that opened the door back for you. It would now seem that is not the case, and in reality, she has a broader hand to play, as do you. As I said before, she is like a muse or a guardian angel of sorts, there to lead your way.'

'I am finding difficult to get my head around always living in this house generation after generation. I keep telling myself that it is no more bizarre than time-travelling. Even so, it is a weird feeling that I am really struggling with.' She paused for a moment. 'I guess in time I will come to terms with it all, but right now...'

'I keep considering the information in the letter relating to your previous existences. I wonder if tucked away in the recesses of your subconscious brain are all your memories of living in this house. Then somehow, they or you convey those recollections into some kind of reality.'

'That is a very interesting perspective on it, Dad. All the same, I don't see how that then takes me back in time. It would be one thing if I were going into a dream-like state, which I am not. I actually go back to different eras in the past.' She squinted, considering her own words. 'I agree completely that all my lives are somewhere in my head, but I don't see how that can transfer into reality.'

'I can't come up with an answer either, and believe me, I have tried. I think, for now, we have to accept it as an unlikely, but nonetheless, fantastical series of real events.'

'Bit like the box magically appearing in the painting, complete with this,' she said again holding up the tiny key. 'And, of course, there's the plaque on Millicent's painting that also changed.

Her father appeared puzzled. 'What do you mean, the plaque changed?'

'Of course, you don't know. When that happened, we weren't on the same page,' she said and chuckled. 'Well, after Millicent's suicide, the plaque on the painting changed to "in memory of Millicent

Black." For the life of me, I can't remember what it said before, but it definitely changed. So if things like that can happen, anything can.'

On the way up to the main house they chatted about how mum was dealing with all the information in the boxes, and that she would need a little more time. They agreed she probably wasn't ready to hear about Rebecca's recent jaunt, although showing her the key wouldn't be too much of a problem.

'Rebecca, before we go in. I am open-minded, although I lost my sight for a long time, until you reopened my eyes. Even with their eyes wide open, looking through a telescope of imagination, the most creative of minds would scramble at your stories. Maybe that is why your Mother needs time. Incidentally, you take all this in your stride, how so?'

'Not sure I do, Dad, especially the reincarnation aspect. You know though, I have learnt to keep my mind open, and I guess to accept it for what it is.' She thought for a moment, 'I don't have a choice, do I?'

'Maybe, after supper, if you feel comfortable, we will try the key in the last box.'

She nodded tentatively, and although she was almost there, she was still not completely ready. Her curious mind wanted to know what the contents had in store for her, but there was something holding her back.

Seemingly aware of her indecision, her father said, 'in your own time, Rebecca.'

As they entered the house, Elizabeth called out from the kitchen, 'Where have you two been? Are we still going out tonight?'

'The restaurant just called me up, and they've had to close tonight because of some electrical problem. So, I thought we could order some food to be delivered, perhaps from that new Indian, if everyone fancies?'

'Sounds good to me,' Elizabeth said, glancing at Rebecca.

'Yeah, sounds great.'

'Tommy won't mind, he loves an Indian, so no need to ask him,' James said.

During supper, Elizabeth, with narrowed eyes, asked Rebecca if she was okay.

Rebecca nodded without answering.

'Have you been up to no good again in the summerhouse, Rebecca?'

'Mum, I did go down there for a look. I found this, which will fit the last box in my room,' she said, holding up the key.

'Oh, will fit, and how do you know that.'

'Well, you know I wanted the magnifier? I used it to look at a box in Meredith's painting. There is a key on top of the box, and this one is the same,' she said waving the key.

'Just another stupid key,' Tommy garbled, with his mouth full of food.

All three of them stared straight at him.

Clearly got the message, because grimacing, he mumbled, 'Oops, Sorry everyone.'

While Rebecca was helping her mum tidy up after supper, she said, 'Mum, I have loved being home. I enjoy uni and all, but I realised yesterday how much I miss our chats and your laugh. We need to sit down and talk again about my stories.'

'Oh bless you, Rebecca, I have missed you also. I am sorry that I have found it difficult to understand everything to do with Meredith and co, but I am getting there. I spoke to Ruth about it all, and she said I should try to remain open. She also said that if I found it difficult, it must be ten times more complicated for you. Moreover, that you have always come to me with your tales, and I should try to be more understanding.' She thought for a moment, 'she was and is right, and I am now ready – almost - to go on your adventures with you, no matter how complex or bizarre they appear.'

'Well, Dad and I were going to have a look in the last box, maybe you could come with us, literally, 'she said, giggled, and held her mum's hand tightly.

They finished tidying up and went to the study to find James.

'Dad, are you ready for box four? Mother and I are,' she said and smiled.

Unsuccessfully hiding his obvious surprise, he stood up, and said, 'no time like the present,' shaking his head, he continued, 'Or past, or anytime Meredith sees fit.'

'Dad, where did that come from?'

He shook his head, 'Not sure where any of this is coming from, but maybe that's the best way. Rebecca, forever, you've been saying that we should keep an open-mind. Your Mother and I are trying to do exactly that.'

Rebecca smiled, realising her dad was pacifying mum.

As they passed the paintings in the hallway, her mum stopped and looked at the Meredith painting. 'I don't remember seeing that box

before. In fact, I was looking last week, and I am pretty sure…
Hmm.'

'We,' Rebecca indicated to her father, 'were talking about this earlier. I think we have to just accept it for what it is, bizarre, but amazing also.'

'Maybe,' her mum said, and narrowed her eyes, clearly unsure.

Entering Rebecca's bedroom, her mother hesitated by the door. She then said, 'is it okay if I stand here and watch. Then maybe later…'

'Mum, whatever makes you comfortable.'

Rebecca and her father sat on the floor next to the box. With the key in her hand, she glanced back and forth between her father and the box. Her father nodded, as she inserted the key into the first hole. Feeling quite peculiar, she turned it slowly, and shivered with anticipation as it unlocked. Holding her breath, she then removed the key, and with a mixture of uncertainty and excitement, inserted it into the other hole. Again, it unlocked easily.

With her emotions in overdrive, she glanced at her mother still standing by the door. She then glanced at her father, who nodded again. Still unsure if she was ready to look inside, she hesitated. With her mind going in circles, she took a deep breath, pushed her shoulders back, and lifted the metal lid.

She lifted out the first batch of papers, which referred to a blacksmith owning the land in 1473, and his building being on the sight of the summerhouse. Rebecca chatted to her parents about these papers, and although interesting, felt there must be something more significant in the box.

Next, she came across some hand-written documents that referred to important building works in the area in 1623. She looked up, and

47

said, 'I don't know for sure, but I believe that is around the time this house was built. The stone flint part of the house at the back matches up with something I found on the Internet.'

'Rebecca, I spoke to Ruth the other day and she mentioned that she'd established there had been a building here since the fourteen-hundreds. Although she did say, it was all a bit unclear. Hey, but we are used to it being unclear,' she said, and laughed in a way that suggested she was a little uneasy.

'Mum, that's brilliant because it does match up with what's in the box. Did Ruth say anything else about the house?'

'Funny enough, I asked the same thing. She said it was again unclear, but reckoned around the seventeenth century, there was some kind of disaster in the North West, which is here, isn't it? I thought that meant seventeen-hundreds onwards,' she said, and lifted her palm in a questioning manner. 'Is that the time the house was built? If so, I wonder what that was all about and if it had any kind of impact on this house.'

'I wonder what sort of a disaster, and as you said, if it affected the house being built. Incidentally, Mum, I get confused by that too,' she said, and turned to her dad. 'The seventeenth century is the sixteen-hundreds. Is that right, Dad?'

He held his thumb up, and said, 'most people are confused by that. The seventeenth century is the sixteen-hundreds.'

'Thanks, Dad.' Rebecca thought for a moment. 'Hmm, I am not sure what to think, because the house is here, so maybe it wasn't a problem.' She thought again for a moment, 'I am certain that if it did have an impact, there would be more information. Hey, I am sure we will find out soon enough,' she said, and laughed quietly.

'So, when you say, "we'll find out soon enough," I am guessing you mean from Meredith,' her mum said, with an obvious tone of hesitancy.

Aware of her mother's reaction, Rebecca glanced towards her dad. 'Mum, are you okay doing this? I know you find it a little uncomfortable. I appreciate your support, but it is okay if... well, we can always tell about it later. Dad and I both find it difficult to comprehend. Incidentally, I meant we may find something in this box,' she said, and pointed to another pile of papers.

'Well I do have a lot of washing from the holiday to catch up on. So, if you don't mind.'

'No, that's fine Mum, besides Dad won't have any Disney shirts to wear to work,' she said, and chuckled.

As her mum headed off, Rebecca smiled at her father, 'I knew mum was getting uncomfortable,' she said, lifting out a large pile of papers tied up with some twine. She started reading, and although she'd had letters from Meredith in the past, this one had a greater impact than the others did. Reading it just moments after her previous meeting with Meredith provided tangible evidence, confirming her episodes with this woman had actually happened. She'd always a nagging doubt. 'These are referring to Meredith's mother and her mother's sister, who was also named Rebecca.' She glanced at her father, and then continued reading. Inhaling deeply through her nose, she breathed out slowly, and said, 'oh my, this is so sad.'

He took the letter, and started reading aloud.

Dear Rebecca,

If you are reading this, you must have found the note in the dandy green dress that I asked you to wear, the first time we met.

My Mother had a sister also named Rebecca. She, like you, could see into the past and the future. She told me of you when I was eleven-years-old, and said that you would visit. If, as I assume, you met me when I was a child, you would have been aware that I knew of you, future girl.

Sadly, my Rebecca talked too often of her insights. Due to her views, seen as obsessive, many considered her foolish and irrational. Madhouse internment was the recommended resolution, although my mother fought hard to find an alternative decree for her beloved sister.

A physician with some insightful wherewithal suggested a lithe approach institution in the Americas. With regret, late in the year eighteen-twenty-seven, the family agreed to her transference.

It is with a heavy heart that I must inform you our dear Rebecca took her last breath two sad years later.

Aside you, she was the only other Rebecca, who could see beyond her years.

I send you this letter, my dear friend, with a painful heart. I hope you continue to see all that is within you. In addition, my prayer is that you never face the ridiculed views that my beloved Rebecca faced. There will be many who fail to understand your intuitive and insightful vision. Be strong.

My love, Meredith

'Oh my, I am all goosy,' she said, and shivered.

'Me too Rebecca, me too.'

'I often wondered if I was the only Rebecca who could see the things I see. I don't understand why just Meredith's Aunt and I have this vision. Surely, if every Rebecca is me, in a different time-zone, they should have the ability to see also.'

'Well, Rebecca, you didn't open your eyes to this until we moved here. Perhaps the opportunity didn't manifest itself for the other Rs.'

'When we lived in Cheshire, I had an inclining something unusual was going on, especially when I visited the whispering pond. Certainly, I was aware that I saw things that others didn't.' She thought for a moment, 'I guess if we had stayed there, I would have only ever seen the fairies and such like, and adulthood could have could have easily put pay to that. Maybe you're right, and the other Rebecca's never had the chance to see their abilities.'

After chatting for a while, they agreed, like the rest of this, there was no obvious answer, and that they could only accept things for what they are, a fantastically bizarre series of real events.

With her father peering into the box, Rebecca lifted out the next batch of papers.

Rebecca carefully thumbed her way through this pile. Much of it was, at best, sketchy information that didn't really add up to much. However, she did find some paperwork that referred to a name change. 'Dad, there is something here that relates to the house name changing to chère à votre maison, sometime after it was taken over by a French industrialist in eighteen-eighty-eight. I know that house name. I found something a while back on the Internet that referred to it as that, although I didn't know anything about the French man,' she said, and raised her eyebrows. 'I am guessing the French industrialist was a man.' She then shook her head.

'Interesting,' he said, still peering into the box, 'no hidden compartments, although we have a lot to take in and consider.' He then raised his eyebrows, 'I suspect there may be more for you to see, and undoubtedly Meredith will have a part to play. It does seem your lady is a key protagonist in all of this. Sorry about the key pun,' he said, and laughed.

They joined Elizabeth and Tommy in the kitchen. Once Tommy had gone to his room, they chatted about the contents from the box. With Elizabeth still obviously a little uncomfortable, they kept it brief.

While packing to go back to University, Rebecca couldn't stop thinking about all the information in the boxes. Now distracted, she decided to draw up a time-line. Slowly, she unpacked each box, and placed every piece of information in some kind of sequence.

With piles of paper all over the floor, her mother popped in. 'Oh, Rebecca, I thought you'd packed that all away.' She shook her head, 'aren't you supposed to be getting sorted to go back to university tomorrow?'

'I know, Mum. I just had to get all this in some kind of order. If I don't it will be playing on my mind. Once I have it sorted, I will tidy it all away and get my stuff sorted.'

'Okay, don't stay up too late, Roxy is coming early.'

Slowly, Rebecca checked the paper trail and started listing everything in sequence. Scribbling on a notepad, she gradually compiled everything in year order.

Chapter 6 - Mrs. Pochard

During the first few of days back at University, with all the information from box four fresh is her mind, Rebecca was finding it difficult to focus her thoughts on studying. She knew she had to put it all to the back of her head, and centre her attention, but it was proving difficult.

One such day during a lecture, she was again miles away. After the lesson, her tutor, Mrs. Samantha Pochard who was a sophisticated woman in her mid-twenties, asked her if she was okay.

'Yeah, sorry, I wasn't paying much attention today.'

'Well, it's most unlike you, especially when the subject is fantasy.'

'Aha, that's the problem. It is a very long story, and one that requires an open mind both from you and me.' Rebecca laughed, wondering if she could, or should confide in Mrs. Pochard, recognising she was someone who'd continued to show a keen interest in her fantasy writings.

With an obvious look of curiosity, she said, 'my mind is open to the extent where I believe most things are possible. It comes from my childhood. When I was young, I saw the world in a way that most would laugh at. I didn't actually care, and I stayed in my world, as long as I could. I lost my way a little as a got older, but forced my way back.' She seemed to think for a moment, 'I actually believed in fairies and such like. I still do, just think most adults lose their ability to see.'

Rebecca shook her head, unable to believe what this woman had just said. 'Wow, I have said the same thing, for as long as I can remember. I so nearly lost my vision, what with common sense creeping up on me, especially being here among inflexible, blinkered individuals. Well, present company accepted.' Now feeling tempted to share her story, she decided to wait a little while longer, and see what else this woman said. Everything was telling her that this woman may be in harmony, and that there may actually be more to her story. 'I am intrigued by what you have said Mrs. Pochard.' Deciding to drop in a taster, she said, 'I believed – when I was young, and still do – that the fairies near my old house pinched my pencil, and they then returned it just before I moved.' Intrigued, she watched Mrs Pochard to see how she reacted.

'First off, please call me Sam. I am not at all surprised you say this, because your written work shows glimpses of your inner thoughts. I also noticed it is more apparent in your notes, and in particular, when you return after a break. I have often thought to ask what inspires your thoughts. For years, I suppressed that side of my beliefs, especially when writing, sadly.'

Rebecca nodded. 'Of late, I have covered up my inner thoughts, and it annoys me to be truthful. This damn rational thinking keeps rearing its ugly head. I'm determined to draw a line under it that's for sure.' Rebecca smiled, 'You seem to be comfortable sharing your views, Sam. I must add that they are views that very few adults are capable of seeing, or prepared to acknowledge. At what point did you find enough confidence to share your views with others?'

'I guess, I was around sixteen, when I told a fairy story at school during an English class. Although some of the boys mocked me, the girls loved my tale. And, that was an inner-city school in London, where peer pressure was everything. My teacher spoke to me after, and he said that with my imagination, I should consider writing fantasy novels, and doing it seriously.'

Rebecca shook her head, 'that is how I ended up here. I had exactly the same thing said to me. I know what you mean about the boys and their negative response. I do think though that it is just because they are scared what their friends may think. Interestingly, although they laughed at me in the open, on the quiet, they owned up to loving my tales.' She shook her head and chuckled. 'It is sad really that they are not allowed to like such things. We went to Disney over Christmas and my younger brother, who is fifteen, was annoyingly indifferent towards the holiday. That was until he found out two of his football teammates were also going. He then paraded around most days wearing a Mickey mask. And that is how blinking peer pressure works. The thing is as we get older, most lose their way, and just clamp down on their imagination. That, I believe, is purely because society says fairies are for children. To my mind that is so sad.'

Over the next couple of weeks, Rebecca kept bumping into Mrs. Pochard, and by the third week, was beginning to wonder if Meredith was playing a part in this. Although she was certain that this woman would embrace her story of time travel, she decided to drop in a leader, to see what reaction she got. 'Have you watched *Back to the Future,* and if so, did you enjoy it?'

'Well, there's a question. I did enjoy it, especially the first one. However, I suspect this is leading somewhere, perhaps into the past or future. Are you a future girl?'

Rebecca gasped, certain now that Meredith had a hand is this. Shaking her head, she could only muster up, 'please continue.'

She smiled, and holding Rebecca's hand, she said, 'Seems I touched a nerve there,' she again smiled, 'I have noticed you plying me with tempters, more so each time we bump into each other, which is often. Why don't you just try me out with your story and see how I respond? What is the worst thing that can happen, I give you a D?' She shook her head, and smiling, raised her eyebrows.

For a few days, Rebecca had been wondering if Mrs. Pochard saw life in a similar vein. After again listening to this woman's carefully chosen words, she felt comfortable enough to share her story or at least some of it. She had trawled the Internet endlessly in search of someone who had experienced something similar to her and now that person was potentially sitting right in front of her. Sam calling her a future girl just confirmed and justified her views and confidence in this woman. She glanced at the clock, and knowing she was due in a lecture soon, suggested they met up for lunch.

'Lovely, I will look forward to hearing all. Just think the onlookers will be able to call you teacher's pet too. What a peer shrinking bonus for them,' she said a laughed. 'Although, I must say, at university that sort of thing is mild by comparison to school.'

All the way through her next lecture, Rebecca asked herself many times if she was doing the right thing. In the end, she decided there was absolutely nothing to fear especially now she was fairly sure Meredith was watching over proceedings. 'Nothing ventured,' she mumbled, as she headed for the door at the end of the class.

She joined Sam in the canteen and as she sat next down, couldn't fail to notice one or two looks. 'Prying eyes,' she whispered.

'I did notice, Rebecca. However, look at them, with their shiny soulless phones glued to the ear or face.'

During lunch, Rebecca went through the first part of her story, starting with the time she found the key, right through to meeting Meredith.

Appearing completely unfazed, Sam said, 'So, if I have this straight in my head, these spiral stairs took you back in time, to the year eighteen-fifty-three where you met Meredith.'

'Yep, in essence, that is it, same thing every time, until recently.'

This time, appearing a little taken aback, she asked, 'So I am presuming there have been more events like this for you.' Narrowing her eyes, similar to her mother, she pouted her lips, and said, 'in your own time, Rebecca. I am sorry if I appear to be pressing you for more information. I am just so excited by all you've said, and actually can't wait to hear more.'

Having noticed the time, Rebecca asked, 'Can we carry this on, maybe after my lectures have finished. I am done by three-thirty.' She then thought for a moment. 'You're not pushing me at all. In fact, it is a joy to have someone, who understands, and importantly, is an open-minded advocate. Incidentally, I don't think we have touched enough on your story, so we can take it in turns,' she said and smiled.

'That would be lovely. Shall we meet back here later? We will almost certainly have it to ourselves, as most students will be off campus by then. That way we can talk without curious ears,' she said and chuckled. 'While we're on the subject, in case you are wondering why I am taking this in my stride, well... let's just say, I have a different, but similarly bizarre story to tell. I use that word for those who can't, or choose not to see the kaleidoscope of life in front of us all.'

Rebecca spent the whole lecture wondering what story Sam had up her sleeve. In the usual Rebecca way, dead on three-thirty, she packed away, and was out the door before anyone had moved. Arriving in the canteen, she was surprised to see the place full. She grabbed a fresh orange juice, and picked a table in the corner. Moments later, Sam joined her.

'Hello Sam, it's rather crowded in here.'

'Oh, they will soon go. So, where were we, with Meredith I believe?'

They continued to chat about Meredith for a while. All the time, Rebecca was wondering about Sam's story.

'So Sam, you mentioned earlier that you had a similar story.'

She smiled. 'When I was nine, my family moved to Sutherland, in Scotland. This felt like it was nearer the North Pole than London, especially during the short days of winter. For me though, it was one big wild adventure. One day, when I was down near a burn, by a waterfall, I noticed something from the corner of my eye.' She then closed her eyes for a second, 'Right in front of me was a group of goblin like creatures. Actually, they were goblins, not goblin like creatures. To me, what little I knew, they were the real deal.' With her eyes closed, as if she were visualising the event, she then hesitated. 'Goblins, for some reason, mostly because of the way they are depicted in books and films, we consider unsociable critters. These goblins were the complete opposite and actually inquiringly friendly.' She paused.

Stimulated by Sam's tale, Rebecca nodded several times, 'cat, curiosity, and all that.'

'There I was staring at them, and there they were, staring at me.' She breathed deeply. 'I have only told this story once, so stay with me. When I did tell my father, he waved his hand away, and called me a stupid child.' She took another deep breath, 'One of them spoke to me.'

'Crumbs, I have seen – at a distance – plenty of fairies, been aware or pixies and elves, but none of them have spoken to me. I have had communication from them, of sorts. By way of the pencil that I mentioned earlier, and when they hid it, so I'd find the key. But I never had so much as a noise from them, let alone a word.'

'When my father reacted that way, I realised then that I was alone in this world.' She beamed a smile, 'until I met you.'

'Did you see them often? And, how tall were they? I'm just curious, because the fairies and such like are tiny likkle things.'

'They are about two feet tall, rotund little individuals. They have pointed, almost witch like features. Perhaps that is why mythology would have you believe they are unsocial creatures. On that subject, do you ever wonder why there are so many tales with reference to this type of critter, and all so similar, yet there's no evidence. Importantly, when anybody talks about such things, the world meets it with ridiculed indifference. Me aside, it seems okay for children to believe in mythical creatures. Indeed, we bombard them with impressions, suggestions, and pointers, through books or the films, and then as they grow older, we pooh-pooh it.' She then hesitated clearly thinking. 'History is filled with references to mythical creatures, outlandish god like beings and so on. People have spent thousands in search of the Yeti, Big-Foot, and Loch Ness, and as soon as there is something even only remotely tangible, it is shot down in flames.'

'I do wonder about such things, and I believe, like you, the people who have seen these kinds of thing are invariably young, with their minds still open. However, when young adults relay their stories, the world treats it with scepticism, and dismisses it as foolish, or childlike.' Rebecca then hesitated as something occurred to her. 'I've just realised something very significant. The people who knock such things are probably in the minority, yet we allow those with a big voice to appear as if it were the view of all. Also, I think another factor is that by the time children reach an age where people will listen, they have lost their own ability to see.' Rebecca thought about her own words for a moment. 'My Mother loved and embraced my tales. Conversely, I was afraid to tell my Father for fear of his reaction. I am lucky, because when I did tell him - because I had to – and that's another story – he met it with an openness that made me realise that I inherited my vision from him.'

'Wow, your views are amazing, and importantly profoundly right. We do listen to the noisy few. The ones who say you can't do this, can't say that, have to think in a certain way, and so on and so on, bla bla bla...'

They sat around chatting until the canteen closed at 8pm. Realising they hadn't eaten, they decided to head into town and grab a pizza. While they sat in the café, Roxy walked in, having noticed them as she passed by.

'What are you two chatting about, I saw you at lunch, and then after classes, and here you are still wagging your lips.'

Grinning, Rebecca said, 'wagging our lips, Roxy. I will never get used to the things you say, but it does make me smile.'

'Okay,' she said and grinned, 'are ya talkin' about Meredith by any chance?'

Shaking her head, Sam said, 'She knows?'

'Yep, she's my true friend and confidante, in spite of the fact that I only understand half of what she says.'

'Likewise, I am sure,' Roxy said, and squeezed Rebecca hand, before bending her finger back.'

'Ouch, bitch.'

'Youz' a bitch, a fairy bitch,' she said and giggled.

'You are so lucky, Rebecca, to have your Mother, Father, and best friend – although that is debatable,' she grinned, 'buy into your tales. I have waited for all my life to find someone I can talk to about this, and then like a London Bus,' she said, and glanced at Roxy,' two turn up at once.'

The three sat around chatting, drinking too much coffee – according to Rebecca – and exchanging stories, although many of Roxy's stories involved boys. At around midnight, Sam suggested it was time to clear out as the waiters were staring. They agreed to meet up Saturday in Roxy's suggested French restaurant in Warwick.

On the way back to halls, Roxy mentioned how lucky Rebecca was to find Sam, with her being open to her tales and such an advocate.

'Yeah, I know, I am lucky. I have you also, and the buy-in from my Dad, and my Mum, although she stands on the other side of the room.'

Appearing curious, Roxy asked, 'other side of the room, what does that even mean?'

Rebecca then explained how her mum had started reacting towards her stories, since they become a little more than just stories.

On Thursday and Friday, Rebecca bumped into Sam so many times that she started to wonder if Meredith was pushing them together and there was more to come from Sam. It was last thing on Friday, and again she saw Sam.

'Do you recall I mentioned a woman named Meredith? As odd as this may sound, I think she has sent you to me.'

'Nothing is odd in my world. I wondered if there may be an outside influence affecting our direction, what with us continually turning the same corner.' Closing her eyes, Sam seemed to go deep in thought – as she often did – and opening her eyes with a smile, said, 'perhaps there is a prevailing wind, or influence at play here.' Again, she closed her eyes – something Rebecca was growing fond of – and then continued, 'Maybe it is indeed your Meredith. I keep thinking that you have more to tell me.'

'I do, and I had already decided to tell all when we meet up tomorrow. Roxy knows all, although I only recently told her the details.'

'Curiosity, along with your cat, is now banging down my door,' she said, with both palms lifted.

'I know, and I am sorry. My tale is so unbelievable that I am struggling with it myself. I guess that is why I am taking my time, getting it right in my own head, before I scramble any other individual's brain cells.'

'It is okay you know. I understand, because it took me six months before I mentioned my tale to my Father. Pointless as it was, I do appreciate how you feel. After all, I was a child, and it should have been okay to be away with the fairies.'

'Yours is a sad tale, and I have thought about it so often since you told me. My Meredith is a good soul, and I am sure she has brought us together for both our sakes.'

'Hey, here we are, you, Roxy, Meredith and I, all on the same London Bus,' she said, and giggled. 'And, it's an open top bus too.'

'I like you; I like the way you think so deeply, the way you giggle, and well… I just do.'

'It is reciprocated, that I can assure you. I feel as if I have waited for ever to meet you.'

As they headed down the corridor, they continued to chat about people's reaction to tales such as theirs.

'Right, I must do some marking. It is okay, I don't think you'll be getting a D, not this time,' she said and laughed.

'See you tomorrow then,' Rebecca said, and blew Sam a kiss.

She woke early Saturday morning to the sound of her phone ringing. 'Hello, Roxy, you're up early.'

'All men are twits,' she blurted down the phone.

'Oh dear, whatever has happened?'

'He has run off with that bird from the girls' soccer team.'

Rebecca listened while Roxy continued to stew down the phone. When she simmered a little, Rebecca asked if she would like to meet up early.

'No, I am fine, well fine ish. I will see you at twelve as agreed.

Rebecca arrived at the restaurant a little early anyway, only to see Roxy and Sam already there.

'You two are early,' she said kissing each on the cheek.

They spent the lunch talking about boys and what horrid creatures they can be. Occasionally the subject went back to Meredith, but it was obvious to Rebecca that Roxy needed some friend time. Later in the afternoon, Roxy made her excuses, having just answered her phone.

'Roxy, promise me that phone call wasn't from that twit of a boy and you're off running after him.'

'No-way-José,' she said, and grinned. 'My Mum is at the train station waiting for me to pick her up. Oops, I forgot, sorry Mum.' She waved her good-bys and headed off. The remainder of the afternoon again involved too many coffees, while Rebecca and Sam talked about the letter from Meredith.

'Let me get this straight, Meredith sent you a letter, from eighteen-fifty whenever, telling you that you have always lived in that house as Rebecca.' She thought for a moment, 'I can understand why your Mum stands on the other side of the room. I have questioned this type of thing and often wondered if it was at all possible. I read a book sometime ago, called *Spirit from the Past* that alluded to reincarnation. Although it was fiction, much of it was written in such a way that it left you thinking the author had some experience.'

'I read that book too, although unlike you, I felt it was a skewed opinion and only that. Purely a work of fiction.'

'Well, you would know best, that's for sure.'

They spent the remainder of the afternoon chatting about the subject, mostly going over Rebecca's story, and her difficulty in getting it straight in her own head.

Over the next few months, Sam, Roxy, and Rebecca met up many times for lunch. The subject was always boys, if Roxy had anything to do with proceedings, although she clearly enjoyed it when the subject turned to Meredith and Sam's goblins. Before she knew it, Rebecca was heading home for the summer break, knowing that she would be 20-years-old when she returned. The day after arriving home, her exam results came through, with excellent marks across the board. To compound her parent's delight, Tommy had become the youngest player – 16-years and ten days – to play a first-team game for Preston North End.

She was sitting on her balcony watching the sun ripple across the lake, remembering the day the family moved here. *Best thing Dad ever did* she thought. Sipping her orange squash, her thoughts briefly turned to Meredith. Since arriving home, apart from acknowledging Meredith on the way in, this woman barely crossed her mind. She suspected at some point that Meredith would beckon her. So far, though, she wasn't getting any type of vibe, and absolutely no sign of the familiar sensation she often felt when something was afoot. This left her feeling a little confused because whenever she'd considered the contents of box four had always felt there were more journeys in front of her.

CHAPTER 7 – WRONG MARRIAGE

It was just after supper, when Rebecca's father asked her if she fancied a chat in the study. Rebecca suggested to her father that it was a lovely evening and a walk down to the lake might be nice. As they approached the summerhouse, he asked what kind of feelings or emotions she experienced when she came close.

'It's odd Dad, because sometimes, like today, there is nothing, not a glimmer. Other days, it is like there's a magnet pulling at my inner thoughts. It is such a weird sensation. I recall the first time I came down here with the key and felt something so strong tugging at me that I couldn't avoid it even if I wanted to.'

'So there's nothing today then? And I assume nothing since you arrived home.'

'Not a sausage, zilch, nout, zip.'

'I can tell you've been around Roxy,' he said, and smiled. 'I love the way she talks. Couldn't understand a word first time I met her. Now though, I find it so endearing. She is a good friend, which is a rare thing you know.'

'I know Dad. I love her so much. Not only is she one of the sharpest pencils in the box, she is honest, and trustworthy.'

'By the sharpest pencil, I suspect you mean intelligent, because she is extraordinarily bright. I recall her asking me about finance, and she just dug so deep, I couldn't fail to be impressed. She had such an understanding. I would love her to work with me when she graduates.'

'Hmm, not sure I see Roxy in the world of finance. Maybe a film star more like,' she said, and giggled. 'Going back to Meredith; I never worry about her being distant, because when the time is right, she calls. I used to try to force it when I was younger, to no avail. Now, I just wait for a message.'

'What kind of message?' he asked. 'On the subject of being younger, twenty this year madam. I can recall you being sixteen as if it were yesterday. Where has the time gone? This has been some couple of years.' He then looked across the lake. 'Thank you for reopening my eyes, dear daughter.'

'Dad, I thank you being there, and able to open your eyes. I have a tutor who has become a friend at uni. Her name is Sam, and she told her dad a story when she was young, and her dad dismissed her out of hand. It shut her up completely, that was until she met Roxy and me. Now the three of talk endlessly about fairies, goblins, and of course Meredith.'

On the way up to the house, they noticed Elizabeth standing by the front door beckoning them.

'Rebecca dear, I have some sad news for you. Mary called,' she said, and gripped Rebecca's hand.

She didn't need to hear any more, because she had known this day would come. With her eyes bleary with tears, and shaking her head, she took a deep breath. She then pointed upstairs, and hurried to her room.

Moments later, there was a gentle knock on the door, and her mum's face appeared.

'Are you okay, sweetie?'

'Yeah Mum. Come in,' she said, sitting up on her bed.

Her mum sat next to her, and without saying anything, comforted her, the way only a mother can do. After a few minutes, Rebecca felt ready to speak. 'Mum, I get where you're at with all the time-travel palaver, but to me, it has been real, and Tabitha was a part of my story. I know what I know, and well…' Wiping her cheek with her hanky, she suddenly realised it was the hanky young Meredith had given her with the key. Taking a deep breath, she showed her mother the hanky, complete with the woven name Meredith.

'Crumbs, where did you find this?'

'Do you recall me telling you that a young Meredith gave me a key?

Her mother narrowed her eyes in a familiar way. 'Yes, I do.'

'Well, the key was wrapped in this hanky. I have only just realised that I had brought it back with me. That is significant, because no matter how many times I tried in the past, I could never sneak anything home. This is the first bit of hard-core evidence.' Still tearful, 'she said, I so don't recall bringing it back. I can't help thinking Meredith somehow – as daft as it may sound - sent it to me, to help comfort me because of Tabitha.' The hanky had briefly averted her emotions, but mentioning Tabitha's name struck hard.

Still looking at the hanky, her mum said, 'oh bless you Rebecca. I don't understand any of this, and am not sure I want to, but it does all seem to link together. I am so glad your Father is on board, and can be your confidant.'

'Mum, you and Dad are my confidants. In your own way, you both bring something different.'

They chatted for a while longer, and then her mum said, 'Right, I must get on with supper, don't want Dad getting huffy.'

'And there you have it; you always make me smile, no matter how down I feel. I love you, Mum.'

'I love you too, sweetie.'

The next couple of days passed quickly, as Rebecca spent a lot of time walking the grounds, enjoying the sunshine. It was Thursday around mid-afternoon, when she ventured over near the old stables. In a flash, memories flooded her thoughts. Although, she never really established anything around the nameplate Nadine, something was niggling at her inner thoughts. She headed back to her room and trawled the Internet, but again came up with nothing. Now though, Meredith was in her head, and she suspected something was about to happen. As tempted as she was to mention this to her father, something was saying don't. The following morning, Mary phoned her and explained that she was too upset to talk to her the other day, hence why she rang Elizabeth. After a brief conversation, Rebecca said she would not miss the funeral for anything. The weekend dragged by for Rebecca, and it was now Monday. Roxy had offered to come with her to the funeral as moral support.

On her way downstairs to meet Roxy, her mum asked if she was okay.

'Yeah, I am fine, Mum. Thank you for loaning me this black dress.'

You look perfect, Sweetie. I hope it goes okay for you. Are you sure that you don't want Dad and I to come along?'

'I am fine Mum. Tabitha lived a great and fulfilled life. I have come to terms with it now. I knew it was coming, but nothing can prepare you, when the news does arrive. I will phone you and let you know I am there and how things are going. I love you, Mum.'

'I love you too, sweetie.

At the funeral, a couple of people enquired as to her relationship with Tabitha. Each time, she said they were friends, explaining that Tabitha grew up in her house.

Over the next couple of days, Rebecca again took to the grounds. Unwittingly, she found herself back by the old fallen oak where she'd first found the key. Today, this area seemed to lack the magical vibe she remembered so clearly. Sitting on the tree, she recalled the sunlight glimmering through the young willows. Now though, the willows had grown and masked the light, giving the area a slight moody feel. Rebecca shivered, glanced down, and noticed the area where she'd found the key, completely overgrown. Kneeling, she removed as much undergrowth as she could, but couldn't see anything. *Well, the tree hasn't moved* she thought. She sat back on the tree and retraced her steps. On her hands and knees again, she knew she was in the right area, but there was no way she was getting her hand anywhere near where she'd found the key. There simply wasn't enough room to poke a pencil underneath, let alone her hand. She considered this for a moment and wondered if Meredith had something to do with this, or... *If she can move a tree, what else can she do?* That then started her thinking about the name plaque changing, the box appearing in the painting, the tablet box, and the silk hanky. If she was ever in any doubt, today she knew for sure that Meredith had, is, and will continue to influence her movements.

With this thought resonating in her consciousness, she took the long way back to the main house. The family was all out tonight at one of Tommy's matches, and this would help, as she needed a break from thinking about everything.

Going to watch Tommy play, was just what she needed to take her mind off Tabitha. Even though, he didn't come on until the eightieth minute, she loved being there. It also helped that they had a seat right behind the dugout. When he did appear from the bench to warm up, she screamed his name so loud, it made all the other players turn around. Tommy glanced back, shook his head, and then put his hands over his face while doing his stretches.

After the final whistle, the manager turned to Rebecca and said, 'you are right to shout your bro's name. He is a class act and we have high expectations for him.'

69

On the way home, Rebecca actually didn't mind hearing all the details. She sat in the back, listening to him talk, while in the back of her thoughts were memories of his younger days. 'If I had known you were going to turn out half decent, I might have let you kick your ball at me more often.'

Tommy grinned, 'moving target, that's all you were.'

'Broken finger, that's all you'll get, twit.'

Elizabeth turned around, and grinning like the cat, she said, 'behave, the pair of you, or no McDonalds. Hey, no Big-Mac for you anyways, Tommy. All this carbo-loading malarkey that your trainer told us about. Seems we have a new diet to look forward too. Yippy,' she said, and chuckled.

It was gone midnight, when they arrived home, and Rebecca headed straight off to bed. As she lay there, for the first time in days, she felt relaxed. She had finally come to terms with Tabitha's death, and although still sad, was now choosing positive thoughts. Next thing, she knew her mum was waking her with breakfast.

'Long lay in this morning, sweetie. You must have been tired. All that shouting, I guess,' she said, and chuckled. 'It did make us laugh, but was lovely what the manager said, and the way he addressed you. Almost makes the scrapes on the knuckles worth it.'

'Crumbs, he blinking annoyed me. All that aside, I am so very proud of Tommy.' She raised her eyebrows, 'maybe a little too loud sometimes.

That morning, Rebecca messed about in her room, going from one thing to the next without actually achieving anything. *Right, let's go for a walk* she thought. She headed downstairs, made herself a sandwich, and told her mum that she would be back later.

'Going to explore again, that's my girl.' Her mum, thought for a moment, 'if you do happen to go into the future, find out if Tommy plays for England.' Shaking her head, and clearly surprised by her own words, she uttered, 'err just forget I said that.'

'Mum where did that come from? Right, I am going for a walk, and only that. I'll be back before supper.' She raised her eyebrows and headed off down the hallway. As she passed Meredith, she said aloud, 'did you hear my Mother? I don't suppose you can tell my mum if my twit of a brother plays for England.'

'Rebecca, sarcasm is worse than swearing, and if you carry on, you'll be showering in carbolic soap,' he mum shouted down the hallway.

As soon as Rebecca stepped outside, an unusual sensation came over her. Unlike the previous times, when the call from Meredith created a recognisable, almost tangible mood, today, she was feeling something altogether different. She decided to take a slow walk down to the lake, consider her mood, and try to understand what was going on. In the past, she'd felt an overwhelming pull towards the summerhouse, today lacked the urgency she'd felt so often before. As she walked along, she wondered if common sense was again affecting the way she was feeling. Just as quick, she dismissed that notion, knowing since she'd met Sam, she'd found a way to avert rational thoughts.

Arriving down by the lake, she looked over towards the jetty and instantly memories of all the fun she'd had with her mum filled her head. Meandering towards the summerhouse, she was aware something was distracting her. She stood there for a moment looking around, but couldn't put her finger on anything. Deciding it was nothing, and returning her attention to the time her and mum visited the bear lodge, she was finding it almost impossible to focus. With something still nagging at her inner thoughts, she narrowed her eyes, looking around again. Without really having a clue what she was looking for, she was suddenly aware there was a light coming from the

71

upstairs room in the summerhouse. 'Can't be, she mumbled, no bulbs.' She shook her head, reckoning her father must have put them in and forgot to turn them off. However, her father was vigilante when it came to turning the lights off, *so it can't be that*, she thought.

Stepping up to the front door, she was getting a weird, uncharacteristic sensation that was a whole lot more than the lights simply being on. This was again unlike anything she'd felt before, and totally different to the sensation that had come over her as she left the main house moments earlier.

Shaking her head, she opened the front door, and stepped inside. Unlike the last visit, she could feel she was still in her own time. Besides, she couldn't smell that unmistakable odour that was always in the air when something is afoot. All that considered she still glanced back outside just to make sure. Nodding her head, she could see everything was as it should be.

She stood there for a few seconds considering how she was feeling. Because her sensations were all so different today, she decided they were probably generated by a mixture of memories. 'Right, turn the light off,' she mumbled, and headed upstairs. When she got there, there wasn't a sign of a bulb anywhere, causing her to breathe in so deeply that her nose made a whistling sound. With her senses suddenly reinvigorated, she decided to try the light switch anyway, even though she knew it was a waste of time. As she expected, nothing happened. Shaking her head, she walked over to the window to see if sunlight was creating the appearance of the lights being on. That notion was instantly dispelled by the tall conifers that were completely masking any light, let alone the sunlight. 'So, that's that out of the question,' she mumbled.

The second she turned away from the window, she heard what sounded like a choir singing. She headed over to the front window, and peered outside, but couldn't see anything out of the ordinary, let alone a choir. *So where's the sound coming from* she thought. Then just as she was about to turn away, something caught her eye. Up by the main house, she could see what looked like a large marquee. With her sensations all over the place, she tried to calm her mood, telling herself she should be used to this. Today though, right from the second she stepped outside, everything had felt different.

Breathing deeply, while still trying to calm her feelings, she opened the window. Instantly, the sound of a female choir filled the room. Leaning out of the window, she could hear the singing was coming from the direction of the marquee.

She was still certain she hadn't gone anywhere, but clearly she had, and trying to steady her nerves, took a deep breath. Regaining her composure a little by assuring herself that Meredith would see her good, she decided the only way to find out what was going on was to go and investigate. Walking down the stairs, her thoughts were all over the place as she looked around for some kind of a clue as to what had happened and where she was. She knew something had happened, but for some reason, she was struggling to take it in her stride. As she opened the front door, she got a quite horrid feeling of heartache and unhappiness. Although, she experienced awful sensations before seeing her mother in the ambulance, this was completely different. It was as if, she was aware something bad was about to happen. Although this sensation was leaving her spooked, oddly, she felt calm at the same time.

Gathering herself, she tried to open her mind and rid it of any balanced thinking, knowing that if she didn't it may affect her ability to see what was in front of her.

Closing the door to the summerhouse behind her, her nostrils filled with that oh so familiar smell of Christmas, and instantly, she knew Meredith was beside her. Instead of analyzing things, she was now back to her old self and ready to take everything in her stride. She paused briefly, feeling certain she was once again in Meredith's era. *Only way to find out,* she thought, *go, and have a look.*

Feeling strangely relaxed and now on a mission, she headed up towards the main house. As she grew closer, a woman and man dressed in what she considered fancy Victorian regalia passed her. She walked close to them, looked straight at them, and nodded, but they reacted as if they hadn't seen her or had chosen to ignore her. *How discourteous* she thought, and then looked down at her clothes and realised they may have seen her as a maid, or helping hand. *Either way,* she thought, *blinking rude.*

On her way towards the marquee, she passed more people, all dressed in a similar way. Again, she acknowledged them without a response. When the fourth couple ignored her, she decided to hell with it, reckoning she obviously appeared too far down the pecking order. *How sad that is,* she thought. Then she passed a pretty, tall slim woman, serving drinks, and reckoning she'd get a response from her, smiled, and nodded. Once again, the woman looked straight through her and acted as if she wasn't there.

Instantly, her thoughts flooded with memories of the time when she saw her mother in the ambulance, and no one was aware she was there. With her emotions now adrift, she stood still, unsure what lay ahead. Somewhere in her mind was an overriding belief that she must be here for a reason. 'Come on Meredith,' she mumbled.

Unlike before, there was no response to her call. Remembering what Meredith had said in her note to follow her instinct, she decided to do just that. *Right,* she though and headed over to the marquee for a look around.

On her way over, she passed several people who again behaved as if she wasn't there. Stopping dead in her tracks, she remembered young Meredith telling her those who needed to see her would see her. With that thought resonating in her psyche, she was suddenly aware that a youthful man, dressed in a waiter's uniform, was looking directly at her.

Heading over, she was aware he hadn't taken his eyes off her, in spite of several guests helping themselves to drinks from his tray. The closer she got, there was something niggling at her inner thoughts. Bizarre as it felt, he looked familiar, and she found herself likening him to someone she used to know at school, even though that was a ridiculous notion. As she approached him, he beamed a vigorous childlike smile. His poorly fitting suit gave the appearance of a child in adult's clothing, and she found herself wondering how old he was.

'Miss, you are looking at me as if you know me. I think you do know me as Richard, and know my age, please don't tell anyone. I will be in trouble if they find that I am twelve. I had to lie, to get the job, and feed me family. I need to work at today's wedding, so please...'

Immediately, Rebecca remembered the letter from Meredith, and that it said she married a Joshua Elm in 1858. As he was speaking, Rebecca was still trying to place him. He had a swagger that was oh so familiar, and his whole demeanour was confident. He obviously thought she knew him, but for the life of her, she didn't know who he was, even though he was so familiar. She chatted to him for a while, and promised not to inform anyone of his age. He dropped a drinks cork, and as it fell, he caught it on his foot, and flicked it back up onto his tray, without blinking an eye. Immediately, she recognised this trait, and knew why he appeared so familiar. *A nineteenth-century version of my twit brother,* she thought and laughed.

'I am sure I know you Miss. Are you not the one getting married this day?'

While he was talking, it was clear he thought he knew her. Considering what to say, an idea came to her. 'The girl you are thinking about is my twin sister, and she is the one who is to be married today. Although we appear similar, she is different from me in a lot of ways.'

'So she is she the one getting married, your sister?' he asked and frowning, he pointed towards the Marquee.

'You ask about my sister's marriage, but do so with concern in your voice?'

'I am not allowed to speak to the people here about. No one would listen to me anyway.' He looked directly at Rebecca, and said with clear alarm in his tone and manner, 'He is a bad man. My mother knows of him from Liverpool.'

'What do you mean, bad man?' Rebecca asked, now believing this may be why she is here.

He is a gambling man, a drinker, and got off a murder. Unlike Miss Meredith, he was guilty, coz he killed my mum's sister because...'

'Because, you said, because. Please tell me more.'

'He was kissing her outside a gin-house in Liverpool three years ago. My mum's sister pushed him away, so he stabbed her with his umbrella. Everyone saw it, but the police don't believe people like us over a gentleman.' He thought for a moment. 'He is not a gentleman; he is a murderer.

Rebecca's head was going in circles, wondering how, or if she should intervene. Now on a mission, she said her good-byes to the young lad, and went in search of Meredith. Somehow, she knew Meredith would know what to do. She searched inside and out of the marquee without any success. Standing there for a moment, she suddenly realised Meredith and the other Rebecca would probably be inside the house. Heading up towards the front door, the entrance was crowded with guests. Despite being single-minded, she had to pause and take in the grandeur of this event. Leading from the front door was an arched trellis, covered in white trailing roses. Red ivy, the likes of which she had never seen before, interlaced with the roses, creating a breathtaking setting. There were many people coming and going, all adorned in colourful splendour. She thought for a moment, and again considered her potential involvement. However, she knew this Rebecca was affectively her, and had to protect her in any way possible. In the back of her mind was this nagging concern about intervening with time, and if it could potentially affect later happenings. As she stood there, her thoughts tangled between the wrongs and rights of intrusion. Considering the information from the boy and the letter from Meredith left her confused. Meredith's letter clearly stated she'd married, had three children, and lived happily, but the boy's view on this man gave a dissimilar perspective and potentially disastrous outcome.

Just as she was considering going inside the house, Meredith appeared through the door. Extenuating this woman's amazing figure was a full-length, lilac dress, with high neckline, fitted waist, and flowing hem. Fixated, Rebecca studied her hair, admiring how neatly is had been tied up, allowing a sprinkle of ringlets to flow loosely from a 'southern belle,' style wedding hat. She took a deep breath, suddenly aware that Meredith was looking directly at her.

Meredith smiled and pointing, indicated to the left. Allowing her to lead the way, Rebecca watched with admiration as this woman moved past her as if she was floating.

Rebecca followed her around the side of the house. As she grew closer, Meredith opened her arms, and said, 'Hello future girl.' She then cuddled Rebecca just like her own mother.

Just as she was about to speak, this woman put her finger to her lips. 'Please let me look at your beautiful face my dear. You changed my life, and I find it reasonable to consider you are here once again with purpose, and almost certainly you possess the wherewithal to change one's destiny.'

'I have missed you dear Meredith and thought of you often. Until a moment ago, I believed I was here just to see my own wedding, which you wrote of in your letter. Thank you for that letter, even though it tangled my senses beyond belief.'

'Firstly, I must say that I do not know of the letter you speak of. I assume I write this in the future.'

Like a bolt of electric, Meredith's word scrambled her thinking further. 'umm, err.'

'There you are umming, and erring again, just as the first time we met three years since.'

'Three years since?' Rebecca asked, now even more confused.

'Why do you appear so befuddled, my dear?'

'Umm, is this the year eighteen-fifty-eight? I ask because in your letter, the one you're yet to write, you said I married in eighteen-fifty-eight, to a Joshua Elm.'

'No my dear, it is eighteen-fifty-six, and my daughter, Rebecca is about to marry Thomas Mier, not Joshua Elm.'

Shaking her head, she said, 'I am trying so hard not to umm and err, but I am so tangled and confused. The letter you will write says nothing of this marriage.' Although her thoughts were more akin to a jack-in-the-box, Meredith's words had given her focus. Her earlier concerns regarding her intervention had instantly evaporated, and she now knew exactly why she was here. *I have to stop this* she thought.

'I find it reasonable to assume the letter I will write has helped you to accept your providence, or you would not be with me once again. It is understandable that your senses are... *tangled*. Your path and existence tested my own consideration for the truth when I first learnt that you would travel to me from the future. My mother's sister, poor misunderstood Rebecca, initially alerted me to your reality.' She glanced down briefly, and smiling, continued, 'I named my daughter

78

Rebecca, in her memory. My daughter is not of your making, and indeed fails to see beyond the very next day,' she said and shook her head with an element of concern.

Realising Meredith was obviously concerned, she asked, 'I detected anxiety in your manner and tone, Meredith. Is there an issue, or problem?' Meredith appeared to be considering her words carefully, something Rebecca had noticed often. She admired this because to her mind, it reflected this woman's integrity.

'Before we talk any further of this day's events, I have much to tell you my dear Rebecca.' She paused, again clearly thinking deeply. 'My Mother's sister, my aunt Rebecca, told me of an occurrence when this house was built. She tirelessly suggested it had ruinous consequences, and that she had to speak with the future Rebecca before the Americas. She insisted you were the only person who would or could act upon her words.' She again paused to think. 'I must emphasize that this was before anyone knew of her impending transference to the Americas. Whenever she spoke, people frowned upon her, mocked her, and treated her words with contempt. Sadly, locking her in her room was their only remedy for someone who they saw as a fool. I, however, trusted her, maybe because I was young and innocent. I was right to trust her, and so you must find your way to eighteen-twenty-seven, and speak with her. I know she will be waiting. Of interest, I have kept my youthful mind always open to an alternate way of thinking, and seeing all that is around us and all that life has to offer. I must say that events such as this day test my outlook.'

Considering Meredith's words carefully, Rebecca now knew that she needed to find her way to 1827 and speak with Meredith's aunt. Still unsure if she was here to intervene with today's events, she decided to tackle things one at a time. 'Your aunt's tale is a sad one, and I am sorry she had such a horrid existence. I, like you, believe that children see the world differently to adults. Of late, I have struggled to bat away common sense, something that rears its head often.' She paused briefly, and continued, 'I will find my way to eighteen-twenty-seven, of that I am sure. With your help, and it would seem with your aunts help too, the doors will open, as they always do. I feel compelled to turn our attention back towards today's events.'

'You said my letter spoke of my Rebecca's marriage in eighteen-fifty-eight. Is that correct?'

'Yes, and it said your daughter Rebecca had a happy marriage and had three children. I might add that the letter spoke of events indicating I married Joshua Elm, which I found a little confusing, but I understood what it meant. What I can say is that there was no mention of Thomas, whatever his name is. Incidentally, what history I have found in my time, tells of this house changing names to Elm Manor, suggesting she married Joshua Elm. So today's events are out of sequence and break the chain.'

'So, it would seem. There is a clear reason you have returned today, and it would be sound to assume it is to again change providence in two separate eras.' She then paused, clearly thinking. 'My disquiet with this man and his marriage to my daughter has held my conscious thoughts for too long.' Appearing tearful, she averted her eyes.

'It is okay Meredith,' she said, holding her hand tightly. 'I know the truth of this man's past. A truth that will bring today's event to an immediate conclusion.'

Appearing animated, Meredith asked, 'may I ask what you know? I know nothing of his past, and it is that which concerns me most. I also have a motherly instinct that something is afoot, which may be disadvantageous towards my daughter. Please enlighten me with all you know about this man.'

'I spoke with a young waiter who was sure he knew me.' She thought for a moment, 'anyway, because he believed he knew me, he seemed comfortable telling me all he knew of this Thomas individual.'

'During our meeting when I was young, I informed you that only those who need to see you actually see you. Therefore, it is reasonable to assume that if he indeed spoke with you, there was good reason, and so it would seem. I have become aware that none of your appearances in my time, or I suspect other times, are perchance coincidental. There is and I believe always will be a profound reason for all events that surround your movements.' She then seemed to think for a moment. 'When I saw you at the front of the house, it was clear that I was the only person who could see you, the waiter aside.'

'Since I spoke with him, and learnt the truth regarding Thomas, I have questioned my right to intervene. I now realise that I must tell you what I have learnt.' She hesitated, looked Meredith in the eyes, and said, 'He is a bad man. Not only is he a gambler and drinker, he murdered a young woman because she pushed him rejecting his amorous approach. The police disbelieved the evidence because the individuals relaying the events were of a lower standing. They, therefore, disregarded the truth, and instead believed Thomas's version, because, he was of a higher standing. A gentleman, hmm…'

'My goodness that suggests my instincts was correct.' She then frowned, and asked, 'how can we change today's events?'

Still feeling a little hesitant, Rebecca thought for moment. Finding reassurance that something would unfold, because it always did, she said, 'One thing is continually evident throughout my journeys, and you intimated towards this just now. One thing stands out through every passage I have made, be it to you and Millicent, or to other events in the history of this house. No matter how convoluted the situation, there has always been an agreeable conclusion. I am sure today will be no different.' Now focussed, she continued, 'if not, I have no doubt that I will return prior to today's events with a resolution to this problem. The one thing I have learnt from all my journeys is that there is always a just ending.'

'I have learnt to trust you my dear Rebecca. So, let us see what happens.' She then looked down, again clearly thinking deeply. 'My complex situation with Millicent's untimely death left me believing my fate was destined towards a sad conclusion. At the eleventh-hour, you appeared with a decree.'

'I know today's events are out of sequence with history. Therefore, I have no doubt today's marriage will not go ahead. I am sure at this point with the marriage being so close that all must seem lost. Remember, I can and will pop back here yesterday, or last week if needed,' she said, and holding Meredith's hand, laughed.

'You seem so assured, and I find that enviable. I am a mother in distress, and my anxiety is complex and overriding my ability to think clearly.' She took a deep breath. 'I said that I trusted you, and I do, so let us see how the day unfolds. Although fretful, I feel assured that if not this day, you will find an answer. As you said, you could return last week if needed.' She then smiled in a way that suggested she'd found comfort in her own words.

Rebecca squeezed Meredith's hand, suggesting they join the guests, and let the day unfold, again reassuring there will be an amiable decree.

As they approached the front of the house, Meredith was instantly in demand. Rebecca stood back aware that again she was largely invisible. Meredith, who was clearly conscious of Rebecca's position turned often and smiled. After a few minutes standing back and taking in the events, Meredith came over, pointed to a tall man in a silver top hat, and whispered, 'that is Thomas.'

He was standing with his back to them, and curious, Rebecca walked over to have a closer look.

Instantly, he turned to Rebecca and with a look of utter contempt, said, 'Do I know you from Liverpool?'

Taken aback, Rebecca breathed deeply, and answered, 'I do not think so.'

Sneering, and waving his arm, he said, 'you sound and look like familiar.'

Instantly, that brought out a side of Rebecca she rarely shows. Certainly, not since a guy at University had pushed her while she was waiting for food. 'Nope, not me, and stop sneering,' she growled, clenching her fists so tight it made her knuckles white.

He grabbed her arm, and pulled her off to one side.

Yanking her arm away, Rebecca said, 'Take you hands off me, or else.'

With a horrid, aggressive look, ha said, 'you are just a maid and you do as you are told.'

Almost on cue, two police constables walked in their direction.

'Thomas Mier, we are arresting you on suspicion of murder three years since in Liverpool. New evidence has come to light.'

Before the policeman could continue, he pushed one of them and turned away.

The two policemen grappled with him and in the ensuing fracas, the three men started to quarrel and fight. Thomas Meir tried to punch one of the policemen, and as he swung his fist, he caught Rebecca's nose with the back of his hand, knocking her unconscious.

CHAPTER 8 - BLOODY NOSE

Sitting up at the front of the house, Rebecca was instantly aware blood was streaming from her nose. Trying to regain her composure, she pinched her nose to stem the bleeding. Seconds later, her mum appeared from the front door.

'Oh Rebecca whatever has happened?'

With her thoughts going in circles, Rebecca realised she was back home. Still trying to regain her composure and reckoning it was best if she didn't mention what had just happened, she forced a smile. 'I tripped over and somehow banged my nose. I know there's a lot of blood, but I am okay, Mum.'

'Let's get you inside and cleaned up,' she said, helping Rebecca to her feet.

As she walked into the kitchen, her father looked up and frowned. The way he looked, she knew his frown was not because of her blooded nose. It was as if he knew something had happened. Showing his concern for her nose, he stood up, and asked, 'were you playing football with Thomas?'

'Honestly James, show a little more concern.'

'Mum, it's just a bloody nose. If I did play football with him, he wouldn't have much joy, and it would be him with the bloody nose,' she said, and laughed. Although it made her smile, her brain was still going in circles. Her consciousness was going back and forth between her struggles with Thomas, the possible ill-fated wedding, and knowing at some point, there was an impending journey to 1827. To compound her composure further, she was trying to appear normal to her parents.

While her mum cleaned her up, she could feel her dad looking at her with a magnified air of suspicion, almost as if he was waiting to get her on her own.

'Right, missy, you need to go and change those clothes. They'll need a good soaking.'

On the way upstairs, something occurred to her, and after changing, she opened the box containing Meredith's letter. Just as she did, there was a knock on the door. 'Come in, Dad.'

'How did you know it was me?'

'Who else knocks and besides, I could see the cat had your curiosity downstairs.'

He sat down next to her and asked, 'where this time?'

'In a minute, Dad, I need to look at something first.' She then opened Meredith's letter and started reading. Shaking her head, she handed the letter to her father and said, 'read the last paragraph.'

He started reading, and as he did, he kept glancing at Rebecca. 'This has changed, hasn't it? I am guessing this has something to do with today's events and your bloody nose.' He thought for a moment and said, 'I need to read this aloud to get it straight in my head.'

Finally, I have my daughter's marriage certificate from eighteen-fifty-eight to a gentleman named Joshua Elm. This marriage was possible only because of your timely intervention in eighteen-fifty-six. Everyone saw Thomas Mier's actions towards you, including two of the local constabulary. Indeed, he was taken to Liverpool directly by the police officers. On his return to court, a gentleman came forward with evidence. It resulted in his conviction for the murder of that poor girl two years earlier. As you said to me that day, there will always be a resolution, and so it proved. In addition, as we know, the individuals that need to see you can and that was, in reality, the scenario. I hope you were not too badly hurt when he punched you. Of interest, I assumed you returned to your time because in your place, a maid appeared. She was remarkably similar to you, and so no one took any account of the change. I cannot, and do not want to explain or understand what happens or happened. As you, I try to maintain a youthful outlook and only be surprised if I am surprised.

My daughter went on to have a happy life with Joshua, and between them, they had three beloved children. This was a credit to and as a direct result of your intervention. Rebecca's children loved her drawings and writings of fairies. I now know my dear future girl have those sentiments within you, although unlike my daughter, you have a yet greater vision. I am sure this letter may change often as events unfold.

We spoke of my beloved aunt, and you must now find your way to eighteen-twenty-seven. Be safe, be well, be happy, and continue to maintain openness towards your farsightedness.

'It has changed completely and Meredith is actually referring to your visit directly.' He shook his head, and said, 'I don't even know where to start.'

Rebecca explained, in detail, the events of the day, including the reason she needed to visit Meredith's aunt. Along the way, she tried to answer her father's many questions. There were times, when she simply didn't have an answer. Although she was frustrated by this, her father assured by pointing out how far she'd come since opening the boxes, and that in time, she will have a greater understanding.

'Good job it's your summer break, because you won't have time otherwise,' he said and laughed.

'Well, here's the thing, Dad, no matter how long I go for it turns out to be only a moment in our time.'

They then went through a few photos, while continuing to chat about pervious events. Before they knew it, supper was ready. Although Rebecca sat talking to her mum and dad about university, her mind kept returning to Meredith. At around ten, she made her excuses and headed off to bed. She lay there going through the events of the day, the changing letter. Often her thoughts deviated wondering if there was a limit to her journeys, where they could ultimately take her, and if they would ever end. She eventually nodded off with Meredith's words resonating in her thoughts, "only be surprised if you are surprised."

The following morning, she woke with her pillow, and hair caked in dry blood. Instantly the events of the day before filled her thoughts. Still trying to her head around how Meredith's letter had changed so dramatically, she started re-reading it, when her mum came in with breakfast.

'Rebecca, look at you. Come on, let's get you sorted,' she said, encouraging her from the bed.

'Mum, I am fine honestly. I just had to look at this...' she said and waved the letter.

After a shower, she changed the bedding, and went downstairs. She then spent the remainder of the day pottering around. On and off all day, she found herself wondering what was so urgent in 1827. That then started her speculating what kind of message Meredith's aunt had for her. She kept thinking that if it was that important, she should be getting an urge to return to the summerhouse. She wasn't feeling anything though, and at one point, started thinking she must have missed something.

This pattern continued for a few days. Often she chatted with her father, who reassured her that as with her previous journeys, the right time would manifest itself, as always.

With her father's words resonating in her thoughts, she sat on her balcony sketching. It was a delightfully calm warm day, and so she decided to head into the woods and sketch the area where she'd found the key. It was something she'd always planned on doing, but never got around to. *No time like the present*, she thought, and packed her art gear into a small rucksack.

On her way down stairs, she popped in to see her mum in the kitchen. Her mum was on the phone, and mouthed, 'two seconds.'

'Okay, let me speak with Rebecca, and I'll call you back in a moment.'

'Mum, I am going to the woods to do some sketching, are you okay on your own?'

'Actually, that was Amanda, and she is meeting up with Ruth in town and asked if we wanted to go.'

'I would love to, but I've been putting off sketching the area where I first found the key. And well, on a mission now.'

'That's okay sweetie. I thought I would offer. I reckon I should be back by five-ish.

'Okay mum, I will see you later.' The second Rebecca walked through the front door, memories of the first time her mum went out and left her alone flashed through her head. As she headed down towards the wood, in spite of those recollections fresh in her thoughts, there was nothing suggesting today would be anything other than just a normal day. She made her way slowly through the woods and on the way noticed a pathway she hadn't seen or been along previously. Deciding to go on a hunch, she followed it, wondering why she hadn't seen it in the past, especially as it was clear and well trodden. A little confused by this, she couldn't help questioning were it would lead her. Just as she was thinking it wasn't actually going anywhere, she noticed a wooden bench ahead of her. Looking at it, she thought, *just plain daft,* knowing she'd searched every inch of this wood and not seen this bench before.

As she approached the bench, she was aware there was something oddly familiar about this place. The bench sat beneath a huge oak, and the only time she'd seen an oak like this was when she was with Meredith. Somewhat puzzled, she sat down, looked around, tried to work out where she was, and if she'd missed something. It looked a little similar to the area where she'd found the key, but this oak was standing, and there hadn't been a sign of a bench. She looked across to the area where the young willows had swayed so engagingly, but in their place stood a huge red flowed rhododendron. Her thoughts returned to the time she and Meredith sat on a bench in these woods. Although this was similar, she was sure this was a different area and besides, this bench was much smaller. Still, all the time, something in the back of her thoughts was telling her she knew this place.

As she sat there contemplating her surroundings, she heard someone in the distance singing a nursery rhyme of sorts. The singing grew closer and as she contemplated this unfamiliar voice, a tall elegant woman, perhaps in her late teens, wandered across the opening. Carrying a bunch of wildflowers, the woman's long brown hair, rosy red lips, and bright blue eyes, radiated an extraordinarily individual demeanour. Although Rebecca didn't recognise this woman, there was an odd suggestion in the back of her thoughts, telling her she should know her. Rubbing her tingling arms, she wondered where she was, and how she'd gotten here, wherever this was. Again, thoughts of Meredith entwined with her already jumbled brain.

She didn't have to wait too long to find out who this was. The woman stopped singing, turned towards her, and beaming a vivacious smile, said with a graceful tone, 'You are my future girl, and I know you are. I have been waiting for you, forever.'

89

Instantly Rebecca knew this woman was Meredith's aunt. 'Hello, Rebecca. I am indeed your future girl, and I too am named Rebecca. I am the one you often speak of and no one believes in.'

'I believe in you, and I don't care what the others think. Those blinkered minds, with their lost vision and discarded innocence, can think what they want. I do not care what they think, because I know what I know. Unprejudiced open minds like ours can see the world with all its twists and turns. They see nothing; we see everything. I love to see the world the way I do, and know you do too.'

'You are right. I do too, and like you, I don't care what others think. Although, in my time the world is a little more accepting of diverse views, and opinions. I am allowed to see beyond the obvious, although sometimes it is met with resistance, but only because they are frightened to see.' Rebecca said, feeling an instant connection with this girl.

'You are lucky, my future girl. In my world, they frown upon me, call me names, and label me. They turn their back because I see the world through different eyes. They are the mad ones,' she said, 'not me.'

The girl sighed with so much pain and anguish it resonated through Rebecca's whole body. Hoping to offer her some comfort, she said, 'I met your niece, Meredith many years from now, and it was her who sent me to you. When I met her, she was an adult, whereas you know her only as a child. She believes you, trusts you, and loves you. I love her too, like a mother. She is my muse, my guardian angel.'

'I also love Meredith, and although she is young, she sees me for who I am. She is the only one who trusts me and doesn't see me as a fool. My heart is heavy, and my soul almost lost. She gives me strength to smile. I know that in the year next, banishment to a cheerless and lonesome existence in the Americas is the only way those around me can deal with my unfastened views. I am sorry for them because their minds are so closed, blinkered, and subjected to

90

onlooker's opinion. I am the mad daughter, and that is my name, to all except my blessed Meredith and you my future girl.'

Feeling this woman's pain, Rebecca stood and compelled to cuddle her, gestured with open arms. The girl responded immediately and squeezed Rebecca so tight. She could feel and hear her wretched soul's pain and anguish within her every move and through her every word. Holding the girl's hand tightly, she said, 'I believe you have something important to tell me.'

'I am okay now you are here,' she said, and again beamed a vivacious smile. 'I can tell of my burden and go forward from this day in peace.' She took a deep breath, and her sigh this time was one fuelled by relief. The building of this house and our subsequent existence are in jeopardy.'

'Even though Meredith had foretold of this message, hearing the words, still impacted on Rebecca. Now with mixed emotions, Rebecca just stood looking at this woman. Feeling her sadness, she found herself wondering if she could, should, or would be able to affect the future outcome for this poor soul.

'It is okay you know. I am destined to go to the Americas. It is part of the plan for me. In time, people will learn from me, and it will then make it okay for future girls, like you, to see beyond normality. Please do not try, or consider changing my destiny. I have accepted it, and so should you. It is, as I am, part of life's coil, as you are also.'

Listening to Meredith's aunt, she felt like this woman was reading her thoughts. 'Rebecca, how do you know all this, and how did you know what I was thinking? Importantly, where do you find peace?'

'In time, this will come to you. I have known of my foresight all of my life. You only became aware when you moved here. You have great capabilities within you that will become normality in time. Many will follow you and be stronger still. Don't ever question it, challenge it, or wonder why. Just accept it. This is how I find my peace.' Again, the woman smiled. 'Some days, even in your future time, people will point fingers, question your way, and consider you out of the ordinary. Let them, and do not care. Find your solace from within. I will be there with you, as will Meredith, through your every turn.'

As Rebecca listened to this woman, she could see why Meredith loved her with such passion. 'I have leant to just accept my life for what it is. On occasions, I find my thoughts confused, but the further I travel along my road, the greater my understanding. I actually embrace it, even when I am told I am dreaming,' Rebecca said, and again squeezed the woman's hand. 'I am lucky that I have found you, have Meredith. Both my parents believe in me too.'

'You are then, further than I hoped. There are many who are close to seeing the way we do. Sadly, life extinguishes their flame with an inflexible hose of exactness that comes with adulthood.'

'Wow, you see so much. I have a friend at University who can see further than most. Although, when I go too deep into her thoughts, I feel her closing down. I have often wondered about this, because she so desperately wants to open the door to her inner sanctum.'

'My society cannot deal with our vision. In your time, you are at the beginning of a new world where people are increasingly open to the likes of our kind. I suggest your friend perhaps had it drained from her when she was young. For you to help her find the way back to that door may be a long road, but will be worth the journey.' She then glanced down briefly, 'as with me, I am part of that journey. That is my peace.'

'My Father also had vision, which he allowed to seep away. My journeys rekindled his appetite. Although, I don't believe he was ever like us, even though his eyes are now fully open.'

'Like many, your Father perhaps had the ability to see beyond his year but allowed it to seep away. Many years after your existence, society, if it hasn't destroyed itself will see our kind as the future and embrace us. You will know all this in time as the doors will continue to open for you. Each time they do you will step forward.'

Again, Rebecca could see why Meredith loved this woman so dearly. 'I have learnt much from you. I will take you with me always within my thoughts. I am sad that I cannot change your destiny. I do respect your opinion towards your own existence, however…'

'I do not want to change my future, and I would not want you to either. My providence is set for me, and your appearance today is part of that destiny.' She then looked down briefly, 'I have just to tell you to find your way to the year sixteen-twenty-three. You must stop a group of workers who arrived on a ship in Liverpool docks. They carried, unwittingly, a plague that will abruptly end the building of the main house, and with it, potentially extinguish our existence. Go with my love and know Meredith, and I will be behind you one-way or the other, for always.' She looked beyond Rebecca, and pointed, 'your time with me is almost up. When you turn, the tree would have fallen, and you will be home.' She then held her arms out.

Rebecca cuddled her, and the tension and anxiety she felt earlier had vanished. She stepped back, looked this woman in the eyes, and said, 'I hope you feel Meredith's and my love, and take it with you always.'

'I do, and always have, and that is all I need. It is your time now, Rebecca. We won't pass again, but I have you now within my soul along with my beloved niece, Meredith.'

'I thank you for your strength, courage, and vision.'

'Go now,' she said, and pointed.

With a mixture of sadness and contentment, she smiled and turned. Before she focused, she turned back, but the woman had gone. Struggling to see through her tears, she could just make out the fallen oak. With jumbled emotions, she took a deep breath, knowing she was home.

CHAPTER 9 - INSIGHT

Rebecca sat on the old oak tree trying to unravel her feelings after meeting with Meredith's aunt. Knowing it was unlikely she would see this woman again left her feeling unusually sad. To compound her already strained emotions, were thoughts of this woman's forlorn existence. As she tried to gain comfort from Rebecca's words of assurance, she knew there was a path for her, and the first step had to be to the year 1623. As the sunlight faded, and long shadows changed the mood of this area, she decided it was time to head up to the main house.

She turned to walk away, and something caught her eye in the undergrowth. As she grew closer, a tingle ran up her back and down her arms. She stood and peered at a piece of white material lying among the nettles. As always, with no regard, Rebecca stuck her hand in and retrieved a silk hanky. Sewn in lilac silk thread was the words, *Carry this with you always, future girl, and I will be beside you. R.*

She held the hanky close to her face and could smell Rebecca's sweet baroque perfume. Somehow, this settled her mood and her anxiety towards this poor woman's existence took a different turn. Breathing deeply, she realised this woman knew she was a stepping stone in humanity's recognition of her type. With the hanky clasped in her hand, she headed back to the main house considering what this woman had said. Wondering what part she would play in all of this, she decided her first action should be to find her way to 1623. Although desperate to get on with it, she knew she couldn't force the issue, and instead had to wait for Meredith or perhaps the young Rebecca to lead the way.

Arriving at the front door, she realised she didn't have her keys and didn't have a clue where they were. Not having her phone with her either didn't help. Not knowing what the time was and not prepared to sit around waiting for her mother, she headed around the back to check the kitchen door.

'Locked,' she huffed, 'and that makes an annoying change.' She narrowed her eyes as a thought occurred to her. Returning to the front of the house, she wondered if not having her keys, and the back door being locked was part of a plan to get her back to the summerhouse. 'And maybe, sixteen-twenty-three,' she mumbled.

Just as she finished speaking, the front door opened and her mum's face appeared. 'You are still talking to yourself, I hear. And how does that go down at uni?' she said and chuckled.

As always, Rebecca was pleased to see her mum, but today more so. One thing she'd realised while speaking with the other Rebecca was how lucky she was to have a mother, who although found her stories difficult to accept, never criticized or ridiculed them. With this thought in her head, she gave her mum a cuddle.

'And what may I ask is that for?'

'Just always being my best friend, always prepared to listen, no matter how daft my tales are, and just always being you.'

'Rebecca, my dear, your tales are never daft, and don't ever think that they are. Anyone who suggests otherwise is well... daft.'

'Bless you Mother,' she said, wondering if she should tell her about the other Rebecca.

'Come and sit in the kitchen with me and let's chat. It is clear to me that you have a tale to tell. I am all ears, bit like Mickey,' she said, and again giggled in a way that always made Rebecca feel good.

'So, I thought you were going out with the girls, what happened?'

'I've been and come back. It is five and I was on my way to look for you. When I opened the door, there you were, with your face telling a thousand tales.'

'Oh right, well that's unusual,' Rebecca said, realising she'd been with Rebecca for the best part of four hours, and unusually that seemed to be four hours in her own time.

'What is unusual?'

'I don't actually know at this point,' she said, still wondering why she'd been gone so long. Especially as she'd only recently chatted to her dad about her journeys taking minutes, even though she'd been gone hours.

Her mum narrowed her eyes the way she often did and putting her arm around Rebecca, said, 'come in, and let's have a chat in the kitchen. It's about time you told me one of your tales. Of late, your Father gets all the details. I know they are a little more complex nowadays, but I am ready to listen. With no agenda, no dream suggestions, and besides, I am jealous.'

'Mum, thank you, and no need to be jealous. What I share with Dad is different to what I share with you. Dad has only recently smelt the coffee; you, on the other hand, have always made the coffee.'

'What does that even mean?' her mum asked, as she sat at the table, and pointed to the seat opposite.

'Mum, it means you have always, and will continue to be there for me, no matter what. Oh, and take your elbows off the table, there's a sweetie.'

Over the next hour, the two sat around chatting. Rebecca explained the situation with the other Rebecca as best she could. She was actually surprised how well her mum was taking it all. That was until she showed her the silk hanky. Although, her mum looked at it carefully, she could see her eyes flickering and knew she'd lost her for now at least.

'Hmm, very sad, and an intriguing tale, Rebecca,' she said, and glanced at the clock. 'My goodness, I need to get on with supper.'

During supper, Tommy's news dominated the conversation. The club had changed his status from YTS, to a full senior contract. Although James had been initially concerned by the money on the table, he had been reassured by the club that only an agreed amount would be available to Tommy, and the remainder be placed in a parent required access account. Tommy wasn't best pleased, but after a lengthy chat with dad and the club, accepted it was the right thing. Several times during supper, her dad had glanced at Rebecca with a knowing look on his face.

When he glanced at her for the nth time, she mouthed, 'I will tell you after supper.'

Later that evening, she went to study and explained that she'd had a chat with mum, and that she'd taken it really well until the hanky. She then told him all about her day with the other Rebecca. She spent a lot of time emphasizing Rebecca's suggestion that in time, society would see her kind as the future.

'Well that certainly puts a different perspective on things,' he said, clearly thinking. 'I read a book sometime back about an individual's spiritual path. At the time, I was wrapped up in my work, but even so, it kind of resonated with me.'

'What exactly did it say?'

'Well, it is only loosely connected. However, it was about seeing the world for what it is, judging people for who they are, rather than their possessions. I am skimming over a lot of it, but I have always been aware that you see the goodness in everyone. Sometimes not Tommy,' he said, and laughed. 'Importantly, you get your energy from the environment and then give that energy freely. I wonder if seeing your fairies and such like was just part of your transition. Ultimately, you were able to see the open door to Meredith and all that has followed.'

Delighted by her father's assuring words, she said, 'that is a very good way of looking at it, and one I hadn't previously considered.'

'I think it is exciting that she said you will learn so much more. Although, I do wonder how much more is there to learn.'

Rebecca nodded. 'I thought exactly that. What I am still struggling with is the idea that I have lived in the house always.'

'I have been thinking about that a lot and think I may understand a little.'

'Cat, curiosity, Dad,' she said, with her palms lifted.

'Well, stay with me on this. Perhaps your genetic spirit is so powerful that it passes from one Rebecca to the next. You know we talked about inheriting eye colour. Well maybe following on from that, each Rebecca inherits a gene so strong that they look, act, behave, and think similarly.' He narrowed his eyes, 'Although you said that Rebecca suggested it was only you two who could see the things you do.'

'Meredith's aunt said something along those lines. I assumed she meant the gene is passed from one generation to the next, which ties in with your idea.' Rebecca hesitated for a moment, considering her own words. 'Even so, how does that make it possible for me to jump back and forth between times?'

'This is just a hunch. Perhaps your genes are powerful enough for you to connect spiritually with the other Rebecca's, and or gene carriers, and their time zones. This then creates some kind of loophole back and forth.'

'That's pretty amazing, Dad. I can buy into that.' She then thought for a moment, and said, 'It would seem you carried the gene to me, and perhaps that is why you can see it all so clearly. And I might add, without a prejudiced opinion.'

'I have thought about your circumstance for a while, and hearing what Rebecca suggested validates my view. Your ability to intervene with potentially negative events in the past certainly would be a way for future societies to see your type as visionaries. Ultimately accept you for who you are, individuals who see the world through different eyes.'

'That's a really good way of looking at it, and one that helps me no end. So thank you Dad.'

They chatted for a little while longer, just covering the same ground. Eventually, Rebecca said, 'right, I must get some sleep as I have a long way to go tomorrow.'

Narrowing his eyes, he asked, 'long way, where to, dare I ask?'

'Well, four-hundred years, that far enough for you,' she said and giggled.

'Oh, going tomorrow are you, well make sure you get the builders to make the kitchen bigger, and maybe take a packed lunch.'

'Oh you make me laugh, Dad. Where have you been hiding for these last few years?'

Nodding, he said, 'behind a blinking financial wall.'

CHAPTER 10 - BOOKSHOP

The following morning, Rebecca woke with her father's words still echoing around in her head. Over the last few months, most of her time was consumed trying to understand the time-travel aspect to her journeys. The recent changes in Meredith's letter had just muddled her thoughts further. As she sat up in bed, she thought about her father's take on it all, and felt it offered up a view that made a lot of sense. Of late, she'd been examining every step with rational thinking and realised that had been closing her mind to the things she readily accepted as a 15-year-old. That common sense was making her focus on analysing everything, which was then making her to look in the wrong places, for the wrong answers. Even though she'd met Meredith twice and Rebecca, questions about its validity had burdened her openness. Even when she was telling her mum or dad about her trips, she'd always tried to find a rational answer, mostly for their benefit. This had infuriated her, to the point where she actually avoided thinking about it too often, and instead, averted her thoughts elsewhere. Between talking to Rebecca, and her father, she now had a clearer understanding, and felt somewhat relieved that it was no longer draining away at the back of her head.

On the way downstairs, she actually felt light headed. Gone were the question's nagging away in the back of her brain. Stopping by Meredith's painting, she whispered, 'I understand now, thank you.'

'Talking to yourself, or Meredith?' her mother called down the corridor.

'Meredith, and morning, Mother. Kiss, kiss, I am famished. Can I have one of those cooked breakfasts you do for Tommy?

'Thinking of taking up footie, are ya sis?'

'Yeah, might do actually; show you a trick or two. Seriously though, I am so pleased that I helped you become such a reasonable player.'

'Reasonable, hmm, well that's a step up from twit, I guess. And, how may I ask did you help me?'

'Being a moving target, that's all.'

'Yep, that's all you were. I guess I was a twit, and I might be sorry, but then again...'

Rebecca looked at her mum, and indicated towards Tommy with her thumb. 'I can hear someone speaking, but I don't recognise them at all.'

'I am not invisible.'

'Sorry dear Brother, I was just surprised by you being, err, nice ish.'

'Whatever,' he said, and headed down the hallway. 'Call me when brekkie is ready, Mum.'

'Please.'

'Sorry, please call me when breakfast is ready, dear Mother.'

With the sound of him thumping his way upstairs, Elizabeth said, 'I don't know what has changed. But changed he has.'

After breakfast, Rebecca asked her mum if she had any plans to see Ruth and Amanda.

'Well, as it is Saturday, and Tommy and your Father are going to football, why don't I give them a call?'

After a few minutes, she came off the phone. 'Right, all set and we are meeting them for lunch down by the river, just as we used to.'

'That will be brilliant; I am so looking forward to seeing them. It has been far too long, what with uni and so on.'

After she'd helped her mum clear away, they said their goodbyes and good lucks to Tommy and headed into town.

'I thought we'd come a little early so we can have a look for some new clothes.'

Rebecca narrowed her eyes, wondering why her mum would want to look for clothes without Amanda and Ruth. Following her mum down a narrow cobbled street, she was beginning to wonder where they were going. She was certain there wouldn't be a department store down here, but followed none the less.

'Here we are,' her mum said, pointing.

'Where are we, Mum?'

'I popped in this book shop last week with Ruth and well... just come in and have a look.'

'What's the deal with tiny doorways in these old buildings?'

As Rebecca entered the shop, her eyes immediately focussed on an elderly gentleman tucked away in the corner. He was dressed in a tweed jacket that had clearly seen better days. The shelves around him were packed full of dust laden books, and next to him were a couple that looked ancient.

Looking up, he said, 'hello, Madam. I knew you would be back, this must be your beautiful daughter,' he said as he lifted one of the books, and carefully placed it on the tiny counter. 'Sorry, not a lot of room in here, but plenty of well versed words. He chuckled, clearly delighting in his surroundings.

As Rebecca read the front of the book, her interest went up several notches. 'Look Mum, this book is titled, The Lakes, sixteen-hundred to sixteen-ninety-nine. This is just what I've been looking for ever since we moved here,' she said, and smiled at the man.

'I have also the seventeen-hundreds and the eighteen-hundreds. Sadly, after that it all went a little quiet. I guess money was the hiding truth.' He then lifted his head in a somewhat accepting, philosophical way.

Rebecca glanced between her mum, the books, and the elderly gentleman. 'I am lost for words. I have been chasing this history forever and found very little. This will answer so many questions.'

'Well, Madam.'

'Please call me Rebecca.'

'Well, Rebecca, as I said to your Mother last week, there is a lot pertaining to your house, certainly in its early years. It seems to go cloudy, shall we say, around twenty years after the house name changed to Elm Manor.'

Doing the maths in her head, Rebecca blurted, 'so that would be eighteen-seventy-seven, no eighteen-seventy-eight actually.' She then grimaced, and glanced at her mum.

'It is okay, Rebecca, he knows all about you.'

'It would seem you are unlike some of us, who are just carriers. You are the real deal.' He said and nodded. 'I have waited all my life to meet you. Sadly, I never married, and therefore my genes will drift away with me.'

Rebecca now had goose bumps on her goose bumps.

'It is okay, my dear Rebecca. You are learning still. You will find in the section marked eighteen-twenty-seven an entry from, coincidently,' he smiled in a way that suggested he knew more than he was letting on 'another Rebecca. I found it impossible to understand this the first time I read it. However, she tells of your visit to my shop. Not only that, even the date is correct.' He shook his head, 'sixth of August two thousand and thirteen. Therefore, by right, these are yours, and I have just been their keeper, awaiting your return. The one thing I ask is that you find some time to talk with me again.'

Unable to believe what she was seeing or hearing, Rebecca opened her mouth, but no words came out. She was aware he was staring at her so shook her head, and said, 'it would be a pleasure.' She thought for a moment, and realised this man may hold some of the answers she'd so long searched for. 'Finally, I get to talk to someone who isn't biased by opinion.' She then turned to her mother, and asked, 'does this gentleman know of my visits to Meredith and such?'

'He is aware that you have met with Meredith, and co.' Elizabeth shook her head, suggesting she was uneasy with what she was about to say. 'He already knew about your journeys when your Father told him all about them,' she said, and shook her head.

'So, Dad has met this gentleman, and knows about the book?'

'He does, and he said you would want to spend time speaking with Mr. Elm, as well as going through the books, in detail. Right, we need to go and meet up with the girls. Then after we can pop back here, pick up the books, and arrange for you to come and visit. Even better, perhaps Mr. Elm would like to come to ours,' she said, and glanced in his direction.

With her mouth open and her palm raised, Rebecca said, 'Mr. Elm. Mr. Elm. By any chance...'

'I am indeed, and we have much to talk about, Rebecca. I would love to visit my ancestors' home.'

'So, you are saying that you are related to?' Before she could finish, he nodded several times.

'Yes, I am indeed related to Joshua Elm, although it was a few generations back. Hey, there is far too much to talk about now. Go and meet your friends and then later we can arrange some time to talk. After all, I have waited for ever to meet you.'

Rebecca said her good-byes, and followed her mum towards the café by the river. With her thoughts all over the place, she walked along without saying anything, trying to take everything in.

'You are very quiet, sweetie, although I am not surprised,' she said, and smiled.

'I really don't know what to say. How long have you known, Mum?'

'Well Ruth likes an old book, and stumbled upon that shop a week ago. She rang me straight away, suggesting there were books that relate to the history of the area and may contain information about our house. Father and I popped in and spoke to Mr. Elm about the books. By chance, he overheard Dad referring to you as Rebecca.'

'So, then what happened, what did he say?'

'Well, he asked if your Dad had just said Rebecca. When we both nodded, he opened the book and showed us the entry made by another Rebecca. I don't know who was more shocked, the shopkeeper, or me. Your Father, on the other hand, took it in his stride, which helped me.'

'This really confirms everything, not that I was in any doubt, but...'
She then thought for a moment. 'Dad has been so comfortable
through all of this, and that has helped me massively.'

'It confirmed everything for me too. Like you, James's openness
has been brilliant. Mr. Elm suggested Dad was the carrier who passed
on the insight to you, if that is the right word. I am not too sure I
understand that yet, but I was a little jealous,' she said, and chuckled.

'Does Ruth know about all of this?'

'Well, here's the thing, your Father suggested we didn't tell her too
many details until we understand it better ourselves. It's not as if it's
an everyday happening, is it? She knows about the books obviously,
and how important they are, but we kept it at that, so when we meet
up...'

Rebecca nodded several times. 'I am actually pleased. I am not
altogether ready to talk to anyone other you and Dad about this. Even
my teacher at uni, Mrs. Pochard, who is into all this stuff, doesn't
know all the details.'

'Oh, look, there are the girls now,' her mum said, pointing.

Although she was delighted to see Amanda and Ruth, she was
finding it almost impossible to focus. The girls asked several times if
she was okay, to which she apologized. Her mum, clearly aware of
the reason for Rebecca's distance, made the excuse that she'd been up
late writing up a project for university. Oddly, this helped her focus
on the girls a little better.

'Oh really, what is that about?' Ruth asked, with Amanda nodding
in the background.

The way Ruth asked resonated with Rebecca, and realising she was
being unsociable, she responded with a big smile.

'Oh, back now are you, Rebecca,' Amanda, asked, 'I was wondering where my girl was.'

'I am so sorry, I have been so rude.' She squeezed Amanda's hand, and blew Ruth a kiss.

'And me, does your Mother get anything, or don't I count,' she said, and giggled in that delightful way, that she seemed to do so often of late.

'Mum, you are always at the top of my list.'

'I know, it's okay, I do know and have always known,' she said, and squeezed Rebecca's hand.

So, I was working on...?' Rebecca said, and proceeded to make up a water-fairy story as she went, all the time thinking she was actually going to write it down when she got home.

On the way home, again Rebecca was quiet in the car. She then noticed her mum glancing at her at every set of traffic lights.

'Mum, can I ask how you felt when you and Dad saw the entry in the book?'

'Well, initially, I felt a little uneasy. Dad noticed this, and reassured me by saying he felt the same, and it was to be expected. He said that the whole notion was beyond any reasonable thinking. He also said something about the most open of minds would laugh this off as ridiculous.' She then nodded several times. 'Mr. Elm said that the first time he read the book, even though he believes in all this stuff, he ignored it. Evidently, he read it a few times and in the end considered it irrational and improbable or words to that effect. Somehow, this helped me. I guess knowing I wasn't on my own, kind of, I don't know, maybe...' she said, and shrugged her shoulders.

After supper that evening, Rebecca decided to go to her room, sit on the balcony, watch the sun set, and write up her water fairy story.

Over the next couple of days, she became so engrossed in her new story that she spent most of the day sitting on her balcony working her way through her tale. She stopped every now and then to give her mum an update on the water-fairies underwater village and have something to eat.

'I don't know where you get your ideas from Rebecca. Can I ask you something?'

'Of course, why do you need to ask?'

'I am struggling to get this business about carriers straight in my head. What do you make of it all?'

'My understanding, and I struggled with this too at first, is that there are many who carry the gene that I evidently have. They then pass it on to their children who just don't quite have the makeup, or ability to understand how to interpret it, or use it. There are many who come close, but they sit on the edge of understanding it.' She thought for a moment, and continued, 'I think most that carry the gene are able to see what they are capable of when they are young. However, as they become older, peer pressure, or blinkered adults chase it away. I have said it before; adults fill children's heads with ideas of fairies, and then extinguish those thoughts with adult reasoning. As the child grows up, they don't know what to think and end up closing their eyes to what potentially lies in front of them. Or maybe what could lie ahead of them'

'I get that, and it actually helps me a lot.'

'I think many children have it within them to see whatever they want to see, and that includes the fairies, but adulthood frightens the fairies away.'

Nodding several times, she asked, 'So, have you thought about going to see Mr. Elm?'

'Yeah, every minute of every day.'

'So, why don't we go today?'

'Love to, Mum.'

'Okay, get yourself ready, and we can spend the afternoon there, and then meet up with the girls after for dinner. Tommy and your Father are at footie tonight, so…'

The two headed into town, parked by the river, and made their way up to the bookshop.

'I called Ruth and Amanda while you were getting ready, and they said they would love to meet up. Amanda suggested a new Thai restaurant in town that's been getting rave reviews. Fancy that?'

'Brilliant, what time, Mum?'

'I suggested about 6pm, give us plenty of time in the bookshop.'

Rebecca stood outside the shop, and glanced at her mum. For some reason, she was feeling a little apprehensive, and it was similar to the feeling she gets whenever she is going on another jaunt. She then shrugged her shoulders back and opened the door.

'Hello, I have been expecting you two, Rebecca, Elizabeth. How are you both?'

'Excited, apprehensive, and…'

'It is to be expected, Rebecca. This day is perhaps the start of a new dawn for you, certainly in understanding your abilities, vision and what may lay ahead of you.'

'That is exactly what excites me and makes me feel a little apprehensive, I guess.'

'Well, I don't intend to influence you in any way, just help a little along the way.'

'Rebecca, I am going to pop to the department store to pick something up for Amanda. I will be back in a while. It will give you some time alone with Mr. Elm.'

'Are you sure, Mum? I am happy if you stay here with us.'

'It's what I want to do, Rebecca. I think it is better all around, and then you can tell me all about it later. I am a way behind you on understanding this journey you're on and will end up asking lots of questions.'

'Okay, Mum, see you in a while,' she said and waived her mum good-bye. She then turned back to Mr. Elm, and still feeling a tad uneasy, said, 'So, best we start.'

He smiled and nodded in a way that oddly reassured Rebecca. 'Indeed. Okay, to start with I have a few things I need to explain to you. In your absence, I ventured a little further and came across a book of prophecies dating back to the twelfth-century. It is written with a mixture of Anglo English, French, and Latin, and that alone makes it a sketchy at best.' He then seemed to consider his next words.

'This sounds interesting, but how does it relate to me?'

'It actually relates to your kind, rather than you as an individual.' He nodded, 'please stop me if I go too quickly.'

'I'm with you so far, and am now kind of excited, because I have looked forever to find something like this.'

'Firstly, the book refers to your gene strain, although it doesn't use those words, and explains that many individuals have it within them. However, most close their eyes to it, and instead rationalise it until it fades.' He smiled again, and nodded before continuing. 'Now, obviously I am using modern-day language to explain this, and you must therefore accept my translation.'

'I realised that and it is just fine. Please don't feel there is a need to explain,' she said, actually smiling inwardly, thinking *oh do get on with it.*

He smiled again. 'Some pages later, it goes further and suggests that it is mostly women who have the ability to see beyond their current life. By that, I understood it to mean backwards in time, as you have. Then it gets very interesting and there is a distinct change in direction, for some that is.'

Shaking her head, Rebecca asked, 'I am not sure I understand that bit. Would you explain a little further?'

'Well, this came as a surprise to me, as I have always had an open mind.' He looked down at a piece of paper with some scribbled notes. He then looked up and nodded. 'The further section refers to some whose gene is so strong it can pass from one to the next without a bloodline. I guess like a soul or spirit. Now this bit I found most peculiar, it refers to your name, in both forms Rebecca, and Rebekha.'

'Well the name thing can be explained as Rebecca is one of the oldest Christian girl's names, so no real surprise there.' Even though, she'd found a rational answer, the idea still caused a tingle in her brain.

'Shaking his head, he said, 'no, it seems to refer to you. It says in the twenty-first-century, a Rebecca will arrive and her gene will be the strongest yet. She will have the ability to manifest herself back to every individual gene carrier who had borne her name or the gene.

She will also have the capacity to see forward to those yet born. She will be the one who changes everything.'

'Well my father and I have chatted so often about this and tried to understand everything, but could only apply guesswork. Whenever we used rational thinking, it took us down blind alleys. What you are saying has some rationality to it but at the same time is way to the left.' She shook her head, 'not sure that many would see it as balanced thinking.'

'This is it though my dear, you can and maybe will change the way people see your type. It would seem you have it all.'

'What do you mean, have it all?'

'The ability to see and go backwards in time, but also forward.'

'Hmm, I have only seen back... hang on, I have been forward, just no one could see me,' she said, feeling a tingle run up one arm and down the other.

'I do not have any answers or explanations for you, only what I have translated and interpreted. However, I would suggest it would be quite improbable that those yet to be born would be able to see you. I also suspect the impact of your involvement in their time could have severe consequences.'

Rebecca nodded, having totally understood his perspective.

'So, I would suggest, you are very much at the beginning of your adventures. May I ask if we move on, Rebecca? I have something very pressing I must show you, and it would be prudent to do so before your Mother returns.'

'Yeah, that's just fine,' she said nodding several times.

He then lifted two of the old leather books onto his desk, and opened them both at the same page. 'These books both refer to the years sixteen-hundred through to sixteen-ninety-nine. The first fifty-seven pages are the same. They then change and go in a completely different direction.'

'I am not sure I understand what you mean.'

'I didn't understand either at first, although I believe I do now. The best way I can explain it, is to suggest they offer up two alternate parallels, or maybe continuations of life in this area.'

'Wow that is a bit extreme. However, I guess no more so than my ability to go back and forward in time,' she said, and laughed feeling a little uncertain.

'He glanced up at the clock, and said, 'we must press on. The books are the same until the year sixteen-twenty-three.'

'I know this year, there was a plague, or possible plague carried in on a ship that arrived at Liverpool docks around that time.'

'There was indeed, and if that plague is not stopped, it will change the whole destiny of this area, yours and my existence, and all the people we know. In essence, all that we know changes.'

'I was told by Meredith and her aunt that I had to go back to this year, intervene, and somehow stop the workers arriving in this area.'

'You know all you need to know then. The two versions of the book run right up to the late eighteen-hundreds and are so very different beyond the plague. One is the life we know and the other is... Let's just say dissimilar.'

Seconds later Elizabeth walked in.

'Ah, Elizabeth, perfect timing. We have just finished our chat.'

'Hello Mum. How was shopping?'

'Good actually, I managed to get myself a new pink dress.' She then glanced at her watch. 'We are meeting up with the girls in half-an-hour, so if you are done, maybe we could head over.'

Rebecca turned towards Mr. Elm.

'We are indeed finished, for now at least. Rebecca, it has been a pleasure speaking with you today, and I do hope we can chat again.'

'Thank you so much Mr. Elm, it has been an enlightening pleasure. I do also hope we meet up again very soon. I will act upon your words.'

On the way to the restaurant, Elizabeth asked Rebecca about her chat with Mr. Elm. She then asked her what she had meant when she'd said she would act upon his words.

'Mum, it was nothing really; just he mentioned something he had found in one of the books and suggested I looked it up on the Internet.'

'Well, it sounded more important than that,' she said and narrowed her eyes it that familiar way.

CHAPTER 11 – RIGHT MARRIAGE

After a late night out with her mum and the girls, Rebecca woke bleary eyed. Moments later, her mum walked in with toast and orange juice.

'How are you sweetie, hang over from your one and only cocktail?' she said and giggled.

'Bit groggy, Mum, but fine, ish.'

'You didn't say much last night about your meeting with Mr. Elm. How did it go?'

Still trying to understand all she'd heard in the bookshop, Rebecca wasn't ready to talk about what she'd learnt. She knew at some point she would be ready to discuss it all, but right now, she was still trying to get all the information straight in her head. 'Yeah it was fun looking through the books that related to the sixteen-hundreds, although it didn't say an awful lot about this house, certainly nothing we didn't already know.'

'Oh, I was under the impression he had a lot to show you.'

'Well he did show me some information that related to the house being built in sixteen-twenty-three, and we spent most of our time looking at that section within the book. We briefly went through some other aspects, but didn't have enough time to go into detail.'

'Oh, I see, well I am sure there is more awaiting you.'

After a shower, Rebecca headed downstairs to join her mum in the kitchen. When she walked in, her mum was on the phone.

She turned to Rebecca with an odd expression on her face, and lifted her hand in a questioning manner. 'Hang on a tick, Ruth. Rebecca, I know this is a daft question, but we did go to the book shop yesterday, didn't we?'

Shaking her head, and with the curious cat calling her, Rebecca nodded, and mouthed, 'Why?'

'I will tell you in a minute. Yes Ruth,' she said, returning her attention to the phone, 'we did go yesterday. I will have a chat with Rebecca and call you back.'

'Mum?'

Raising her eyes, Elizabeth said, 'Ruth walked past the bookshop this morning on her way into town, and it wasn't there.'

'What do you mean, it wasn't there,' she asked, with her head going in circles.

'Ruth said that there was no sign of the shop, the old man, or the books. "Greyed out windows and the door boarded up" is what she said. That was it.'

'That's plain daft. He couldn't have cleared all that lot out over night.' Rebecca shook her head, 'unless there was a fire in the shop,' she said a shivered. 'We need to go and check.'

'Let's go now; I need to change my pink dress for a smaller size.'

On the way to the car, Elizabeth called Ruth and arranged to meet her outside the bookshop. When they arrived in town, they met her in the car park and headed for the shop.

'See,' Ruth said, pointing, 'it actually looks like it's been empty for ages.'

Rebecca stood outside shaking her head, at a complete loss as to what to say or think. She looked at her mum and Ruth, who both looked equally puzzled.

'Let's ask next door, and see if they can shed any light on the matter.'

'Good idea, Ruth,' Rebecca said, pushing at the front door of the coffee shop. Rather than just asking about the book shop, she reckoned it would be polite to have a coffee while they were there. 'Mum, Ruth, fancy a coffee while we are here?' They both nodded. 'I'd like two cappuccinos and an iced latte please.' Shaking her head, still unable to believe what happened to the bookshop, she asked, 'the old bookshop next door, did anything happen?'

'I am not sure I know what you mean, Miss,' said a tall Italian sounding elderly man.'

'Sorry, I didn't explain my question very well. Did anything happen in the bookshop last night?'

'I am still at a loss, Miss. There hasn't been a bookshop next door for many years.' He turned and shouted, 'Maria,' and then said something in Italian.

A woman's voice called back, again in Italian.

'My wife, Maria, said it is ten or more years since Mr. Elm died and there hasn't been a bookshop there since.'

With her mouth open, Rebecca turned, looked at her mum and Ruth, and lifted her hand. Although she wanted to say something, no words came out.

'Ruth smiled at the man, as he placed the coffees down, and said, 'Thank you for the coffee. We thought the bookshop was there recently, obviously not,' she handed over some cash, 'keep the change.' Turning to the girls, she said, 'let's sit in the corner by the window and have our coffee.'

As they sat down, Elizabeth said, 'Wonderfully amazing if you ask me.' She seemed to think for a moment, and said, 'although, that's par for the course with you Rebecca.' She then smiled, but couldn't hide her bewilderment.

Rebecca could see her mum was ruffled. 'You are right, Mum it is amazing. I have learnt to expect the unexpected since we moved to our house, what with Meredith, and so on.' She reckoned it might be time to tell the story Mr. Elm had shared with her yesterday. She was now beginning to wonder if the shop was there just to make sure she went back to the sixteen-hundreds. Over the next hour, another coffee, and the most delightfully light Cassatta, Rebecca explained all she had learnt in the bookshop, including her impending jaunt to the sixteen-twenty-three. Ruth asked several questions, and seemed to be accepting everything in her stride. However, her mum, although listening, only nodded, and occasionally forced a smiled of sorts. Although Rebecca wanted her mother to be engaged, she knew it would take time and was happy with her just listening.

Just as Rebecca was about to ask her if she was okay, Elizabeth said, 'Well that's it, we have no choice other than to accept the whole thing, no matter how outrageous, or irrational it may seem. It will always be madly bizarre, but I now know it is real, if that is the right word. I am actually looking forward to seeing where it takes you next. I am now wholly on board, Rebecca,' she said, and nodded several times while gripping Rebecca's hand. 'It has taken me a long time to accept everything, but with all this evidence, it would be foolish to ignore it or dismiss it out of hand. The bookshop disappearing, Mr. Elm passing away ten years ago, even though we spoke with him yesterday, is all the evidence I needed.'

'Me too,' Ruth said, 'it is a remarkable series of events for you Rebecca. No matter how incomprehensible it may seem, it is a journey that we can, and will continue to learn from.'

'I guess what I am most bothered by is that I didn't find out anymore from him.' Hearing her own words, although disappointed, Rebecca realised she had probably learnt all she needed to. 'Mr. Elm and Meredith both told me that in time, society would learn to accept my kind and see us as the future. As you said, Ruth, learn from it.'

'What does that even mean?' Elizabeth asked.

'Well, the way I understood it, is that I am just the beginning and many more people with this fantastically bizarre ability to travel, for want of a better choice of words, will follow in my steps. I was told that people in the future would have a greater control over their ability to see beyond their years. I know that I have a better grip compared to the first time I met Meredith. I am certainly more relaxed when the unexpected happens. For sure, I am still a little uneasy, but I settle down a whole lot quicker now.' She thought for a moment as something occurred to her. 'Just thinking out loud here, if I do go back to sixteen-twenty-three and change events for the better, I could also go into the future and change potential disasters.' A chill went up her spine, as her words triggered memories of the incident with her mother and the boiler.

As James and Tommy were again at football, the girls decided to have another evening out, this time in their favoured Italian restaurant. On the way home, Rebecca fell asleep in the car, and woke just as they pulled across the gravel drive.

With her head thumping, Rebecca said as she entered the house, 'Ouch, my head hurts. That is the last cocktail I am having, it's mocktails in the future for me.' She then kissed her mum good night and headed upstairs.

Half way up the stairs, she called out to her mum. 'It is madness mum, bookshops don't just disappear.'

Her mum stood at the bottom of the stairs appearing a little vague. She seemed to think for a moment, and said, 'I think the thing that I struggled with most is that Mr. Elm died ten years ago, and yet we saw him yesterday. I guess it is a bit like you seeing Meredith the first time, and she died over a hundred years ago.'

She nodded, 'good way of thinking about it, Mum,' she said, and headed upstairs, pleased with her mother's improved acceptance and understanding of events.

The following morning she woke to the sound of her mum opening the balcony door. 'I am never drinking again,' she said, rubbing her forehead. 'Bit like boys if you ask me, give you a head ache.'

Her mum narrowed her eyes, 'boy friend on the scene?'

'No, Mum. Well only a guy at uni who I went for a coffee with on a kinda blind date that Roxy set up.' She then raised her eyebrows. 'He was a twit and probably always will be.'

Over the next two days, Rebecca, her mum, and dad, talked a lot about Mr. Elm along with the bookshop's disappearance. On the third day, they all met up with Ruth in a café in town. Having considered every reasonable aspect relating to Mr. Elm and the bookshop, they all agreed there was no rational explanation. Her mum, who suddenly seemed remarkably relaxed with the whole concept, again suggested it was par for the course. Just as her mum finished speaking, an idea popped into Rebecca's head.

'Mr. Elm said he was a carrier, and that he wasn't like me. Perhaps he was like me after all, and could actually travel backwards and forwards in time. He could have manifested himself into our time, just to speak with us. I guess conceivably he could have been here offering some kind of reassurance that this journey I'm on isn't so mad.' She shook her head, but that doesn't explain how the bookshop would have suddenly been full of books.' This then reopened her memories of her mum and the boiler incident. Thinking about it, she realised the bookshop was probably no different in that it appeared purely to send her a message of sorts. 'I guess there will never be a rational answer to any of this, and we have to accept it for what it is. At least now, we all know it's real, and maybe that is why Mr. Elm appeared in our time.'

'That's a reasonable conclusion, Rebecca.' Her dad glanced toward the others and said, 'I must say, it's been a long time since any of us have doubted, or questioned your adventures. The bookstore appearance, as bizarre as it is, just affirmed all we knew. It is unbelievable, but it happens and we have to accept it for what it is.'

'Thanks, Dad. I need to hear that every now and then. It helps me to focus and comprehend what's going on. Perhaps I should say it helps me accept it for what it is, an unbelievable, nonetheless, tangible series of events.'

'Your Father is right, sweetie. We all know and accept the reality of this amazing adventure of yours. Only yesterday, Ruth was saying how difficult this must be for you, and that we all need to support you.'

She held her mum's hand, and gave it a squeeze. 'Thanks Mum, Ruth, and you Dad.'

'I think that Mr. Elm was here to reassure you, but also to make sure you continue onward. Thinking about everything he told you would suggest you have an important role in helping society to accept your kind as a way forward.' Her dad seemed to be thinking deeply, then looked up, and said, 'Perhaps, in time there will be no limits for you and what you are capable of achieving.'

Rebecca nodded several times. 'I get that, Dad, especially if I could travel into the future. It is frightening to think that I could actually prevent a war or something like that.' She then considered her own words, sending a tingle up her back. 'Crumbs, that alone would be a good enough reason for Mr. Elm to visit our time.'

On the way home, they chatted about the bookshop, Mr. Elm, and Rebecca's part in all of this. Having thought too much about what may be ahead of her, Rebecca's head was at bursting point. However, as she opened the front door and saw Meredith's painting, she found comfort knowing this lady would guide her forward.

The following morning, she joined her mum, dad, and Tommy outside for breakfast.

'Morning, sweetie, how did you sleep, considering yesterday's events?' her mum asked with a relaxed tone.

Taken aback and still getting to grips with her mum's obvious acceptance of her situation, she smiled and nodded. 'Yeah, great actually, thanks, Mum.'

'Mum, ask her,' Tommy said, pulling at Elizabeth's sleeve.

'Tommy, you're too old to be pulling on my sleeve. Besides, you ask her.

'Bex.'

'What?' she said, and glared at him, then grinned.

'Umm, I am playing in a football tournament in Belgium next week. Do ya fancy coming? Mum and dad are,' he said, with the most annoying grin on his face.

Instantly, Rebecca's brain went into overdrive. Although she was proud of the twit, the thought of a week watching him play football was a step too far. 'Would love to, but I have a university project that has to be submitted in ten days.'

'Oh that's a shame,' her father said, with a knowing look on his face.

'Will you be okay all alone, sweetie?'

'Yeah, Mum. I will ask Roxy over for a few days as she is doing the same work,' she said, while kicking her father under the table.

'Oh, okay. Well we are due to leave later this afternoon. Are you sure you're okay with this, Rebecca.'

'Mum, I am twenty in a few weeks. In Meredith's time, I could have been married with two children.' She then turned to Tommy. 'Are you okay Tommy, me not coming along. I will be thinking of you and cheering you on.'

'What's she on about, Mum, and who is Meredith?' Tommy asked appearing blank.

'Just the woman in the painting, nothing for you to worry about, Tommy,' her mum said, and glanced at Rebecca.

'Bex, it's all cool, just don't cheer too loud, and embarrass me again,' Tommy said and laughed.

The morning seemed to drag by for Rebecca as she pottered about in her room, pretending to work on a project. Around one in the afternoon, her mum popped into her room.

'We are off now, sweetie. I could see in your eyes, the last thing you fancied was a week of football, but the least you can do is come down and wish him luck.'

Turning away from her laptop, she said, 'I know, Mum. And thanks for not letting on in the kitchen.' She then followed her mum downstairs.

As she was waving good-bye, the car window opened. Her mum leant out, and said, 'please, Rebecca, be careful if you go anywhere.' She then nodded knowingly. 'Call Ruth if there are any issues.'

'I will, Mum, and thanks. Have fun,' she said, and blew everyone a kiss. 'Tommy, do well, although you always do.'

On her way inside, she looked at Meredith's painting, and mumbled, 'where next?' Although she knew 1623 was on the agenda, there was this weird feeling nagging at her thoughts, suggesting something else was afoot.

There was no answer, there never was, but it made her feel better. On her way upstairs, she started getting an odd sensation that was all too familiar. 'That's was quick,' she mumbled. She went up to her room, closed the laptop down, and went outside on the balcony. Glancing towards the summerhouse, it looked oddly different, but for the life of her, she didn't know why. *Right, better go and investigate,* she thought.

As she opened her bedroom door, she could hear music. *Odd,* she thought, *don't think mum left the radio on.* Just as she was thinking it, she got a most peculiar sensation that sent a shiver the entire length of her body. She closed her eyes, and rubbed the back of her neck. She gasped, as her fingers touched what felt like lace. With her eyes still closed, she turned towards the full-length mirror outside her room. With every part of her body tingling, she slowly opened her eyes.

In place of her jeans and tee shirt, was a shimmery, full-length lilac dress. She stepped up close to the mirror, looking herself up and down. Although feeling a little edgy, she realised she was possibly back in Meredith's time. From her previous wedding visit, she recognised this style of dress, with its high lacy neckline, nipped in waist, and long flowing hemline. She smiled to herself, thinking how girly she looked. She then glanced down at her feet, and instead of her pumps, were a beautiful pair of delicate, lilac satin shoes.

'Don't look half-bad, if I say so myself,' she mumbled.

'Are you talking to yourself again?' a voice asked from Tommy's room.

'Yes I was, Meredith,' she said, instantly recognising this familiar voice.

'I knew you would be here for this day,' Meredith said, as Rebecca opened the door.

She smiled, thinking how much better the room looked without Tommy's football posters. She went over to Meredith's open arms and cuddled her. 'Wedding day, I suspect by this regalia,' she said, and held Meredith's hand, while admiring her dress. 'You look so beautiful, Meredith, but then you always do.'

'So do you my dear Rebecca, which makes a pleasant change from the usual farm style attire you are more often than not wearing.'

'Umm, err,' she muttered.

Beaming a smile, she squeezed Rebecca's hand, and said, 'some things never change, umming and erring as you always do. I would not have you any other way, and have missed your distinctive choice of language.'

'I do have an excuse though. There I was in my bedroom, minding my own business, when boom, I am back with you, wearing this dress. You said you knew I would be here today. So, why am I here?'

'Due to your favourable intervention, my Rebecca is marrying Joshua Elm this very day. The man she was to marry two years since is in prison, rightfully so. I would suspect that you are here, as a guest today. This I surmise from your apparel, and I suggest all will see you this day. You, I am sure, will consider your words carefully, and be mindful of others interpretation.'

'I will,' she said and nodded. Then in an attempt to reassure Meredith, she said, 'I will carry forward, with pertinent wherewithal, considering my expressions carefully, thereby avoiding disconnection with the guests.'

'Well said, my dear Rebecca. Shall we join the other guests? On the way, you can enlighten me with all that has occurred since our last encounter.'

On her way downstairs, Rebecca explained the sequence of events, and all that had happened right up to and including the bookshop.

'I would suspect, Mr. Elm was there, as you suggest, purely as a reassuring presence. I would also consider there was an advanced pressing reason for his timely intervention.'

'I did consider this myself, and believe it is to ensure that I go to sixteen-twenty-three, the time of the plague.'

As they arrived at the foot of the stairs, amid a multitude of beautifully dressed guests, Meredith turned to Rebecca, nodded, and smiled. She then turned to an elderly gentleman and said, 'Aha, here is Mr. Elm senior. Let me introduce you. Mr. Elm, this is my niece, Emilee. She has travelled from afar this very day, specifically for the wedding of your grandson to my beloved daughter, Rebecca.'

The tall, silver-haired gentleman bowed, and offered his hand. 'Emilee, it is a pleasure to meet with you on this fine day. I thank you indeed for the long journey you have undertaken to be here this day.'

The best way she knew how, Rebecca curtsied. She took Mr. Elm's hand lightly, and said, 'I declare that my journey for this day is insignificant aligned with the merriment that I will gain from being here.' She then smiled inwardly, pleased with her first encounter. Looking at this man, and seeing his remarkable similarity to the man in the book shop, further stirred her already stimulated senses.

As she moved from one guest to the next, she found herself enjoying picking her words carefully and the subsequent positive reaction she was getting.

Meredith introduced her to several more guests, and then turned to Rebecca, and indicated that she needed to go and join her daughter. She squeezed Rebecca's hand tightly, and said, 'I need not have concerned myself with your choice of words, dear Rebecca. You have handled yourself delightfully, befitting of your charming character. While I am with my daughter, please feel at home, and embrace all that this day brings. Importantly, know it has only been possible because of your intervention.'

'Before you go, Meredith, may I ask you something?'

'Why of course you can, please ask anything of me.'

'All of my previous visits have been for a reason. Do you believe this is the case today? Alternatively do you, like me, believe I am here to witness your daughter's wedding and only this?'

'I have asked myself this many times, even before you arrived at my door this very day. I have considered the justification of your presence, and believe, as with the bookshop, it is purely to help you understand and accept this journey you are on.'

'I did wonder about that, and I came up with the same reasoning.'

'I suggest today is purely to show you what you are capable of, and the influence can and will continue to have. The guests here are mere mortals. You, however, are from an elevated level of consciousness.'

'To me, you are more than a mere mortal, Meredith.'

She nodded, smiled, and said, 'in the scheme of life, and all its turns, we are just that. You however, are the way forward. You will grow, and become stronger with every turn. I have seen such change within you since our first encounter. I believe there will be many events for you that will help you grow further still. There is a lot in front of you. Go, and delight in today's proceedings, and be assured, I will never be far from your side.'

Rebecca enjoyed the remainder of the afternoon and stayed focussed on her new vocabulary. Choosing her words carefully, she occasionally pitched in the odd modern word just to see what reaction she would get. At three in the afternoon, it would seem her day was culminating in the wedding of Meredith's daughter.

After a delightful wedding service, she sat back in her chair, considering everything, and kept asking herself why she was still there. Just as she was thinking there might be more to come, Meredith approached her.

'Hello my dear Rebecca. I hope you have enjoyed this day. I am a little surprised to see you still here.'

'That is exactly what I was just thinking,' she said, and narrowed her eyes. 'Hmm, I wonder.' Just as she said it, a scruffy man came over. Just as he was about to speak, two smartly dressed, burly men hurriedly approached them and gripped the frail, bedraggled man by the arm.

'You need not be here Mr. Smith, and this we told you an hour since.'

As they were about to lead him away, Meredith intervened. 'It is okay. He is here to speak with my niece and me. We have already approved this.'

One of the men, bowed, and said, 'I am sorry Madam. We know this man as a vagabond from the village, and believed he had no part here.'

'It is okay, please be assured.'

As they left, Mr. Smith, with his bedraggled appearance ruffled further, turned to Rebecca. 'Ya know me son Richard, and spoke with him at last failed wedding two years since.'

Rebecca nodded, and said, 'I do know him well.' Aware this man was still occasionally looking over his shoulder, she said, 'it is okay for you to be here, and they will not trouble you again.' With her head now jumping from one idea to the next, she took a deep breath. Realising that this might be why she hadn't gone back to her own time, she asked, 'Is there a problem with Richard?'

'Miss, he is ill, and cani get from his bed. We cani afford to see a doctor.'

Rebecca turned to Meredith and lifted her hand.

'My doctor is present as a guest. I am sure he will tend your son.'

'Fanks Misses,' he said through his tear-covered lips. 'Can we's go to him now. I am sorry I 'ad to see you Miss, there was no one else.'

Meredith turned to Rebecca and said, 'I will take you to Dr. Darroch and we can ascertain if he is free and will oblige.'

After a lengthy discussion, the doctor agreed that he and Rebecca would go to the aid of Richard. On the way to the doctor's carriage, he explained that there had been a diphtheria virus around the town since March, and the physicians locally had found it virtually impossible to treat.

Immediately, Rebecca's head started jumping ahead of her, knowing there was a relatively straight-forward treatment commonly available in her time. She instantly recalled a project at school that she'd completed about such viruses, including a lengthy section that focussed on the impact such infections had on small farming communities. She had particularly enjoyed this subject and established that with the increased availability of penicillin in the nineteen-twenties, the problem disappeared virtually overnight. She reckoned her visiting with the doctor would only serve to make sure Richard was constantly rehydrated. She was now certain the wedding was a roundabout reason for her presence, and so considered her next move carefully. In the back of her head, she could visualise some unopened penicillin antibiotics sitting on the table in the kitchen. They were intended to be for a cough that her father had. As always, he had refused to take them, suggesting fresh air was the best solution. 'How do I get those,' she mumbled.

'I am sorry Miss, did you say something?'

'No, no, just mumbling, sorry.'

As the doctor spoke, she started wondering if it was right for her to introduce a tablet that wasn't due for general release for another seventy years. More so, she didn't have a clue how she would get them to Richard. Just as she was thinking this, Meredith came over.

'Dr. Darroch, may I suggest you go with Mr. Smith alone. My niece is needed here.'

'That is absolutely fine, he said, as he helped Mr. Smith into his carriage.

Dr, Darroch, may I politely suggest that you are sure to give Richard plenty of fresh cool water. A relative of mine was consumed by this disease, and he was helped by continuous hydration.' Although he narrowed his eyes, he nodded several times, and it was clear by his tentative reaction that he had not come across this virus before. Knowing time was of the essence, Rebecca called out, 'cool clean water and plenty of it please.'

As they pulled away, Meredith turned to Rebecca. 'I could almost feel you thinking my dear. I sense you may have a conundrum, and if appropriate I would like to enquire as to its difficulty?'

'We have medicine in our time that will treat young Richard. There is some of this medicine on my table at home. I now have two issues. The first problem is how to get my hands on the medicine when it's in my time.' She took her time thinking carefully about the next point and before she had time to consider it any further, Meredith spoke.

'What may I ask is the second consideration you mentioned? The first will as always unravel itself. If it is meant to be, there will be a conclusion.'

'Well, I know there is always a way forward, but my second issue is an ethical one, and I am not altogether sure how this will work itself out. The problem is that the medicine will not be available for many years. As such, do I have the right to introduce it now?'

Meredith nodded. 'That question is easy to answer. I would suggest that individuals such as you have always introduced new discoveries from the future. Ones that are seemingly beyond their years and by example consider the railways that now connect one county to another. Next, we will be able to travel to London in just a day or so, and who know what will follow.' She then laughed and said, 'please do not tell me and spoil all the fun of invention.'

Rebecca narrowed her eyes, and instantly her head filled with a discussion she had at her university about computers. They had questioned how one day computers were the size of a house, and the next you could lose them in your pocket. She nodded to Meredith. 'Hmm, I am still not convinced that it is right to introduce a medicine from my time, but nonetheless, I take your point.' In the back of her head, she was beginning to understand her possible role in all of this.

'May I suggest you go alone, sit in a room upstairs, and consider your choices? You could give the medicine to young Richard's father after the physician has left. That way, no one needs to know where it has come from, and importantly, no explanation will be demanded. You could say it was a concoction from France, and Mr. Smith would be none the wiser. I would suggest, without sounding too churlish, he would have forgotten your words by the morrow.'

Rebecca agreed, and although still somewhat undecided, she headed upstairs. She arrived in what she thought was her room, only to be greeted with a huge four-poster bed, and a wall racked with a myriad of leather-bound books. It instantly reminded her of Mr. Elm's shop. She started looking through the books, and in the corner by her feet, something grabbed her attention low down. She knelt and instantly her eyes settled on to a well thumbed book. It was *Emma*, by Jane Austin, the same one she'd found in the summerhouse the first time she'd visited it. With her neck tingling for the nth time today, she took it from the rack, sat on the bed, and started reading.

CHAPTER 12 – PENICILLIN

Bleary eyed, having fallen asleep, Rebecca sat up on the bed. She was instantly aware she was home, and the only sign that she'd been anywhere was the Jane Austin novel lying next to her. With the dream notion going around in her head, even though it hadn't raised its head for some time, she made her way over to her cupboard to see if she now had two of the same book. As she started looking for the books that she had found all that time ago, something was telling to her look again at the one on her bed. As her eyes settled on it, she gasped. She knew she should be used to these surprises by now, but this was a different book. In place of *Emma* was the novel *Persuasion*. She thought for a moment as the pieces started to link. Emilee was the name Meredith used to introduce her to the other guests. Now wondering if there was a hidden message within this different book, she started looking through the pages. As she did, an instantly recognisable piece of hand woven paper fell on her lap. She knew this was Meredith's paper, and with her head again focused, she opened it and started reading.

Dear Rebecca,

This, I suspect, finds you again in your own time.

It is your judgment alone that will decide if you should intervene with young Richards' infirmity.

I propose that you will naturally know, in time, the right choice to make. In addition, I also offer that if the door opens for you, that is within itself an indication as to your movement's correctness.

Be strong, step forward, and maintain your openness.

My Love, Your Meredith

Rebecca sat back, twiddling the letter. After re-reading it a couple of times, she decided to go and look for her father's antibiotics. On the way downstairs, she started thinking about the times she tried to take something with her from her time, or bring something back. Now Meredith's words were starting to mean something. She felt comfortable in the knowledge that the door would remain firmly shut if it were at all wrong. She then realised her father's medicine might not actually be penicillin, which will put pay to it once and for all.

Entering the kitchen, she could see her father's medicine right in the middle of the table. She picked it up, and started reading the small print. 'Penicillin, she read aloud. *Right, now where,* she thought as she headed upstairs. As she arrived back in her room, memories of the young Richard filled her head. With her thoughts distracted, she tried to think about her next steps. Part of her was still feeling a little uneasy, but there was also this underlying urgency running around muddling her thoughts. All of a sudden, her head cleared, and she knew to make her way down to the summerhouse to where she first met Richard. With her attention now alertly focused, she put the tablets in her pocket, and headed off.

Although she knew she was doing the right thing by Richard, there was still a tiny element of uncertainty surrounding her movements. Now standing in front of the summerhouse, she was unusually hesitant and unsure what to do next. For some reason, she decided to head around the back, and as she did, immediately spotted a man sitting on the door step at the rear of the building. *Now this is getting bizarre* she thought, knowing she hadn't actually done anything this time other than walk up to the summerhouse. To compound her confusion, the summerhouse was showing signs of her father's refurbishment, yet here she was looking at Mr. Smith from 1858.

As she approached the man, he stood up, bowed, and said, 'Meredith told me to wait on this step for ya Miss.'

Trying not to show her confusion, Rebecca thought for a moment. 'Did the Doctor help Richard?'

'Na, he said there was nout he could do. He would not go close to me son. I gave him lots of water, as Miss said. I spoke to Miss Meredith, and she said you'd know what ta do.'

Rebecca smiled, and after reassuring him that things would turn out okay, she handed him the bag containing the tablets. 'You must be very careful with these. Do not let anyone else see them, no matter what. You must promise me that you will follow these instructions.'

'I will Miss. Will they help me boy?'

'They will indeed. He must take one in the morning and one in the evening with lots of water in between. Under no circumstances tell anyone where or how you came by these.'

'What's circus stanses?'

She smiled, and said, 'Just tell no one. You must promise me.'

Nodding profusely, he said, 'I promise Miss. I does. Where did ya get this stuff from may I askt'?'

'I came by these during a trip to France. Right you must go to your son now, Mr. Smith. Please say to Richard that he will be well soon.'

'I will Miss. What is France? Thank you muchly Miss,' he said, again nodding profusely.

'France is a place a long way from here that you need have no concern for. You must go now.'

He nodded, turned, hurried away, pausing only to turn back and wave.

As she watched him vanish into the woods, memories of her first time here filled her head. She headed towards the front of the summerhouse, and was aware of an odd feeling suddenly consuming her thoughts. While speaking with Mr. Smith, she briefly considered how she got to him without noticing a change in her surroundings. She shook her head, and opening the front door to the summerhouse, instantly spotted new spiral stairs. Realising she hadn't actually been anywhere and seemingly never left her time, made her feel quite peculiar. Considering this, she speculated where this twist on proceedings could take her. The more she thought about it, the further perplexed she felt, now wondering if Mr. Smith had somehow manifested himself into her time. She quickly dismissed that idea, reckoning she'd stepped briefly into his time, without noticing a change, and then back again. For all that, she still had an odd sensation going around at the back of her thoughts.

She briefly looked around inside the summerhouse, and felt there was nothing more here for her, not today anyway. With her stomach rumbling, she decided to head back up to the main house for some food. When she got there, she looked in the fridge, and not in the mood to cook, decided on a pizza from the freezer. *Sort of thing Tommy would eat* she thought, as she placed it in the oven.

Even though she enjoyed it, she was still cross with herself for being lazy. Heading upstairs, having decided to read Persuasion, she mumbled, 'unless it's changed again,' then laughed aloud.

As she entered her room, an idea pooped into her head that if the medicine had been successful, perhaps Meredith's letter might have changed to reflect this. Reading, she felt a little miffed that it was still the same. Now with concerns for Richard bumping around in her head, she found it impossible to focus on the book. Booting up her laptop, she decided to do some research on the area, to see if anything pertained to a virus around that time. After a couple of hours, the only thing she found out was that penicillin still became available in 1928. She sat on her bed and although still concerned for Richard, felt oddly relieved that she hadn't changed anything by introducing the medicine.

At a complete loss what to do, she decided to give Roxy a call, and see what she was up to.

'Hello,' Roxy said, 'I was just going to ring you. What are ya' doin'? I am at a complete loose end, and thought I might invite myself over for a couple of days.'

Rebecca was so relieved to hear her voice that it made her a feel a little emotional.

'Is ya okay sis?'

'Yeah, just tired. Mum, Dad, and the twit are in Belgium for ten days, and I am... well, let's say, I would love you to come over. Maybe we could go out tomorrow, perhaps into town.'

'On my way, and how about we go into Liverpool for some retail therapy. Sounds like you could do with it too.'

An hour later, Roxy came in through the back door, shouting at the top of her voice.

Hurrying downstairs, Rebecca called back, 'I am coming, stop shouting.' As she arrived at the bottom of the stairs, she pulled one of Roxy's headphones out and whispered, 'stop shouting.'

The two went to Liverpool the next day. Because they had so much fun, they chose to stay for a couple of extra nights. Arriving home mid-evening, three days later, and worn out, they decided on an early night. Roxy was due back at her parent's house tomorrow.

The following morning, Roxy and Rebecca said their good-byes. As Rebecca waved her off, she was wondering what to do with herself for the next couple of days. There was no sign of Meredith, and although the 1600s were nagging at the back of her thoughts, she felt that was a way off.

CHAPTER 13 – MR. JEFFREY

For the rest of the morning, she sat around, reading a few pages of *Persuasion*. In between, she searched on her laptop trying to find anything relating to the 1600s. Around lunchtime, she had a sandwich and decided to go for a walk.

Ever since she'd lived here, each time she arrived at the lake, she always turned left towards the summerhouse. Standing at the water's edge, there was something telling her to go right today. She stood there for a moment, considering this, and deciding to follow her instinct, made her way along the shoreline.

Although there was a path of sorts, it was clear no one had been this way for a very long time. It was an unusually hot day, and the shade from the huge ancient conifers came as welcome relief. Making her way along the increasingly shadowy pathway was leaving her feeling a little spooked and the narrowing, overgrown trail was compounding her mood. Just as she was considering turning back, the path headed away from the water's edge, and again responding to her gut instinct, she followed it into the woods.

The further away from the water's edge she got, the darker it became, to the point where she had to watch her every step. Clambering over a few fallen branches, and brushing her way past waist-high nettles, made her question her decision and again consider turning back. She paused for a moment, wondering how far her father's land stretched and if this path was actually taking her anywhere. Squinting ahead, she could see a small ray of light in the distance. Guessing it may be opening somewhere behind the stables, she left the pathway, and headed in that direction.

She struggled her way towards the light, but it just didn't seem to be getting any closer. Again, she paused, turned, and looked back.

Just to compound her indecision further, a nettle she'd trodden down, sprang up and wrapped itself around her arm. Between huffing and cursing, she spat on the nettle stings, which helped a little, just as her Nan had told her it would all those years ago.

'Right, enough of this indecision,' she mumbled, and continued towards the light. As she waded through the undergrowth, something at the back of her head was asking why she felt different. In the past, she'd have delighted in this environment, but today, she was feeling a tad uncomfortable. Thinking about her emotions, she stopped looking where she was going, and again brushed the same arm through some more nettles. 'Damn and damn,' she blurted, wondering if Meredith had sent her this way.

Just as that thought entered her head, she noticed something that looked like stonework off to her left. Pushing her way through the undergrowth, trying to avoid the nettles, she headed in that direction. She was soon halted by a mass of head-high brambles, that was inconveniently entwined through the branches of a larger than average hawthorn. Looking around, she knew she had to find another way. She peered through the twisted branches, and was taken aback to see a tiny cottage nestling beneath a canopy of young oak trees.

Briefly, she wondered if her father knew of this building. She then headed back and rejoined the path. Now excited and with renewed enthusiasm, she tried to find a route towards the cottage. Trampling down the undergrowth, she soon arrived in the small clearing. Through the brambles, she'd only seen one cottage, but she was now standing there looking at a terrace of four. To confuse her further, these cottages looked remarkably new. The windows were all intact, and the doors looked as if they'd just been painted. She then glanced up at the roof and was shocked by its spotless appearance.

She stood back and wondered how this was even possible. To her, the buildings looked new, even though she knew that was unlikely. She decided to have a look around the back, half-expecting to see a mass of undergrowth. Instead, she came across two old-style carts

140

laden with bricks. Behind these carts was a well trodden path heading, she suspected, in the direction of the main house. Looking at the rear of the cottages and seeing they were in the process of being built, left her utterly bemused.

As she stood there trying to get her head straight, she heard men speaking. The voices seemed to be coming from somewhere up the path and appeared to be getting closer. Just as she was trying to make sense of the broad accent, three men appeared in front of her.

A short, portly man approached her. He was wearing a straw hat, a dirty white linen chemise, knee length baggy green cords, and a pair of enormous tan boots. ''Ello, Miss. Wasany' exspectin' you down 'ere.' He offered a shallow bow, struggling to bend. He then turned to the other two, and said, 'This be Miss Rebecca. She is the Master's girl.'

The other two younger men, dressed similarly, bowed.

'Wots' bringin' you this way?' he asked, while grimacing as he rubbed his back with one hand.

Trying to hide her difficulty understanding him, Rebecca smiled. Realising she had again moved seamlessly from her own time to another, and wondering where she might be, she was suddenly aware the man was staring at her. She nodded, and said, 'I am here to check on the work. Are you gentlemen working on these houses?'

The man started shaking his head. 'Err, I is not a gentle man.'

Rebecca smiled, 'to me you are, until I know otherwise.'

'Well thank you Miss. I is not been called that before, even by me spouse.' He said and grinned in a child-like way. 'We is near finished the workers cottages, Miss. We has worked as 'ard as we can.' He then nodded several times.

'It is okay, I am not checking up on you, just enquiring how the work is going. May I enquire as to your name?'

He nodded again, and said, 'I is Mr. Jeffrey, and these two is helpers from the village. They is named Jimmy and Scotty. We will be ready for the workers from the ship, Miss. We is workin' as 'ard as we can, Miss. I know they is arriving in two week at docks in Liverpool.'

Rebecca took a deep breath, and trying to hide her astonishment at what he'd just said, she turned away and coughed. Regaining her composure, she smiled and said, 'the workers that you spoke of, the ones arriving at Liverpool docks, are they scheduled to work hereabouts?' By the man facial expression, Rebecca knew she had to use short sentences and pick her words carefully. 'The workers from the ship. Are they going to work here?'

He nodded several times, and said, 'Yes Miss, on 'da big house.' He then indicated over his shoulder up the path.

Although Rebecca had an idea where she was in relation to the house, she now knew for sure. 'Can you show me where the house is?'

With a heavy, quizzical frown, he said, 'Not built yet, Miss.'

'Sorry, I meant will you show me where it is to be built?' she said, realising how stupid that must have sounded.

'Yes Miss. May I set these two lads at work first?'

She nodded and watched as he showed the two lads what to do with some roof tiles. After a couple of minutes, he turned to Rebecca and indicated for her to follow him. A little way along the path, having seen him rub his back again, she asked, 'May I ask if you are okay, Mr. Jeffrey?'

He nodded sheepishly. 'Yes Miss, just the man makes us work eighteen hours day and only 'nuff food for one, and we sleep on the ground.'

Frowning, Rebecca said, 'May I ask who makes you work eighteen hours?' Shaking her head defiantly, she immediately started planning how she would change this.

'The man, Miss. You may see him.' He said, and pointed in the direction they were walking.

'Does he control all the work, the food, and so on?'

'He does, Miss.'

After just a hundred or so yards along a rough sandy road, she arrived in an open area. She stood and looked around, trying to get her bearings.

The man turned and pointed, 'it is to be built here, Miss.'

She felt odd, knowing this open area was where her home would be, and although unrecognisable, it had a strange familiarity. As she was considering these emotions, an extremely tall, smart man approached them. She glanced towards Mr. Jeffrey, and he nodded. With a peculiar arrogance, the man walked up to her. She had already made her mind up that she didn't like him because of the food situation. That emotion was now compounded further by his disdainful, loathsome demeanour.

'Good day Madam, he said, with an ugly exactness. He put one hand on his hip, holding back his long green velvet jacket. He then placed one foot forward, and brandished a surly bow. Again, showing tangible haughtiness, he said in a distasteful tone, 'I do not recognise you, Madam. May I enquire as to why we have the indulgence of your company and the reason for your visit?'

Wide eyed, she knew she had to come up with something quickly. The man turned and addressed the worker, allowing her more time to think.

'Time is of the essence Mr. Jeffrey. You should be working on the roof for the cottages.' Then pointing dismissively with the back of his hand, he indicated back down the lane.

Mr. Jeffrey nodded to Rebecca and hurried away.

She guessed this man might be a foreman of sorts, especially as he was the one setting the long hours and food rations. Still annoyed by this man's presence, and manner, she decided to take control of the situation, recalling that Mr. Jeffrey had earlier referred to her as Rebecca, the Master's girl. 'I am the daughter of the house,' she said, briefly making eye-contact and then averting her head away with as much arrogance as she could muster. For some reason, she felt an anger towards this man, the like of which she'd not felt before. His tone with Mr. Jeffrey had just intensified her sentiment towards this man, and she felt intent on bringing him down a peg or two.

He again bowed, 'I am sorry that I failed to recognise you, Madam. Please feel free to ask anything of me, your humble servant.'

His slimy manner and unprincipled eye contact made her skin crawl. She was now on a mission. Without looking at him, and pointing to where she assumed the house was to be built, she said, 'Workers, when are they due to arrive?'

'I believe they are due in two weeks, Miss. One hopes that the ineffective worthless locals, including Mr. Jeffrey, will have the cottages finished in time.'

'Enough,' she said, staring directly at him. 'What is your name?'

Seemingly unruffled, he narrowed his eyes, and said, 'Master Jeremy Smithe.'

Reckoning his name was as slimy as he was and trying not to grin, she steadied herself. 'Well Mr. Smithe, I urge you to reconsider your references towards the hard-working locals. You set them outrageous targets, and expect them to work with little enough food for one man, let alone three.' She then looked again directly at him. She knew this approach towards labouring workers maybe normal in this time. However, although she was probably misguided to intervene, felt the need to do something. As he went to speak, she held her hand up. 'Where is the Master?'

Still unruffled and now appearing creepier – if that was even possible - he pointed towards the building area, and said. 'Madam will find Sir, your Father, in the wooden cottage behind the spruce trees.'

Without making eye contact, she headed off in the direction he had indicated. As she approached the building plot, it was virtually impassable, so she made her way around to the left and towards some tall conifers of sorts. After a few yards, she could see a log-style cabin to her left. As she approached, an obese man opened the door. Although his clothes were that of a gentleman, his appearance was scruffy, dirty, and unkempt.

'Have you been interfering? I was watching you talking with my Brother, and you were waving your arms again. You may be my wife's daughter, but you are no daughter of mine. Therefore, you have no business involving your nose in works that do not affect you.' He then licked his lips in a distasteful way and burped. 'If it was not for your Mother's money, I would rid you from my life forthwith.'

Rebecca's brain was now in overdrive, and was trying to digest all this man had said before she responded. Just as she was about to speak, he started waving his arms, intensifying her mood even further.

'It is a shame you did not go with Victoria, your Mother to France this past day.'

'How long will it be before my Mother returns?' she asked, trying not to swear.

'You know she will not be back before the house is built. She left me in charge and responsible for all works. Therefore, you have no business involving yourself.'

She knew she was here only to stop the workers arriving from Liverpool, but wanted to give this man a piece of her mind, before she did anything else. Although, going by his manner towards her, she reckoned whatever she said would probably be ignored. At a loss what to say or do, she started wondering why Meredith had sent her to this exact time. Infuriated by these two men and the situation, she decided to head back down to Mr. Jeffrey. He was the only one who treated her with any level of respect, and she felt if nothing else, he would be honest with her. She had always been instantly sensitive to people's moral fibre and was sure he was a good man. As she turned to walk away, she decided she wanted to give this man a shot across the bow. 'I will be back, and when I am, you will find your involvement in these proceedings would have changed.'

Growling, he sneered, waved his arm dismissively, and said, 'that I doubt, now be gone with you.'

She headed down towards Mr. Smithe. As she approached him, he was again leering. Ignoring him, she walked past him without making eye contact, and on towards the small cottages. She wasn't sure how Mr. Jeffrey would help her, but as soon as she saw him, felt at ease. Going on a hunch, she greeted him and asked, 'Did my Mother have a favourite place here about?'

'Yes Miss, your Mother did have one place. It is the hut down by stream that runs into the lake near to the Oaks. She goes to there when she goes away from her husband.'

She reckoned she knew what he was saying, but felt the need to dig a little further. 'To get away from her husband, what do you mean?'

146

Recognising the man's hesitancy to answer, she said, 'it is okay to speak. I will not repeat anything you say, and that I promise you. I need a truthful answer and trust your opinion.'

'He nodded, and appearing a little more comfortable, said, 'He is a nasty man, and she needs to go to her place away from him.'

'Thank you,' she said, reckoning she'd heard enough. She bid her good-byes, assuring him that upon her return, she would improve his working conditions. Rebecca reckoned she knew exactly where this hut was, even though she hadn't seen any signs in the past. She wasn't at all sure what she'd hope to find there, especially as the woman she was looking for was in France. Regardless, and going on a hunch, she decided to go and look for the hut.

She then headed in the direction of where she'd originally found the key. Going by what he'd said, she guessed the hut might not be too far from there. This time, she waded through the nettles as if they weren't there and soon arrived back at the water's edge. Weighing up everything, she was now wondering if there was more for her to do here other than just stop the plague. She felt odd, walking along the bank not seeing the summerhouse, and this mood was intensified knowing her home hadn't been built yet.

As she made her way to where the summerhouse would eventually be, she couldn't help wondering what it would be like not living here. For sure, her thoughts occasionally went back to the whispering pond and her old house, but living here had offered her so much.

Just to compound her reflective emotions, there was no path to follow. Looking out towards the island to gain her bearings immediately brought back memories of the time she'd spent in the boat with her mum. Now feeling a little wistful, she headed into the woods hoping to find at least the big oak. She knew oaks lived for centuries and so felt reasonably comfortable she'd find that and could then use it as a land mark.

On her way through the woods, she started thinking about her new ability to jump from one era to another without taking to the spiral staircase. Wondering if she could start to control this, she lost track of where she was. Looking around, the woods in front of her were dense, and she was unable to see further than a few yards. She paused, unsure which way to go, and then decided to follow her instincts, reckoning if she got lost, Meredith would guide her.

After a few yards, clambering over some fallen branches, she arrived in an area that looked oddly familiar. To her left were some youthful willows swaying in the gentle breeze. As she grew closer, she was getting a weird sensation. These looked like the willows she'd seen the first time she ventured into the woods. Unsure what was going on, she hesitantly turned to her right, and there was her fallen oak just as it was the day she'd found the key.

She headed over to the tree and although everything appeared exactly as it was all those year ago, there was something not quite right. She perched herself on the trunk, and looked around. At a loss what to think, she hitched up her legs, leant her back against an upright branch and closed her eyes.

Chapter 14 – Which Way Now

As she sat there with her eyes closed, she thought about the day she found the key. Her memories were bright and vivid, and even though it was five years ago, it felt like yesterday. She then started thinking about Meredith, who suddenly seemed so close it was as if she could smell her sweet lavender perfume.

'Hang on a minute,' she blurted, I can smell her perfume.

Slowly, she opened her eyes and glanced around. Nothing had changed, but it sure felt as if something was different. She was convinced something was going on, so stood up, and again looked around. As she stood there, the aroma of Meredith's perfume filled her nostrils.

Even though her surroundings hadn't changed, and she was still seemingly in her time, going on gut instinct, she called, 'Meredith, are you there?' Even though there was no reply, she was sure something was going on.

Just then, she heard some rustling in the trees behind her, so called again. Still there was no answer. Then she heard an almighty bang that sounded like a shotgun. With her nerves jangling, but curiosity calling, she shouted, 'Who is there?'

Seconds later, a tall elegant man, dressed in an upper-class Victorian outfit appeared through the trees. 'I am so sorry. I did not know anyone was in the woods today. I am here hunting the wild boar with a few friends. Thank heavens our shots didn't hit you.'

Trying not to show her tangled thoughts, Rebecca smiled. 'I am the one who should be sorry. I went for a ramble and ended up here. Now I may be lost.' As she smiled, she heard an instantly recognisable voice. 'Meredith,' she called.

'Madam, are you an acquaintance of Meredith?' She has travelled here from the Americas where she lives with her Mother and Aunt Rebecca.

Just this one sentence had scrambled emotions and unable to hide her surprise, she blurted, 'what, Meredith lives in the Americas?' Now with so many questions converging on her thoughts, she sat there staring into space. Suddenly, she noticed the man's expression, and realised she must have been pulling faces. She smiled, and said, 'sorry if I seem vague, I think it must have been the gunshot.'

He narrowed his eyes, frowned, and said, 'Yes, and she has lived there these past ten years. You appear to know her well, and yet you seemed unaware that she lives in the Americas. Let me call her,' he said, turning. 'Meredith, come hither please my dear. There is a lady here who knows you.'

Seconds later, Meredith appeared through the woods. Rebecca stood up to greet her, but was instantly aware that she had a distant, somewhat bemused appearance. As she looked at her, she could see the woman's brain working. Meredith tentatively offered her hand, and Rebecca knew there and then that something significant had changed. It was her Meredith okay, but clearly, this woman didn't recognise her.

'I believe that I know of you. You are familiar. However...' she said, with her head slightly to one side, and her eyes uncharacteristically narrowed.

Although Rebecca could sense something wasn't right, she didn't feel at all uneasy certain there would be a simple explanation. She stepped forward, and offered her hand. 'I am Rebecca. I too know you, although I now believe our paths may have only crossed gently.'

Meredith smiled. 'Rebecca, you share the same name as my beloved aunt. I must say that I adore the expression you used - our paths crossing gently.' The woman glanced to the ground, clearly thinking. 'I know of you, although until this day, you were only a story.'

The gentleman looked confused, and noticing this, both Rebecca, and Meredith went to speak at the same time.

'You go first Meredith.'

Turning to the gentleman, Meredith said, 'my aunt Rebecca told me of this meeting some years earlier. Harold, you know well that many persons dismiss her stories as just that, stories. I, on the other hand, have always engaged and cherished each one of her tales. It would seem, as is often the case, her telling of future events was again accurate.' She then turned to Rebecca and said,' we have a lot to discuss my distant friend. We are to have luncheon by the lake, and I would be delighted if you joined us.'

Although the man nodded, he was clearly perplexed.

'I will explain all, Harold, in due course.'

As Rebecca was trying to work out what was going on, a bizarre thought consumed her consciousness. 'This might be an absurd question, Meredith, but I need to ask. The big house on these grounds is there, isn't it?'

Shaking her head, she said, 'I do not know of the house you speak. There have not been any dwellings here about since a horrid plague took many lives. The unfortunate souls were buried within this land, and there was a covenant setting it as a sacred site.' She narrowed her eyes, and said, 'Although, I suspect you are aware of the plague if my aunt's words are true. At this stage, I have no reason to doubt they are.' She squinted, and with an unusually hesitant tone, she whispered, 'Future girl.' Again, she appeared deep in thought. 'There is an aspect that my aunt spoke of that I found confusing. She recommended I show you something in the stream, and assured me that you would understand.' The woman then stood and offered her hand to Rebecca.

On their way to the stream, Rebecca's curiosity was at bursting point. 'Did your aunt say anymore?'

Nodding, the woman said, 'I will explain when we arrive by the pool in the stream.'

From the way that Meredith answered and by the look on her face, it was clear to Rebecca that this woman was as confused as she was.

A moment later, they arrived by the stream, and bizarrely it was the exact point where Rebecca had cleaned the key she'd found all those years earlier. Chilled by this, Rebecca turned towards Meredith not knowing what to expect. She lifted her palm in a questioning motion.

The woman pointed towards the pool, and said with a distinct air of uncertainly, 'Please, Rebecca look at your reflection in the pool.'

She clambered down the bank, just as she did all that time ago. She then leant forward, and with a deep intake of breath, shrieked. The reflection was not hers. Unsure what to think, she twiddled her hand through the water, and again stared at the distorted reflection. Now at a complete loss what to think, or say, she turned towards Meredith.

She beckoned Rebecca to join her. 'I am not sure that I will ever understand this. However, my aunt said that if you had failed to avert the plague in sixteen-twenty-three, your appearance would change. Clearly that is the case, as we know the plague took many lives.' She again seemed to go deep into thought. 'She explained to me that your Mother's family were affected by the plague, and subsequently, your father married a different woman. Although you are clearly Rebecca, the mother you know was never born, and therefore, your appearance is dissimilar. Now the next part, I did not understand, so please forgive my attempt to explain.' The woman appeared to be considering her words carefully before speaking.

Distressed by this woman's words, Rebecca took a deep breath, and tried to control her emotions. Eager to know more, she said, 'It is okay, Meredith. I am certain all will become clear.' Although troubled, she was sure there would be a resolution, there always was. Even though this was not her Meredith, she could feel the same goodness of character and was reassured by this.

'As I alluded to a moment ago, I am not sure I will absolutely comprehend my aunt's words. I will, however, attempt to relay her message.' Once again, she averted her eyes and seemed to go deep into thought. 'My Aunt said that a lady named Rebecca will appear one day, and that she will be from the future. She explained that you have a unique ability to travel back and forth between eras.' Again, she paused. 'So, the next part I am not sure I grasp completely. Evidently, you have the capacity to travel to specific dates in the past and once there, avert tragic incidents, such as the plague. She explained that if you appeared, and I didn't know you, then I was to show you your reflection in the stream. If you appeared different to yourself, you would have failed to avert the plague. She also said that I must reassure you that not all is lost. Your ability to travel is passed to you from your father, yet your appearance in from your mother.'

Rebecca's emotions were now all over the place. Unsure what to say, she stood there staring at Meredith. Previously, she had wondered if she had the right to intervene with events in the past. She now knew she had to find her way back to 1623, before Victoria goes to France, and attempt to avert the plague. Although in the back of her thoughts, she knew everything would be okay, she still felt tearful. Looking towards Meredith for some kind of reassurance, she held her hand out.

Meredith moved forward and cuddled Rebecca. She whispered, 'it will be okay, and you will avert these events. I understand your sadness. My aunt assured me that you would come to me today. She also explained that the reason for your visit was to assure you that intervention was of the utmost importance. I hope you are now clear that your mission is to avert the plague.'

Nodding, Rebecca gripped the woman's hand. Whispering, she said, 'you are my Meredith, just as I know you, all-be-it, in a different existence.'

Over the next few minutes, Rebecca tried to explain all about Meredith's alternate life. Although occasionally, Meredith appeared perplexed, she seemed to understand.

Then as if everything had fallen into place, her expression changed. 'My Rebecca told of this life. Although I was comfortable with her atypical tales, this one seemed somewhat implausible. I believe and understand everything a little clearer.' She appeared to consider her own words, then looked up, and smiled. 'I know why you are here now. The plague that I spoke of was devastating to the North of England, and took several thousand lives in its wake. I believe you are here to learn of the impact, and be reassured of the significant importance of your proposed intervention.'

'I was initially unclear of the part I should play in this, and indeed if my intervention was justified. However, speaking with you has made my mission clear and even more important.' Rebecca took and deep breath, digesting her own words.

'My Rebecca told me to say to you that your mission is indeed clear. That you must find your way back and avert this plague.' She paused briefly. 'I will, of that I am sure, see you again, and our lives will have trodden a different path. Although, I believe your path is set.' She then rummaged in a heavy cloth bag and produced some paper. Opening an envelope of sorts, she handed Rebecca a handwritten document. 'I have carried this with me every day since my aunt emphasised its importance to you, and said that you would need it in the 1600s.'

Rebecca carefully opened the document and started reading. It referenced the impact the plague had in this area, and how it was carried to these shores. 'This will indeed help me, and I thank you.'

They chatted for a little while longer and although Rebecca wanted to stay and talk some more, she knew she had to get going. Heading off back towards the lake, she wasn't at all sure which way to go, or what to expect. One thing she had learnt through all her journeys was to expect the unexpected. Deciding to head back towards the small cottages, she came across a large marble plinth by the lake. Etched into one side it simply read "In Memory of the Many." Focussed, she headed along the shore, and back towards the cottages. As she entered the woods, she was certain that she was still in Meredith's time. The nettles she had flattened earlier, were standing and although robust plants, she knew this wasn't possible.

After again wading her way through the undergrowth, she soon found herself back at the cottages. Mr. Jeffrey was on the roof fixing tiles. He turned and as if he didn't recognise her, greeted her.

'Hello Miss, Canna I help thee?'

Rebecca waved and called out, 'Thank you. Do you know where Victoria, the owner is?' Although a little unsure, she suspected that she was in 1623, and was hopeful it was prior to Victoria's departure. 'I was hoping to see the lady who is responsible for these works.'

He smiled, and pointed towards where the house was to be built. 'She will be with Sir up yonder.'

As she made her way along the muddy path, she wondered what lay ahead. However, unlike her previous trip to this crossroad, she felt oddly confidant that she could do what she was here to do.

She turned into the opening and could see Mr. Smithe, standing beside a woman. As she made her way over, she could feel her skin crawling and found herself cringing, knowing how uncouth he was previously.

The woman turned and greeted her, clearly indicating she knew her. 'Rebecca, there you are; I have been looking for you. I need to speak with you before I travel to France in the morrow. I need you to take control of the building works in my absence.'

As she finished speaking, Mr. Smithe, appearing annoyed, interjected. 'I am in charge while you are away, not this girl.'

'I have informed you before. This is my family home and as such, the control lies only with my family. Rebecca is my beloved daughter, and you are at best an outsider looking inwards.' She then glanced at Rebecca, before averting her attention back to Mr. Smithe. 'As I explained only this last day, if that does not fit with your plans you can depart.

Looking irate, he pushed Rebecca away, and standing close to this woman, said, 'I am in charge and that is the end of the matter.'

'I warned you previously about your behaviour toward my family members. You are here purely as a kind gesture from my deceased Father. He felt he owed it to your grandfather who helped our family long ago. I was never content with this arrangement, as well you know. You have now taken a step too far.'

Snorting, he replied, 'I do not care what you think, believe, or say. I am in charge. He then raised his fist.

Seconds later a tall youthful man, perhaps in his twenties ran over. Shouting, he hollered, 'Sir, do not raise your hand to my Mother, or Sister.

Mr. Smithe turned towards him, and once again, raised his clenched fist. Before he could strike the young man, the woman stood between them.

'That is enough. I am not going to France, and will instead stay here and control proceedings. You, however, are to leave forthwith.

'I am not going anywhere,' he replied, suddenly appearing a little uncomfortable, but nonetheless arrogant.

My Uncle, the Major, is arriving this next day, and you will be escorted from the premises forcefully. So, you have a choice. You pack and are gone today or...'

He sneered at all three, and skulking, turned away, heading towards a horse and carriage.

The woman turned to Rebecca. 'Rebecca, I would suggest that is the last we will see of him, for now at least. His behaviour has been turgid for too long and today was the day for him to go.'

'I must say, you dealt with him with strength and verve.' In the back of her head, she was wondering how to address this woman. Again, she found herself unsure if she should call her mother, or Victoria.

The woman narrowed her eyes a little, and asked, 'You clearly have something to say my dear Rebecca. In addition, I do not know how many times I have said that you must address every individual by his or her name. That includes me, your mother, and Thomas, your brother.

Thrown a little by that, Rebecca went to speak, but no words came out.

'Please Rebecca; say that which is on your mind. I have no time for this as we have many issues to consider before the workers arrive at Liverpool.'

That was the inroad Rebecca needed. She carefully produced the document from the inside of her light jacket. 'This, Mother is of the utmost importance. You must read it and act upon the information within.'

The woman read carefully, occasionally glancing up at Rebecca. When she had finished, she said, 'Because it is signed by our King James 1st, we must act upon this forthwith.' She then turned to the young man and said, 'Thomas, please make ready my carriage. To Liverpool this day, we must haste. Rebecca, please stay here and preside of events in our absence. Your great Uncle, Major Sutherland will arrive tomorrow.'

'I hope you are successful and avert the impending danger. May I ask if we can allow the workers down by the cottage some more food? Their rations are meagre.'

'That will be that Mr. Smithe's doings again, I suspect. Yes, upon my return, I will arrange appropriate provisions. Before I go, I must ask where you obtained this information.'

At a loss what to say, Rebecca stumbled, 'err, I got it from a man whose name eludes me.'

'There you are erring again. Please Rebecca, try to remember and inform me upon my return. It is important that I know where you came by this letter from our king. More importantly, it would appear that this letter refers to events as if they already occurred.' She then looked again at the letter. 'It is not dated; however, it did seem to refer to the plague in a past tense. I am not sure how this is possible. I will, nonetheless, act upon its information and stop the workers arriving from Ireland.' She again glanced over the letter. 'I am hopeful you have the wherewithal to offer a robust explanation.'

They bid their farewells. Rebecca stood there watching them leave, unsure what to think or do. She knew she had completed all she needed to here. It was just a matter of again following her instincts and seeing where it led her.

Making her way down towards the lake, she was feeling satisfied that she had done all she could, for now at least. Deciding to head back towards the oak, again on a hunch, the intense hot sunshine was making the lake water appear increasingly inviting, having not had a drink all day.

No, she thought *I should be home soon enough.* Entering the woods, she made her way back towards where she'd met Meredith earlier on in the day. She didn't know why she was heading this way, but just felt she was going in the right direction. She stopped still, realising she was actually following the tracks she had trodden down earlier.

'This jumping from one time to another is becoming a little weird,' she mumbled. It was now actually making her feel a tad vulnerable. In the past, although she hadn't any control over what was happening, at least she knew something was happening. Now though, she wasn't getting any warning. There were no indicators, no smell of almond, nothing to suggest she was going anywhere. One minute she's in the 1600s, and the next who knows where, and the fact that it was all occurring without any warning was making her feel a tad uncomfortable. She kept trying to reassure herself that in time, she might have some control over her path or movements. That thought though wasn't helping her, and she was feeling increasingly uneasy. Thinking about it as she walked along, she wondered if meeting up with the aggressive Mr. Smithe had led her to feeling this way. But then her Meredith wouldn't let anything untoward happen, 'would she?' she mumbled. She smiled to herself, and as she did, heard a heart warming, familiar voice.

From behind some dense evergreens, Meredith called, 'Rebecca, where are you?'

That is it, she thought, *every time I think to myself that Meredith will help me, she appears.* Maybe that is my way of controlling things, by thinking it through,' she mumbled. The second she said it, a hand touched her shoulder. With or without the perfume, she just knew this was her beloved Meredith, and with open arms, turned.

'I see you managed to avert the plague, my future girl. And again, you are talking to yourself. You are right that the control lies only within you. In time, it will be easy, for now though, allow it happen.'

Slightly stumbled by her words, Rebecca was unsure what to ask first. 'Err, umm.'

Beaming a vivacious smile befitting of this woman's gentle personality, she said, 'My dear Rebecca umming and erring again. Take your time, and ask all you need one question at a time.'

'Good advice, something my tutor is always telling me. How do you know that I averted the plague?'

'We are here, are we not? Our shared home is there. If you had not succeeded we would not be having this conversation.'

'When you put it like that, I guess it is obvious.'

'Remember, I learnt much about you and your type from my aunt. Even though I was young, her words still resonate with me. I feel that I am perhaps the link between you and her. You had your mission, and that was to obviate the plague. You were successful. I suspect there will be further missions for you in the future. My task, I believe, is to support you until are able to step forward alone.'

'When I first came to see you, it was via a staircase in the summerhouse. That is the building by the lake, where you lived for a time. My route was the same, irrespective of the time and people I visited. I climbed a spiral staircase, opened a door into a bedroom, and there I was, in another era.' Rebecca thought for a moment, trying to heed Meredith's advice and ask one question at a time. 'Recently, I have found I move from my own time to another, without noticing. I don't understand this.'

'In time, you will be able to move freely between eras. You have already begun to move from one period to the next without knowing

160

you have done so. As you become more comfortable, and confident, you will have total control over where you go.'

'Earlier, I was thinking that if I thought of you, or called you, you would help me. Is that not the case?'

Smiling, she said, 'No it is not, although I delight in the idea. When you call me, or think of me, you are actually focussing that part of your brain, which helps you move freely.' She squeezed Rebecca's hand. 'I will always be here when you need me, although I believe you are close to finding your own way.'

'You are important to me and my soul. I will always need you. However, you are saying I can move freely on my own?'

'In time, in good time, you will have complete control over your movement.' She then thought for a moment, 'bless you my dear Rebecca, you remind me so much of my beloved aunt. You two are akin in so many ways. I love your visits for many reasons.'

'Many reasons?'

'It vindicates my aunt's taunted views, which she endured, pretending she didn't care. She did of course care. Furthermore, I know you are my aunt's flagship, and her tormented heart and spirit, although heavy, smoothed the way for you. Importantly, I love to speak with you and feel your inner strength.'

Rebecca and Meredith chatted a while longer, mostly about her aunt, but also about Rebecca's abilities to move freely.

'Go my beloved Rebecca and know our paths will cross again soon. Remember, you are in control now, although I will always be here whenever you need me.'

Rebecca arrived back home, not having a clue how she'd gotten there. With Meredith's words ringing in her ears, she kept wondering how she would get to grips with controlling her direction and movement. In the past, she'd gone on a vibe and followed her gut instinct. Meredith had put forward a completely different perspective on things. As she was making supper, she remembered the list of incidents compiled after visiting Mr. Elm's bookshop. She sat down to eat, reading her notes. She was aware that she wasn't feeling any of those familiar vibes that always filled her head when something was afoot.

She considered Meredith's idea. *If she is right,* she thought, *it is up to me to choose when and where I go.*

With her head at bursting point, she decided to give Roxy a call to give her mind a breather. She chatted about Roxy's new boyfriend for a while, which helped. After she came off the phone, her alarm started going, reminding her that her parents were due to arrive home in the morning. With the kitchen more like a bomb-site, she started tidying up, which seemed to take forever. A couple of hours later, and exhausted from all the events of that day, she headed up to bed. As she lay there with Meredith's words ringing in her ears, she thought about everything that had happened. The way she felt right now, she couldn't see how she would ever get used to events like today. As far as being in control of when and where she travelled seemed a million miles off.

CHAPTER 15 – BACK TO UNIVERSITY

The following morning, she was up early, and ready for her parents and Tom's arrival home mid-morning. They sat around chatting, mostly about Tommy's football. Her dad seemed to recognise that Rebecca had heard enough, and suggested Elizabeth showed her the photos they took of Ghent and Brussels on a day off from football.

Tommy flicked his eyes, and said, 'right, gonna go clean me boots.'

'Thomas, they're my boots, not...

Pulling a silly face, he looked at his mum, and laughed. 'If they are your boots, you can clean them.' Again he laughed.

Twisting Tommy's finger, Rebecca said, 'Touché Tommy, not so much of a twit after all.'

'Moving target,' he mocked, and again pulled a silly face. 'Right, gone...'

Rebecca spent the remainder of the morning looking at photos with her mum.

Over the next couple of months, she split her time between sharpening up a short story for university, and going out with Roxy. On one of her trips to London, to celebrate Roxy's 20th birthday, Sam, her tutor, who had driven down for the party, asked Rebecca when she would be twenty. Rebecca sat staring at Roxy's birthday cake, not knowing what to say. Over the summer break, she'd learnt to keep common sense in check and found a way back to seeing the world through youthful eyes. The idea of this milestone birthday came as a bit of a shock to her.

'Umm, I think I am going to hide my birth certificate and give the adult bit a miss. I tried being grown-up for a while along with rational thinking, and it's just not my style. Besides, if being an adult means I end up closing my eyes to Meredith and co, then I am definitely not going down that road.' She laughed, realising that although Roxy and Sam, knew all about Meredith, the other guests – who were appearing somewhat bemused – didn't. She turned toward the others, and said, 'it is just a story thing Sam, Roxy, and I have been working on.' She glanced at Sam, and said, 'scarily my birthday is in three weeks, but shush, keep it quiet.' She again laughed.

'Rebecca, age is just a number,' Roxy said, with Sam nodding, 'and you can be whatever age you want in your head. Look at my Granddad on the dance floor,' she pointed. 'He is seventy-something, but inside, as he often tells me, he is twenty.'

'Couldn't agree more,' Sam said, 'look at us three, who would know I am a million years older than you two.' She leant across, squeezed Rebecca's hand, and giggled.

Over the next couple of weeks, although Rebecca's focus was on preparing herself for year-two, she occasionally sat on her balcony sketching. Often Meredith came to mind, and although her memories were clear, her last visit felt particularly distant.

On a bright sunny day, she decided to go and sit down by the summerhouse. She sat there recalling everything that had happened during the summer break. Unlike in the past, where her memories tended to quickly fade, of late they had remained fresh. For all that, though, Meredith felt unusually distant. Thinking about what Meredith had told her about being in control of when and where she travelled, she was finding it difficult to see how that was ever going to happen. Miles away, she was staring across the lake when her father came and sat next to her.

'Rebecca, we haven't chatted for what seems an age. What with Tom's football, I feel like I've been ignoring you. Your twentieth birthday is coming up, so do you have any ideas what you would like to do?'

She laughed, 'yeah, give it a miss. Dad, you've not been ignoring me, besides, I've been so busy with uni-work and Roxy.'.'

'I've not heard any mention of Meredith lately, any reason?'

Over the next hour or so, Rebecca went through everything that had happened in detail. Regularly, her father asked poignant and insightful questions, which pleased her. Frustratingly, she didn't have an answer to many of his questions. Her father, showing remarkable understanding, assured her that her guardian angel would help her and in time, her sight-line would be clear.

'Guardian angel, Dad?'

He smiled, 'your girl Meredith. It strikes me that she is your guardian angel.' He smiled again, and said, 'Come on, let's take Mum out for dinner.'

They headed up to the house, and on the way decided on the Elizabeth's favourite Italian.

During the next week, Rebecca finally came to terms with her birthday. The day before, she was actually curious with excitement, suspecting something was being arranged. More than once, she had walked in while her mum was on the phone to Ruth, Amanda, or Roxy, and each time she'd turned away being suspiciously secretive.

On the morning of her birthday, her mum woke her with her favourite breakfast, with Tommy, her Dad, and Roxy – who had secretively arrived the night before – all singing happy birthday in the doorway.

Her mum suggested going for lunch with Roxy, which was a nice surprise. When they arrived, Ruth and Amanda were waiting in the restaurant and again they all sang happy birthday.

On the way home, she mentioned several times how pleased she was with lunch, but was surprised by her mother's indifferent reaction. Pulling up in front of the house, she was a little taken aback to see Tommy and her dad waiting at the door. To add to this, the door was covered in balloons. When she got out the car, Tommy was acting suspiciously making her think something might be afoot. Even so, no

165

amount of suspicion could have prepared her for what was awaiting her in the kitchen. As she entered, she was greeted with a chorus of happy birthday. There were several of her relatives, both Nans and Granddads, two of her old pals from school, along with Sam from University. Seconds later, Ruth and Amanda walked in with the biggest cake she'd ever seen.

She had a brilliant evening, and although still a little uncomfortable with being twenty, realised nothing had changed. The following morning, with an alcohol fuelled headache, she told her mum, she was never drinking again. Suggesting this time she meant it.

'Whatever,' her mum said, and chuckled.

Over the next couple of days, she spent most of her time getting ready for her second year at university. She knew this year was going to be a whole lot more intense, and if she was going to do well, she needed to avoid any distractions. The idea of being serious and grown up left her feeling a little put out. However, she knew what she had to focus on to do well. If that meant Meredith had to take a back seat, then so be it. With her intent straight, she headed back to university and remained on track.

Before she knew it, she was home with her family for the Christmas break, and heading off for two weeks in Aruba. This time, much to Rebecca's delight, Roxy, and her parents joined them. She had a brilliant time, even though she had a little too much sun by the second week.

Rubbing an aloe-vera plant on her sore skin, she muttered, 'no alcohol and no sun.'

'Yeah right,' Roxy said.

She stuck by her words, although on the last night, with her arms peeling from her sunburn, drunk a little too much.

In the blink of an eye, she was home and again heading back to university. The intensity of work seemed to crank up this term, and although she often chatted to Roxy and Sam about Meredith, the events of the previous year, all seemed like a distant memory.

Standing with Roxy in the corridor, awaiting the year-end results, she said, 'Where has this year gone?' and shook her head. 'I was just getting used to being twenty, and it's twenty-one for us soon, I guess we should act like adults. I remember my Nan saying, "As you get older, the years fly by in the blink of an eye." I never knew it would be this blinking quick. When you get really old, like forty, years must last around fifteen minutes,' she said and giggled.

Sam, who was standing behind her said, 'Excuse me, forty is not old, and I will be forty well before you two. Besides, at that age, a year lasts at least twenty minutes.' She said, and chuckled. 'Here're the results coming now, not that you two have anything to worry about, wink-wink.' She then patted Rebecca on the head, just the way her mum always did. 'In all seriousness, you two have shown me that it is okay to be of a certain age, and still see the world through youthful eyes. And, by that I mean, see what you want to see.'

Moments later the results were pinned up on the notice board. As expected, both girls gained fantastic scores.

'See, I told you with a little focus you can achieve anything.' Sam said and patted Roxy on the head this time, which made them all laugh.

Arriving home, and after seeing the results, James and Elizabeth suggested a trip to London to meet up with Roxy and her parents to celebrate. They ended up staying for a week, taking in one of Tommy's football matches. This time, much to the delight of everyone, he was playing for England under-18s at Stevenage F C's ground the Lamex Stadium. They won the game against a youthful French team by two goals to one, with Tommy scoring the winner with seconds left on the clock.

The summer seemed to fly by for Rebecca, which included her first holiday away without mum and dad. She and Roxy had spent a week in Majorca, where a combination of too many Sangria's resulted in them often not getting out of bed until lunchtime. When they did rise, they over indulged themselves sunbathing, which left them with sore arms and a headache. On the plane on the way home, the girls decided it should be an annual event, although they both also agreed to buy some proper sunscreen, and learn when to draw a line under the alcohol.

With a ton of work to catch up on, both girls spent the remainder of the summer break working. They did take it in turns staying at each other's house, which seemed to help enormously.

With just two days to go before Rebecca was due to head back for her final year, it was her 21st birthday. As with the previous year and still recovering from Roxy's 21st, Rebecca's parents laid on a lavish event. A few of Tommy's teammates turned up, much to her dismay, although one of the players was a little too cute for her liking.

Towards the end of the evening, Roxy whispered in her ear, 'Flip he is dishy.'

'Who are you talking about?' Rebecca said, knowing very well whom she meant.

'Leave off; you have been speaking to him for the last two hours, to the point where I was feeling decidedly ignored.' She then squeezed Rebecca's hand and giggling, said, 'go girl.'

The morning she was due to head back to university for her last year, she was daydreaming, sitting on her balcony waiting for Roxy. Unexpectedly, Meredith came into her thoughts. Although she had fleetingly thought of her from time to time, it had always felt like a distant, almost inaccessible memory. Today though, she was there, right at the front of her thoughts. Just like so many times in the past, it was as if Meredith was calling her. She sat there for a few seconds, but couldn't ignore this feeling. She recognised this sensation and knew a visit to the summerhouse was her only option. At the bottom of the stairs, just as she was going to see her mum first, she stopped to look at the painting. Frozen to the spot, a familiar chill went up and down her back. Unable to look away, something was holding her ridged. It was as if she was in the painting, standing next to Meredith.

Then she heard a whisper, "Do well, be your best, I will see you soon enough."

With her nerves jangling, she felt quite peculiar, but at the same time, remarkably calm. She considered speaking to her mum about it but as she hadn't really said much about Meredith for ages, decided to keep it to herself. Besides, she knew what the message meant. She went back upstairs to wait for Roxy, and give herself a little thinking time. Whenever the subject of Meredith had come up, either through her own thoughts, her dad, Sam, or Roxy asking about it, she'd felt disenchanted with how vague it had all felt. It had always seemed so far away, and she often found herself wondering if there was any more for her. On many occasions, she'd thought about Meredith's words, and tried to control her thoughts and somehow manifest herself somewhere, anywhere. Every time though, she'd drawn a complete blank. As much as she felt an urgent need to visit the summerhouse, she guessed the whispered words from Meredith actually meant for her to focus on her work, and in time, she would be back with her.

CHAPTER 16 – FINAL YEAR

With Meredith's whispered words still resonating in her thoughts, Rebecca arrived back at University, knowing exactly what she needed to do. With her head on straight, she focused every ounce of attention on the job in hand. Occasionally, she allowed herself a little down time, and this invariably involved going for lunch with Sam and Roxy. On one such day, Sam asked about her adventures, and if she'd had any further interactions with Meredith.

'Interesting you should ask me that, I was only thinking about her this morning. Just before I came back for the start of this year, she spoke to me.' She then went on to explain about feeling as if she was in the painting with Meredith.

'Well, as daft as that would sound to most people, we know differently,' Sam said, with Roxy nodding in agreement.

'I did wonder why you hadn't mentioned her, and how you were managing to focus so much on your work. To be frank, I have been struggling to keep up,' Roxy said.

'Haha, Frank, it is everyone else who needs to keep up with you.'

With Rebecca totally focussed of her work, the year seemed to fly by. It felt like déjà vu, as she once again stood in the corridor with Roxy awaiting their results. Although she was confident, she was a little apprehensive haven gone very left field with her dissertation whilst discussing the book publishing world.

'Been a great year for you two,' Sam said, 'any thoughts what you'd like to do now?'

'I want to teach,' said Roxy, 'and hope I can be as great as you, Sam.'

'Bless you, Roxy. Thank you, although with you two, my job was made easy. Besides, I now have two friends for life. How about you, Miss Adventurer, what do you have up your sleeve?'

'I think I am kind of ready to write about Meredith. I was thinking I could perhaps do it as a fictional time adventure story. It is difficult though because it's so personal. Don't get me wrong, I want to do it, just keep finding excuses and end up putting it off.'

'Well, I cannot wait to read that,' Sam said and then nudged Roxy's arm.

Moments later, their results were posted on the board. Deciding to hold back and let it calm down, the three stood around chatting.

After the mass had cleared, Sam said, 'shall we have a look?'

Roxy walked up to the board and immediately started screaming with delight, 'First,' she hollered. She then turned to Rebecca and held her hand up in a questioning manner. 'Cat normally has your curiosity, has it got your tongue too?'

Nodding, and holding Roxy's hand, she said, 'seems we both did well. I got a first too.'

'You look very deep in thought, Missy,' Sam said.

Rebecca responded with a smile. 'I guess getting a first means I have to write about Meredith now, whether I am ready or not,' she said and laughed.

The girls decided to go to town to celebrate. As they sat in the bar, Sam turned to Rebecca.

'So, why are you not ready to write about Meredith?'

'I think, but am not sure, that there is a lot more to come with her.' She then went on to tell Sam and Roxy all what Meredith had said about being in control of her destinations. 'It is odd, but as soon as I finished my last piece of work, it was as if Meredith was knocking on my door. I hadn't really thought much about her, and then bam, there she is, just the way she so often was in the past, right at the front of my thoughts. It is like she is calling me.'

'Well, that's brilliant, surely?' Roxy said.

'It is, but I am... I don't know how I feel. Perhaps it is because it's been so long since I had any contact. I guess I am scared it has gone from me, and I can't see anymore.'

'What do you mean, can't see anymore,' asked Sam.

'I mean, I am not able to see the openings when they are there.'

'Didn't you say that you just walked down near the summerhouse, and boom; you were suddenly in another time?'

'Yeah.'

'Well, surely it will still be the same. You have always said that it happens when it's meant to, so why would it change. And, besides, you said that Meredith said she'd see you soon enough.'

The girls spent the rest of the afternoon chatting about Roxy teaching and that Sam had been offered head on English at the University. Sam also suggested that when Roxy was ready, she could take a role here.

Picking up a newspaper, Sam said, 'Have you read about this horrid virus called Bazanty that is taking hold in the Middle and Far East. Evidently, it started years before in the foot-hills of the Himalayas and went largely unnoticed. That was until now, and it has grown to epidemic levels. Poor souls, I so wish there was something I could do to help.'

They spent the next while talking about the subject of aid in this type of situation. Sam suggested that one day she would volunteer to go and help with something like this, having always felt it was in her make-up.

Roxy said, 'why not go for a few weeks now. I am sure if it is that bad, they'd welcome your help.'

'Might just do that,' Sam said, nodding while clearly considering the idea.

Around 6pm, Roxy and Rebecca headed back to Rebecca's house. Roxy's parents were going to visit tomorrow and both families were going into Liverpool to celebrate the girls finishing university.

CHAPTER 17 – MAPLE LEAF

Rebecca and Roxy arrived home around 10pm and spent a couple of hours with James and Elizabeth, with the occasional interruption from a particularly noisy Tommy. Around midnight, the girls headed off to bed.

'The look on your Dad's face when you told him you got a first. He looked like he was going to burst with excitement. Mind you, your Mum was also beside herself with joy. Ha, even your twit of a brother seemed to be pleased for you. I must say, he is getting rather cute.'

'Don't even go there, or I might have to strangle you, or him, thinking about it both of you.'

The two girls lay in bed chatting, and laughing every time Roxy teased Rebecca about her brother. The following morning, with Roxy still asleep, Rebecca crept out and sat on the balcony watching the sun cast long shadows across the water. In a flash, she was back to the first day she sat here, and again, Meredith was close to her door.

With Roxy still snoring, she headed downstairs for a coffee. As she entered the kitchen, her mum was just putting some coffee beans in the machine.

'Coffee, dear?'

'Love one, Mum. And can I have one sugar, had enough of this avoiding sweet things. Life's too short.'

'Oh er, that's a change from miss high and mighty, sugar is no good for you,' her mum said, and chuckled in that way that always made Rebecca feel good.

'I love you Mum.'

'I love you too. Where's madam, still sleeping? That girl likes to get some bed time,' she said, and giggled again.

After having a coffee with Roxy, once she finally got up. She said her good-byes and arranged for her to come back tomorrow evening. Once she'd gone, Rebecca decided to go for a walk down near the lake. On her way along the hallway, she stopped to look at Meredith's painting. Again, she felt transfixed, as if Meredith was standing next to her. There was something stirring for sure, but whatever this feeling was, today it seemed different. As she closed the front door behind her, she reckoned she probably only felt this odd because it had been so long since she'd trodden this path.

The second the front door shut, she had the most peculiar feeling. Again, following her gut, something was telling her to go back inside to see her mother. 'Mum, I went without saying goodbye. Sorry, I'm just going for a walk. See you shortly. I love you Mum.'

'I love you too sweetie.'

Feeling better, she headed down towards the lake, wondering why she'd felt such a strong need to say good-bye to her mum. She shook her head, unable to work out how she was feeling. There were all the familiar signs that something was going to happen today, but this was different, very much so. She actually felt a little uncomfortable, but not enough to stop her following her instinct.

As she arrived by the lake, she could smell something most odd. She knew the smell for sure, but couldn't put her finger on it. It wasn't the usual almond smell she got whenever something was about to happen. Then it came to her. It was maple syrup. Well at least, that's what she thought it was. Just as she was about to go and have a look inside the summerhouse, she heard some voices cheering. It was boisterous, somehow reminding her of one of Tommy's football matches. She took a deep breath through her nose and held it for a second before turning towards the sound. She had been down this road before, but no matter how many times it still sent a shiver running up and down her spine.

She turned slowly and could see countless people, standing around tables at the front of the house. As she grew closer, she could see a lot of men in uniform, intermingled with women, also wearing uniforms that were oddly familiar. Around the exterior, she could see many children playing around a maypole. To her, it appeared as if they were celebrating something. Getting closer, her attention was drawn by one particular woman. Trying to work out why she recognised her uniform, the penny dropped. The woman was wearing a uniform similar to the one Judith had on when she was here in 1943. The mood during that visit was tangibly sombre, whereas today's mood was the complete opposite.

She started looking around at the other people, when a voice behind said excitedly, 'Rebecca.'

She instantly knew this voice, and turned. Judith was standing there with her arms out, beckoning her towards her.

'Dear, dear, Rebecca, we thought you were dead. Heavens above, I am so pleased to see you. Come and join us celebrating the end of the war. Your boyfriend, Etienne will be so pleased to see you. He has been distraught with sadness, as we all have, since we had news that you had been killed in action. It is perfect that you should return from your nursing duties this very day.'

With her brain scrambled, her thoughts jumped between France, Etienne – whoever he was – and the war being over. Racking her head, she reckoned it must be 1945. At a loss what to say, she cuddled Judith, realising that this woman believed she was her actual daughter. Judith responded, with teary eyes, cuddling her so tightly, her relief was tangible.

'So, what happened to you Rebecca? The information we received said you ventured too close to the front line and were presumed missing in action. In fact, I have your tag.' She then produced a silver disk from her pocket. 'Here,' she said and handed her the disk. 'It was only two days ago that we received the sad news. Everyone will be so pleased to see you. This is truly a joyous day. Come and join the others,' she said, pointing back towards the proceedings.

As she followed Judith, she was trying to work out what she should say. As she approached the crowd, a man in a light-brown uniform, a neat black cap, bearing a gold maple leaf shaped badge, approached her. By the look on his face, Rebecca suspected this was Etienne.

'Ma'am - am I pleased to see you, hooray, and thank God for your safe return.' he said with an unusual tone and dialect.

Although she had worked out he was Canadian, he sounded like a mix of French and American. She actually found his appearance, manner, and dialect, pleasing on both the eye and ear. *Okay, I best say something* she thought.

Before she had a chance, both he and Judith started talking at once.

'You First Ma'am.'

'Rebecca, tell us all about what happened. How is it that they presumed you lost in action, and by that we assumed you were dead?' She glanced at Etienne, and continued, 'How on Earth did your tag end up back here?'

She'd had enough time to make her mind up what she was going to say, but needed to be careful. Again, she was about to speak, when Etienne started talking.

'My Major informed me directly that you were seen to be shot. Indeed many witnessed this sad event. None of this makes any sense, my amoureux. I was informed that they even buried you.' He shook his head, 'all that matters not a jot, you are here my Cheri.'

Rebecca was thinking she needed to be careful, or she could get used to his mix of languages and his oh so sexy voice. *Okay, out with it*, she thought, reckoning that their Rebecca perhaps had sadly lost her life. 'I went to the aid of some wounded soldiers with another nurse. We were very similar to look at, and that is where, I believe the mistake was possibly made. Sadly, my colleague was shot.' She could sense a little tension, and seeing an element of confusion, decided they needed a little more. 'Our soldiers were gaining ground quickly, and I stayed to help the other nurse, as they pushed forward.'

'Oh my, Ma'am, you saw some goddamn conflict. Thank heavens you were able to dodge the Jerry's bullets. I am thanking the Lord that our mighty Red-Devils pushed on, and thereby saved you. Louer le seigneur.'

Smiling, Judith said, 'Praise the lord. Hey, listen to me, I sound like Etienne. As for him mixing his language, I am sure you'll soon become reacquainted with him jumping from English to French and back again.'

Rebecca found herself now wondering why she needed to become reacquainted with his language change if he was her boyfriend. She didn't have to wait too long to find an answer.

Holding out his hand, and gently squeezing Rebecca's hand, he said, 'I know we were only together for a month before you gallantly went from us a year since, to help our mighty Canadian Red-Devils. The day we met, I knew you were the gal' for me. My heart's flame burns for only you. These two days past, I believed I could no longer live without you, as I could no longer live without air.'

Warmed by this man's words, encapsulated by his eyes that seemed to be watching her soul, she was at a loss for words. Having never felt anything like this before, she mumbled, 'err, umm, thank you for those kind words.'

'Come along with you now Etienne, let our dear girl have some time to think. Besides, look we are not the only ones who are delighted to see her.' Judith said, indicating to the others watching on.

As Rebecca glanced up, she was aware that pretty much everyone was standing, and staring. As she looked around, she could see Christopher, Judith's husband, Rebecca's father, approaching slowly with the aid of walking sticks. As he drew closer, she could see his eyes filled with tears. 'My beloved girl, you have come home to me to save my heart. I lost one of my girls and could never stand to be without another. My beloved Judith has given me strength throughout, but life without you would have been a sorrow I could never endure.' He then turned, gripped Judith's hand, and letting go of his stick, he gripped Rebecca's hand. 'Both of my girls are home to stay.'

Rebecca looked around and one by one, her eyes settled on familiar faces. To her delight, in the distance, she could see a young Tabitha playing, seemingly oblivious of her presence. Off to the left were recognisable faces of land girls. Unlike the first time she met them, they were all smiling. As drenched as her brain was, she felt calm and oddly at home among these people and knew she was loved by this family. There was warmth here that went beyond their obvious joy at seeing someone they believed they had lost. As strange as this was, she actually felt like she fitted. Just as she was considering this, Meredith came to mind. Feeling puzzled, it played on her mind for the next hour or two. She tried to stay focused as she went around greeting everyone, often telling the same story again, but something was nagging at her inner thoughts. Once she was sure she had greeted everyone, she went over to Judith. 'Judith, I feel I need to go for a walk alone. To be straight, I feel a little overwhelmed and a few minutes alone.'

Judith squeezed her hand and said, 'I could see you were a little at sea. Go, I suspect towards the summerhouse, and we shall see you in a little while.' Oddly, her tone was questioning as if she knew something. 'May I have a cuddle before you go? I hope we will see you back here soon.'

She nodded, cuddled Judith, and said, 'I promise I will be back.' She didn't know when, but she felt oddly certain it would be soon. As she made her way towards the summerhouse, her mind was going in circles. If she were to go to her time now, all these people will again be stricken with grief, having only just gotten their girl back, for her to vanish once more would be so harsh on them. As she made her way up towards the summerhouse, which was, just as he remembered it, she was feeling a most peculiar sensation. The front door was oddly locked, so she made her way around to the back. On her way, it felt as if something had changed, but instead of feeling uneasy, she was actually comfortable. Seconds later, she heard a voice, and instantly recognised it as Meredith. She turned and greeted a somewhat serious looking Meredith.

'I must tell you, that although in the coming days you will feel distressed, unable to find your way home. It is for a good reason. I will be back with you again soon. Future girl, please be happy with the environment you find yourself in on this day. I will be here when you need me most. Conversely, I cannot help you back to your period. In time, everything will unfold, and one day you will be home again. For now, you have a lengthy mission. Be happy, be loved, and be strong.'

Before Rebecca could say anything, Meredith backed away into the trees and seemingly melted away. Breathing deeply, she tried to digest all that this woman had said. Shivery and unsure what to do, she slowly made her way around to the front. A short distance away, she could see Judith approaching her. Moments later, the woman stood in front of her.

'I know who you are, and why you are here. I don't know why I know, but I do. I believe, and again I am uncertain why or how I know, that you are with us for some time. I briefly thought earlier that you would not stay, and I suspect you picked up on this.'

Nodding, Rebecca said, 'I did, I did. I didn't realise that you knew of me, where I am from and...'

'All I know is that you are not my Rebecca. I knew this the first time we met two years since. I am the only one who knows. I believe your initial time with us may be distressing for you. I do not understand how or why I know this. I just do.' The woman gripped Rebecca's hand. 'Know I will love you, as will Christopher. I also believe Etienne will love you too. Know this, and find your solace and peace through being loved.'

With Rebecca's head going in circles, she was beginning to feel a little fretful. In the depths of her brain, was a weird feeling that it would work out. Right now though, she was wondering how long she would be here. To compound her torn emotions, she now knew why she'd felt the need to go back and say good-bye to her mother.

CHAPTER 18 – HOW LONG

Over the coming days, although Rebecca felt comfortable amongst these people, in particular Etienne, she was constantly wondering how long she would be here. The days turned into weeks, and those weeks turned into months. Often, when alone, Rebecca would sob uncontrollably, fretting for her real family. Surprisingly for her, she found solace in Etienne, and although she fought hard against her emotions, she was falling in love with this man. No matter how low she felt, he lifted her with his presence. One such day, when she was feeling particularly low, having again unsuccessfully tried to find her way home, he joined her by the lake.

'My distant Cheri. I feel you carry a weight that none of us could possibly understand. I sense your anguish and all I can offer is my mortal soul, my heart, and my endless affection. Je t'aimerai tourjours.'

Rebecca turned and holding this man's hand, she replied, 'one day, I too will love you always. Please understand that right now I carry heaviness in my heart. In time, I know it will ease. Be patient my dear Etienne.'

Over the coming months, Rebecca often searched for a way home always hopeful Meredith would guide her. One such day, having again been unsuccessful, she sat by the lake, considering her future. Trying to find some comfort, remembering Meredith had told her she was here for a reason, she mumbled, 'what is that reason.'

'Future girl, I am here.'

She turned knowing it was Meredith, but was shocked to see an extremely elderly woman standing in front of her. Nonetheless, she was both delighted and relieved to see this woman, so smiled, and held her hand out, trying to mask her surprise.

Meredith stepped forward and in spite of her frail body, cuddled Rebecca in an enchantingly familiar way. Although she was overjoyed at seeing Meredith, her emotions were mixed with a deep rooted sadness, being reminded of her real mother. The two sat and chatted for an age about Rebecca's current mission with Etienne and Judith's family. Often, she asked how long she would be here. Each time though, Meredith seemed to avoid the question.

Having chatted a little more about Judith, she felt compelled to ask once more when she would be home with her real mother. This time, Meredith stood back.

'My time here is short, and you will soon find yourself without me. My spirit needs to rest now. One thing you must know before I go. Between us, this time, our mission is one that will bring salvation to many. You are here for several years. Fear not though, in time all your questions will be answered. Go gently through this life, and smile always, mostly be happy, love and be loved. The day will come, and you will be back with your family as if this never happened. So, please live the life you find yourself in and allow yourself to be unafraid. I must go, but know you have brought joy to my life where there would have been pain. For that, I love you my future girl.' She then cuddled Rebecca, again reminding her of her real mother.

With tears streaming from her eyes, Rebecca could feel this woman's frail body slipping away. She stood and watched as Meredith, with her hand held out, gently faded into the evening air.

Rebecca sat silently, with her heart in turmoil. Meredith's kind, reassuring words were conflicting with her anguished thoughts of not seeing this woman again, a woman she'd become dependent upon. Her despair was compounded further, stuck in this era, and unable to find her way home. At least now, she knew that one day she would be back with her real mother. An hour turned to two, and trying to focus her thoughts, again considered Meredith's words. She'd always known Meredith's departure would come, but right now, it offered little solace. Trying to be positive, she wondered what kind of salvation she was referring to and how it would involve her. In the past, she had always drawn comfort, knowing that Meredith would be there guiding her way. She was gone now, and Rebecca knew she had to find her own way. She knew that Meredith would have wanted her to be strong and feeling a little easier, she consoled herself, knowing she had a new mission, albeit unknown.

A moment later, Etienne walked towards her. She was surprised how pleased she was to see him, and unable to contain her feelings, stood and cuddled him. He cuddled her back, and it was just what she needed. She had never felt this kind of emotion towards a man, other than her father, and occasionally Tommy. This though, was a completely different sensation. She stood back and holding his hand, could see and feel his selfless compassion.

'Hello my Cheri. Judith and I were troubled by your absence. Are you okay?'

Unexpectedly, he'd lifted her pain immeasurably, and still holding his hand, she said, 'You are the person I needed to see. Thank you for finding me.'

'I suspect your words cover the pain you feel this day. I can only offer my love, and hope in time you will find a way to love me also. I understand you have conflict that you must deal with first. I offer you my shoulder, if needed. Know that I am, and will always be, at your side.'

She didn't know if it was his carefully chosen words, or the way in which he said them, but it lifted her spirit immeasurably. Without thinking, she uttered the words, 'I love you, and my heart has known this since our souls first met. My brain has stopped me saying these words, words I saved for my parents alone. You have my heart dear Etienne, and always will. We need to start living now and leave behind the demons of war.'

Over the coming weeks and months, often she would think about her mother, father, and Tommy. She was now comfortable amongst these people, and in particular, enjoyed having Tabitha as an adopted sister. Her solace though, on sad days was Etienne, and whenever she

184

saw him, he lifted her. One such day, as he approached her while she was sitting at the back of the house, enjoying the morning sun, she thought of Roxy. *She would be so jealous* she thought. From behind his back, he produced a birthday cake and seconds later, the whole family appeared through the kitchen door. Although elated by this, it reminded her of being at home. Seeing the number twenty-four on the cake, came as shock, realising she had now been here for two years. The kindness these people brought quickly dispelled her grief. She knew that she was here to stay and as if suddenly escaping a slumber, her eyes widened.

Etienne placed the cake on the table and bent on one knee. 'My beloved, we have seen the bad times and have cast them from our lives. We have done this together. I could not imagine my life without you.' He then produced a small box from his pocket, and opening it, he said, 'Will you, my Cheri Rebecca, stay with me always.'

Without thinking, and holding her left hand out, Rebecca nodded. 'I will and I promise you all of me.' Her thoughts immediately went to her real mother. Hiding her emotions, she brushed away the tear, and stood, looking towards her new family.

Her marriage to Etienne was a fabulous affair on a lovely summer's day. An open-air marquee set by the side of the lake, was as she had planned one fun day with Roxy. Over the coming months, she settled into married life, and before she knew it, she was heavy with child and facing her 25th birthday. Being so close to child birth again brought thoughts of her real mother. Although that deep sadness would be with her forever, she was facing her new life with open arms. Her adventures with Meredith now seemed so far away, and although thoughts of this woman came to her occasionally, she believed her journeys were a thing of the past. Over the coming years, she went on to raise two beautiful boys. One was particularly interested in law and gained a position at a law firm in Liverpool. The other, James Thomas, went on to take a doctorate in tropical diseases. The day James returned from University, he said he planned going to

Himalayas to help a challenging virus named Bazanty that was gaining momentum.

Suddenly, her thoughts went back to university and a conversation she'd had with Sam and Roxy about a virus in that area. Although it was in her distant past, she remembered the name. Then a penny dropped, and she considered what Meredith had said about salvation on the night she left her. She now felt close to her beloved Meredith, as if she were once again by her side. She now believed her time here was purely to bring James into the world so he would go on to find a cure for this dreaded virus.

On the 22nd of July 1971, now 48-years-old, Rebecca waved her son good-bye as he left on his adventure. Although she was sad, everything made sense. She understood her reason for being here, and although she loved Etienne, and her boys dearly, her thoughts returned once more to her real family. Over the coming weeks and months, she often wondered if the door would open and take her back to her world, and if so, how she would deal with the emotional turmoil.

Entering her fiftieth year, Rebecca received news that her son, James's time in Asia had been successful, and he was returning home. She and Etienne arranged a sensational event for his return. The day before his scheduled arrival, a woman appeared at the door. A chill ran the length of Rebecca's body, as Etienne passed her in the corridor as if she wasn't there. He then greeted this woman as if it were she. Although feelings of loss were again consuming her every breath, she knew her job here was complete, time was up, and was on her way home.

The following day, she took a backwards step, aware that once again, she was seemingly invisible. With tears filling her every thought, she watched her son's joyous return, from a distance.

She knew it wouldn't be long now, and found herself wondering what her life would be like returning home as a 50-year-old woman. She ambled down towards the lake realising her parents would be old or worse still, dead. Heavy with mixed emotions of sorrow and hopeful expectations, she sat by the lake. As she looked across the water, she remembered the fun she'd had with her mum. She was finding it difficult to understand her emotions, although she loved Etienne and the boys, there was a void in her heart. She couldn't understand why she was racked with anguish. She leaned back against a fence post and closed her eyes wondering what tomorrow would bring.

Chapter 19 – How Can That Be

She opened her eyes, feeling remarkably alert and sprightly, and reckoned she must have nodded off. With a cool summer wind chilling her face, she looked around. Glancing down at her legs, she rubbed her eyes. She couldn't believe what she was looking at. Instead of the tweed pleated skirt she had on before she'd nodded off, she was now wearing the jeans she had on the day she met Judith all those years ago. She touched her cheeks, and was more than a little shocked to feel how smooth they were. Unsure what to think, she upped and ran to the lake edge to look at her reflection. With a strong wind blowing in, the waves made it impossible to see properly.

Remembering the day when she was with Meredith and had seen her reflection in a pool in the woods, she headed that way. As she entered the woods, although still uncertain what was going on, there was a real hope that she was home and perhaps young again. She clambered down the bank and peered at herself unsure what to expect. Gasping breath, she looked again, and trying to hold together her frail emotions, she ran towards the house.

As she approached home, Tommy was kicking his ball against the garage door. She had never been so pleased to see him, and unable to control her emotions, ran over and kissed him on the cheek.

'Err, get off,' he said, rubbing his face.

'Twit.' She smiled to herself, having not called anyone a twit for years. Seconds later, she heard her mum calling her.

'Rebecca, where have you been? I've been looking for you all morning. Well for the last ten minutes.'

Seeing her mum instantly filled Rebecca's emotions to bursting point, and trying to fight back her tears, cuddled her tightly.

'From the way you're cuddling me, one would suspect you've been with Meredith again. Come and have some lunch with Dad and me and tell us all about it.'

Hesitantly and as considerately as possible, Rebecca went through her story gradually. She was only too aware how obscure and ludicrous it would sound, but importantly was mindful of her parent's reaction when they found out she'd been married and had two children. Over the next couple of hours, although deeply saddened by the thought of not seeing Etienne, or her boys again, she felt inexplicably okay. Bizarrely, her story seemed like one of those dreams you have that you just can't remember clearly. The more she talked about her life with Etienne, the further away it drifted, and it was beginning to feel like a distant memory. As she explained about being married and having two sons, although her parents were clearly a little surprised, at the same time, they both appeared to take it in their stride. In particular, her mother was noticeably relaxed.

'I am not altogether sure how I feel,' Rebecca said, 'it seems, and feels like a story that I read in a book a long time ago. It is all rather odd, and if I didn't know any better, I would say I imagined the whole thing.'

'Well it is a remarkable episode of events, Rebecca.' Her dad shook his head, seemingly unsure what to say. 'I seem to recall you saying Roxy's father is a therapist and or hypnotist. Is that right?'

'He is, and although I have considered that, it's a no...' She narrowed her eyes, 'for now at least'

'I just thought that with your memories being so distant, that maybe...' He then seemed to consider his words carefully. 'Perhaps none of it actually happens to you. Somehow, you are able to manifest into their lives, and then see their world through your eyes.'

'I've thought that Dad. The thing is though, what happens to my body while my consciousness is in their head?'

Frowning, Elizabeth said, 'Do you remember that day down by the lake with Ruth and Amanda, when you said you'd been gone for ages, and actually it was no time at all? Perhaps that's what happens every time. Maybe you or your subconscious brain travels wherever it is, and your conscious brain believes you have been there for however long. In actual fact, in real time, you've been gone for seconds. That way, your physical body doesn't actually go anywhere.'

'That sounds very plausible, Mum and a brilliant notion. Rebecca then thought about what her mum had said, and added, 'Like reading a book.'

'I'm not sure that I understand the book's relevance,' her mum said, with a quizzical look on her face.

'I do,' her dad said, 'you can read twenty years worth of goings-on in just a few pages. With a good book, you feel like you are there. In no time at all, you've lived every word with them.'

'I'm loving that idea, Dad. Maybe I am tapping into a part of my brain that most people can't or don't use. I remember Sam, my tutor saying that when she writes, her characters lead her. She also suggested that she was using a part of her brain that's beyond conscious thought.'

They continued to chat for a while longer, having all agreed that was the most sensible answer to this completely mad series of events.

Feeling a whole lot more at ease, Rebecca spent the rest of the day pottering around. Waking early the following morning having slept like a log, she decided to do some research on her computer. After trying every spelling of Bazanty that she could think of, nothing came up. Having thought about it, she realised that if James's work had been successful, there wouldn't be any records. Just as she was about to close down her laptop, she decided to try one more approach, and typed Himalayas 1970s. After scrolling through some unrelated articles, she eventually found something close. Carefully she read

190

through, and in time unearthed some circumstantial evidence that related to a doctor from the UK working in this area on virus prevention.

That was all she needed to know. Although it was many years since she'd considered her trips being a dream, this last episode had seemed as though it could have been. She closed her laptop, and headed downstairs, feeling quite pleased and satisfied. On the way past Meredith's painting, she nodded.

She joined her mum in the kitchen, sat at the table, and said, 'Mum, that idea of yours was amazing. I actually believe that is exactly what happens.'

'Well it dispels the dream notion once and for all. Oddly, it makes me feel a whole lot better about all the events surrounding your trips. I loved what your Father said about reading a book. I think Ruth would call that layman terms.'

'Actually that is perfect, layman terms. I feel a whole lot better today. I was engulfed with concern that I had married, had two children, and couldn't remember any of it. I think the thing that really bothered me, was not being upset. I mean, I was upset, but nothing like I should have been. I don't miss them or feel the anguish I should. If what you suggest is right, that I just see their world through their eyes, then I wouldn't feel any pain.'

'Well, Roxy coming over later, which will help take your mind of it all.'

'Bloody hell, Mum. Bloody hell.'

Waving the soap, her mum said, 'Not too old for this missy, and they'll be no supper for you tonight.' She then giggled, and asked, 'Why did you swear anyway.'

Laughing and coughing at the same time, she could barely get her words out. 'I made arrangements with Roxy thirty-odd years ago.' And again, she laughed to the point where she couldn't even look up.

Appearing completely bemused, Elizabeth said, 'what are you on about?' Then putting her hand on Rebecca's shoulder, she laughed as if the penny had just dropped on her head. 'Of course you did, that must feel so weird.'

'I don't know what it feels.' She shook her head, 'boy is she going to be in for a shock. Oh, Roxy, since I saw you yesterday, I've been married, had two children and am back for supper. Beat that if you can.'

Both, Rebecca and her mum laughed on and off all afternoon. When Roxy did eventually arrive, neither could get a word out through laughter.

'You go first Mum, coz I can't breathe at the moment,' Rebecca blurted.

Taking a deep breath and trying to keep a straight face, Elizabeth said in a solemn tone. 'Did you know madam here has been pregnant,' she then indicated to Rebecca with her thumb.

Roxy, clearly unsure what to say, flicked her eyes back and forth between them both.

Unable to contain herself, Rebecca started to giggle.

'You sod. You can go off people you know, although you would have needed to like them in the first place,' she said, and laughed.

The three sat around chatting for the remainder of the afternoon. Around five, Rebecca and Roxy offered to cook supper.

'Hang on Mum, the food is probably off because the veg I bought was in err umm 1971,' she said, frowning. 'Oh my goodness, what a thought that is.' She then burst into tears, as her emotions tumbled around her.

Both her mum and Roxy comforted her, and slowly over making supper, Rebecca explained to Roxy all that had happened. Although Roxy asked many questions, just like Rebecca's mum, she seemed to take it in her stride.

The following morning, they decided to go into Liverpool with their CV's and see what was in the offing work wise. Having visited three agencies, they felt it only right to make an evening of it. Arriving home around midnight, there was a note from Rebecca's dad on her bed.

Dear Rebecca and Roxy,

I know you girls have your focus towards the literary world. I would like to support that adventure, and ideally offer you the opportunity to pursue it with ease.

Therefore, I would like you two to work at my offices for two days a week, and that can be any two days you choose. I will pay you what I suspect you would earn as a newbie in another job working five days.

Please understand that this is not just a fatherly offer. I have high regard for you both intellectually. Therefore, I am paying you an amount to show that worth.

Dad/James

'What do you think, Roxy?'

'I am cool if you are. I guess it depends what he wants us to do, because numbers bore me, unless it's page numbers,' she said, and laughed.

'Yeah, that's my view. I am also a little concerned working for my Dad's firm. Nepotism can be a poison chalice, and am concerned how others will react. I think it is best we speak to my Dad later when he gets home.'

'I would think he has thought about all that, to be fair to your Dad.'

'Yeah without doubt.'

The girls sat around chatting for the rest of the afternoon. Mostly, the subject returned to Rebecca's most-recent trip. Although she was a little surprised how Roxy seemed to take everything in her stride, she also realised she'd had a long time to get used to it.

After supper, the two girls spoke to James about working for him. He explained that he'd lost a major player from his administrative team, and felt it was a role perfectly suited to the girls. When the subject of money came up, he said he had looked into the going rate for an admin team leader. He went on to suggest that even if he only split that between the girls, it would be more than they would be paid as a new entrant elsewhere. He also said it was for as long as the girls wanted.

The following morning, the two girls went with James to his offices to have a look around. At lunch, they both agreed it would be a good opportunity, and would help them both pursue their writing careers. Rebecca was still a little uncomfortable with the idea of working for her dad. However, after chatting to Roxy about it, they both agreed that only time would tell.

CHAPTER 20 – A NEW DAY

Both Rebecca and Roxy agreed that Thursday, and Friday would be the best days to work. Their primary motive was so they could go out on the town after work, especially on Friday.

After lunch, they spoke with James, who suggested the girls started working around the time they would have returned to university. What with both girls 22nd birthdays coming up, and another week's holiday planned in two weeks time, they all agreed on a mid September start.

The summer seemed to fly by for the girls, and before they knew it, they were heading home from their holiday. At the airport, the girls said their good-byes, with Roxy heading home to London to spend a couple of weeks with her parents.

Rebecca, now at a loss what to do, sat on her balcony, working on an illustrated fairy book she'd started at university. One particular afternoon, with her mum, dad, and Tommy in Scotland for a football match, she was unsure where to take her story. She decided to head down for a walk in the woods to find some inspiration. As she headed towards the lake, she wondered why her earlier trips seemed so distant of late. Other than talking about Judith, and Etienne, there was very little occupying her thoughts. In the past, every moment and event consumed her consciousness as she went through every detail over and again.

Briefly, she thought about Meredith. Although she still felt a strong emotional attachment, she wasn't too saddened by her not being around, anymore. Although surprised by her feelings, she'd always known she wouldn't be there forever, and this helped her understood her feelings. She had forever believed that Meredith had led her way, and wondered if her passing had created a void and if this was the reason that she'd had no inclination to go exploring.

She sat down on the veranda at the front of the summerhouse considering her emotions. As thoughts of Meredith, Judith, and Etienne consumed her, she felt a tap on her shoulder. Knowing she was alone, she took a deep breath and turned, but there was nothing. A little uneasy, she stood up and looked around, but there was no one there. She sat back down at a loss what to think. Briefly, she considered it was a leaf reminding her autumn fall was here, and another year had passed. As quick, she dispelled that thought, knowing it defiantly felt like a hand on her shoulder. A little uneasy, but not too perturbed, she wondered what that was all about, and if it was one of Meredith's messages.

She sat there trying to remember where her thoughts were. With her mind a little blank, she peered across the water and wondered what lay ahead of her, if anything. Although her time with Judith and Etienne now seemed a distant memory, there were still emotional remnants niggling in the back of her thoughts. Her mood was compounded further knowing Meredith was gone. That got her wondering what would happen if she went back to a time when Meredith was alive and what reaction she would be met with.

Briefly, she thought about her dad's hypnosis idea. The more she thought about it though, the further away she moved from that suggestion. Although it made sense, and perhaps would help her understand how things were working, she couldn't help feeling adverse to the concept. She knew what she knew and besides, if she knew too much, it might actually affect what was going on, and may lead her down a wrong road. She got out her notepad and started scribbling, but couldn't focus. She sat and stared at her pencil, remembering the day she found the key. Although it was an age ago, oddly it felt so close. Considering this, she wondered why on one hand some of her journeys seemed distant and yet, memories like this were right at the front of her brain.

As if she was getting it for the first time, she realised memories such as the key were tactile and actual events, while her journeys, although real, were locked in the depths of her subconscious mind.

Finally, she felt like she was getting somewhere with this whole thing, and was starting to understand how it all worked.

She headed back to the house, wondering about the hand she'd felt on her shoulder. With no reasonable explanation, she decided to put it down to another one of those events that are seemingly impossible to explain or understand. No sooner she thought that, she reckoned it was time to put her knew understanding to the test.

She headed up to her bedroom to check on some notes that she made relating to events surrounding the house's history. Right at the top were comments relating to 1878 when a French industrialist took ownership. Her notes were brief, and although they referenced the year, there were no exact dates. Just as she was considering this, she read her notes a little further and realised it had happened after Meredith's husband, George, had died suddenly. She realised she might get to see Meredith again, all-be-it as an elderly woman. In an instant, her thoughts filled with the day she saw a frail Meredith seemingly for the last time.

Trying to focus her brain, she was a little unsure what to do next. She looked at the clock and realised it would be getting dark soon. As she wondered if she had enough time to go and try her new-found focus, she realised that time didn't actually matter. Deciding there was no time like the present and as time would always be on her side, she headed off outside and down towards the summerhouse.

On her way, she wondered how, or if she could focus sufficiently, not having a specific date to aim at. *Oh, well, I'm sure either it will happen, or it won't* she thought.

As she arrived by the summerhouse, there were none of the vibes that were always there whenever she was about to go on another jaunt. With the evening sun slipping from sight, she looked up at the early stars. Remembering what Meredith and the man in the bookshop had said to her, she wondered if this was the time to try to make something happen. As the thought entered her head, she again felt a hand on her shoulder. As before, she didn't feel at all uneasy, and instead found it strangely comforting as if it was a new kind of message.

Although, she was tempted to look around to see if there was anyone there, instead, she closed her eyes and tried to focus her thoughts towards Meredith. Alas, she wasn't getting any kind of sensation. Somewhere in the back of her thoughts, something was telling her to visualise an elderly Meredith, or perhaps George. Still nothing was happening. She peered around in the fading light, and all at once, an idea came to her. Repeatedly, she muttered the French name for the house, 'chère à votre maison, chère à votre maison.'

With her senses suddenly heightened, finally she felt as if she was in control, and knew something had happened. Importantly for her, she was confident she had forced the issue. As she got to her feet, she was immediately noticed the air was filled with the smell of something burning. Looking around in the late evening light, she could see flames coming from near the front of the main house. Alarmed by this, she hurried in that direction, and as she grew closer, she could see a middle-aged man stocking a huge bonfire.

Approaching the scene, she could see two young men heading towards the fire with two large paintings. Recognising these paintings as those of Meredith and Millicent, she called out, 'What are you doing?' Not one of the men blinked, turned, or acknowledged her. Instead, they started speaking to one another in French. Suspecting, as with other trips, she might be invisible to these men, she, nonetheless, hurried towards them, waving her arms and calling out. Still completely oblivious to her, they carried on talking as they launched both paintings on the fire.

Both saddened and alarmed at what she was seeing, and at a loss what to do, she started searching for Meredith. After several minutes of running around, there was no sign of her. Now feeling angered by the burning paintings, and distressed at not being able to stop it, she headed towards the main house. She entered through the front door, and inside, was shocked to see the house ransacked, which only served to heighten her anger more so. She headed to the kitchen calling as she went, still hopeful of finding Meredith. There was no sign of her anywhere. Deciding to check upstairs, she turned and spotted an intriguing pile of papers on the table. Although these were in French, Rebecca had become entirely competent in this language, having lived with Etienne for many years. Although still stressed by what was going on, she realised her time with Etienne was continuing to bear fruit, made her smile.

Animated, and a little more relaxed, she scanned through the top paper, which turned out to be Meredith's daughter death certificate. It indicated that Rebecca Jane had died on March 4th 1888, while in France, having fallen from a cliff. The cause of death was stated as being accidental. *Hmm,* she thought, feeling a little concerned by this. For some reason, it just wasn't sitting comfortably with her.

The second paper, which was in English, was also a death certificate. This one was for Meredith, indicating she had died of old age. The date of death was February 25th 1888.

Immediately, Rebecca's brain started going in circles. She had never been one for conspiracy theories, but this was too much of a coincidence. Now alarmed by her suspicion, she started going through other papers. The next she came across was a French newspaper, which was dated 19th March 1888. Underneath this was an English newspaper. Because it was seemingly new, with no dog ears, she suspected it was only a day or two old. Doing some easy maths, she knew that both Meredith and her daughter had died within the last month, and yet the house was being ransacked already. With her conspiracy notion heightened even further, she continued to search with a renewed determination.

The next few papers appeared largely inconsequential, which was a little surprising, but nonetheless, helped her focus with a clear line. Then, just about to head outside, she noticed a brown official-looking envelope. With narrowed eyes, she opened it and started reading. This was part French, part English, and as she went through it, her alarm bells stopped ringing and instead started clanging.

The first paper was Meredith's will and testament - in English leaving the house solely to Rebecca Jane, her daughter. It was dated 6th June 1886. It indicated that Meredith's husband, George had died two years earlier, along with Rebecca's husband Joshua, in a tragic fire in a hay barn, in 1884.

The second paper was Rebecca Jane's will, dated March 3rd 1888, and it indicated all properties were to be left to Monsieur Jon Renaulds.

'That's the day before she died,' she mumbled. With so many dates now going around in her head, she narrowed her eyes and tried to focus. If she had suspected foul play before, she was now certain something untoward had happened. Again, she started looking through the other papers. She then came across something that stopped her dead in her tracks.

These papers indicated that on the 15th December 1885, Rebecca had entered into an agreement with Monsieur Jon Renaulds, and Monsieur Pierre Renaulds to establish and fund for an orphanage in the Midi-Pyrenees region of France. The papers went on to say that if in the event of Meredith's death, all funds would be maintained by Rebecca Jane, and if in the event of Rebecca's death, all UK properties would pass to The Renaulds' family.

With her lips pursed, and her head aching with anger, Rebecca gathered together every last piece of paper. At this point, she was too annoyed to know what she would do with them, but something she would. With her hackles up, she headed to the front door. As if she wasn't already heated enough, she overheard two of the men speaking as she passed.

One of them was saying how effortlessly this family had fallen for the contrivance. The other one, adding that it was easier than the Dutch family they had swindled four years earlier, and how easily they had got away with it, even though the local law enforcement had all the evidence they needed for a prosecution. The third man smugly offered up how easy it was convincing the Surete that Rebecca Jane had fallen from the cliff. Now, she wasn't certain, but seemed to recall the Surete being a nineteenth-century name for the French police.

Seething, she stood a listened, hoping they may indicate something else she could use as evidence. Earlier, as she was collecting papers together, she wondered how she would be able to convince anyone of her story with only papers relating to the future at her disposal. For sure, she knew that Meredith would understand, but what if her relationship with her was actually over, and she was now invisible to Meredith. Just then, one of the men mentioned that he had the Dutch paperwork in his holdall in the hallway, and that he was going to frame it and put it up on display after they've moved on to their next victim.

Rebecca didn't need an invitation, and hurried back inside, searching for anything that might contain more paperwork. Seeing an attaché case lying on the floor in the hallway, she grabbed it, thinking it was actually working out very useful being invisible. She opened it and it was full of paperwork written in a language she didn't recognise. She wasn't sure if it was the right case, but seeing a Dutch flag at the top of one of the papers, suggested it probably was right. Besides, it was the only case around, and she had no choice. On her way out, and without glancing back towards the men, she sped towards the summerhouse. On her way, she was thinking all this legal paraphernalia would be right up Ruth's street, and reckoned speaking to her should be her first move.

With so many dates in her head, she focussed her thoughts on the date Rebecca Jane had signed the orphanage agreement. Over and again, she mumbled to herself, '15th December 1885.' Arriving by the summerhouse, she was still saying the date to herself. She didn't know why she was focussing so heavily on this because after all, she had all the paperwork, complete with dates. Something though, was saying it was the right thing to do. She didn't need to consider this for long, because turning towards the main house, could see she was home.

'That's it,' she mumbled, 'it's as simple as that, know where I want to go, and make that is my sole focal point.'

CHAPTER 21 – LEGAL RUTH

Arriving back in doors with her head full of dates, first thing she decided to do was to lay out all the papers on the kitchen table. The more she read the papers, the angrier she became. Although, she knew that time would always be on her side, she felt she needed to do something sooner rather than later.

With paperwork everywhere, and still fuming, she needed to focus. She took a deep breath, and methodically put it everything together a sequential list of events, and started compiling a date-line.

1884 – George and Joshua die in fire

15th December 1885 – Meredith's daughter, Rebecca Jane signs agreement for orphanage fund

6th June 1886 – Meredith's will

25th February 1888 - Meredith's death

3rd March 1888 – Rebecca Jane's will

4th March 1888 – Rebecca Jane's death

19th March 1888 – Date I was there

Next, she turned her attention to the attaché case. Opening up her laptop, she started doing some translation. There was far too much to translate all of it, but at least she knew it was in Dutch and she'd established a definite date, so she added this to her list.

16th June 1884 – Papers relating to Dutch events.

With her head at bursting point, she sat back and tried to come up with a plan of action. Her mum, dad, and Tommy not due back for a couple of days, so she decided to give Roxy a call. After going through her story over the phone, Roxy suggested it was something Ruth could help with, being a legal buff and all.

'Problem is, Ruth's new office is in Liverpool, and I am not paying for a cab,' she said, and laughed. 'I did think it would be right up Ruth's avenue though. If she can't sort it out, no one can. I think I know what I need to do, but it helps having a second opinion.'

'No prob, I was planning on ringing you anyway, and asking if ya fancied a night or three in the pool. Give Roofy a call and see if she can meet us for lunch tomorrow. Then call me back in five.'

After arranging with Ruth, she called Roxy back.

'I feel like I've hoodwinked you into coming over, Roxy.'

'Don't be daft; I wanted to come over anyway. Right, babe, see ya later tonight. I am already on my way, on speaker in me new Mini.'

'Oh you got it then?'

'Yeah, lovin' it. Soon R.'

Around nine that night, Roxy arrived. The two spent a couple of hours going through the paperwork, until Rebecca couldn't keep her eyes open any longer. The following morning, they headed into Liverpool. Ruth had called and said she had most of the morning free, so they met up for a coffee around ten.

After their coffee, they headed to Ruth's office where she started putting everything in order. When she came across the Dutch paperwork, she said, 'I just need to pop next door, be right back.' Moments later, she returned. 'This is Mila; she is Dutch and is going to help us with this paperwork.'

Mila started going through the papers, often glancing up and frowning. After a few minutes, she looked up and said, 'This is one unpleasant gang on individuals. According to these papers, they convinced a Dutch family into aiding an orphanage. Then once the family had signed away all their positions to this gang, they were murdered.'

'That is exactly what they did with Meredith's daughter,' Rebecca added.

'What is of major concern is that there seemed to be enough evidence to convict the men. Bizarrely, there were never any challenges, accusations, or arrests made. It smarts of a corrupt police individual or individuals if you ask me.'

'How so?' Ruth asked.

Mila then frowned as she read some more. 'Well, here's something in particular,' she said, holding up official looking papers. It is in English. Its target audience was the British police and was compiled by the French police. It warns of a family named Renaulds that they believed were looking for targets in the North of England. It specifically names Monsieur Jon Renaulds and Monsieur Pierre Renaulds.

Frowning, 'That is the same men that bloody murdered Rebecca Jane,' Rebecca said. 'And burnt Meredith's and Millicent's painting.'

'The ones in your hallway, Rebecca?' asked Roxy.

'Yep.'

'But they were there last night.'

Rebecca shook her head, 'it is sometimes almost impossible to understand, but as with the plague and the house not being built, I can change the sequence of events and actually stop them from occurring.

The simple fact that the paintings are there now, would suggest I was successful in stopping these men.' She then thought for a moment, 'however, if I fail, as with the house, disaster.'

Mila was looking totally bewildered, and Ruth clearly aware of this said, 'Mila, I will explain later. It is a long and convoluted tale.'

Mila nodded, but still appearing confused returned her attention to the papers. After a few deep breaths and the odd glance in the direction of Ruth, Rebecca, and Roxy, she said, 'reading through some of this hand-written stuff, it seems these papers were intercepted by a certain Dutch official. Therefore, that may be why they never arrived at its correct destination.' She then frowned. 'If these papers were presented to the current police forces of all countries, there is sufficient evidence to pursue a post-event prosecution and conviction. In the right hands, these papers would be damming to the Renaulds family, all be-it several generations removed.' She then looked up, appearing angered. 'I am not altogether sure how this family got away with this, other than to say it was during a period when law enforcement liaison was at best, fragile. This one paper alone,' she said, holding up the letter from the French Police, 'would be sufficient to open an investigation.'

Glancing towards Roxy and Ruth, Rebecca said, 'That is all Meredith needs, just that one paper.'

With her eyes wide, Mila, again appearing baffled, asked, 'I keep hearing that name, who is Meredith?'

'Of course,' Ruth said, glancing at Rebecca, 'you don't know about Rebecca's story. Meredith is one of Rebecca's old family members.'

Mila asked if she could keep copies of the paperwork, saying that she has always kept a keen interest in historical cases such as this.

'I only need the letter from the French Police,' Rebecca said. She was actually feeling excited now, knowing that even if she was invisible, all she had to do was find her back to a date prior to Rebecca Jane signing the orphanage agreement, and make sure these papers were seen.

Mila made copies of all she needed. After lunch with Ruth and Mila, Rebecca thanked them for all their help. Her and Roxy, then headed into town for some retail therapy. The two girls had a fun couple of days in Liverpool. Back in doors, and just as Roxy was heading off home, Rebecca's mum, dad, and Tommy turned up. Roxy ended up staying on for a while, chatting mostly about Tommy's football. The two girls had decided not to mention the events of the last couple of days, for now at least. In the end, Roxy ended up staying over for another night.

The following day, Rebecca found a good opportunity to chat to her father about the Renaulds family. Tommy was out with Elizabeth at a school event, and this has offered up an ideal time.

'It strikes me, Rebecca that your mission is clear and it is to stop events in the past from turning fowl. In fact, the more I think about it, the more I am convinced of that.'

'You said something about that yesterday babe, and I wasn't sure what you meant,' Roxy added, appearing a little perplexed.

'What Dad said, is exactly what I've been thinking of late. Often, I have wondered if my intervention in the past would adversely change events in the future. With these events, in particular, and those surrounding the building of the house and the plague, I now believe that my job is to stop things from going wrong.'

'So, what you are saying is you stopped the plague and thereby the house was built. I thought that was what you meant when you talked about it the other day, although I guess the penny never really dropped. Oh my, that is a scary thought. If you hadn't stopped the plague, then there would be no house, no Meredith, no French s-bags, and maybe no you.' Roxy narrowed her eyes, the same way she did when her boyfriend at university ran off with a cheer leader. 'Wow that is a heavy load for you. How do you deal with all that pressure?'

'I don't know that I have ever thought about it like that. Every situation that arises, I've managed to take it in my stride, maybe. Well, not that simple, but it is always one thing at a time, maybe.' Rebecca thought for a moment. 'I guess when you put it like that, it is a heavy load.'

'I am so sorry; I didn't mean to make you feel uneasy.'

'It is not a problem really and actually helps me understand my role in all of this.'

'I suppose if you are indeed capable, which it seems you are, of preventing horrid incidents, then it is no wonder society will see you kind as a way forward,' James said, appearing a little serious.

'That is exactly what I was thinking, Dad. Thank you Roxy, you views actually have helped me take another step forward towards understanding my role.'

They sat around chatting until Elizabeth and Tommy returned. Roxy ended up staying over again, with her and Rebecca having their first day at work the following morning. Although both found it a long day, they enjoyed their time in the office. Their next day, which was a Friday, they decided to stay over in town and have a night out spending the money they'd earned.

Although Rebecca enjoyed work and the night out, she was finding it difficult to think of anything other than getting back to Meredith. Saturday morning, Roxy headed home for a few days. Once she'd gone, Rebecca's turned her attention to Meredith. Although she was feeling an overwhelming need to get back, something was telling her to wait. As in the past, she knew that when the time was right, she'd know. Instead, she decided to improve a process her father had shown her while she was in work. Both she and Roxy had felt they could develop the current process, and so she set about making some simple but affective changes.

Monday came and went, and by the evening, she was bored trying to get an excel programme to do what she wanted it to. She joined her family for supper with her thoughts once again back with Meredith, having again stopped by her paintings in the hallway, wondering what it would be like if it wasn't there.

Her dad seemed to notice this. 'You are very quiet, Rebecca. No need to ask what you're thinking about.'

'Well yeah, and no. I have been working on that excel spread sheet for the last couple of days, but am struggling to get it to do what I want.

'You really don't need to be doing it at home, Rebecca.'

'I know, Dad, but I just wanted to do it, and well...'

'I know the difference between you thinking about work and something completely different,' James said, and laughed. 'I suspect you're away with Meredith somewhere, especially after all that happened the other day.'

'What happened the other day?' Tommy blurted.

'Yeah, is there something I don't know about?' Elizabeth asked, narrowing her eyes.

'Tommy, it is nothing for you to worry about, and, Mum, I will tell you later.

After supper, Rebecca went through her latest tale of events with her mum. Once again, her mum seemed to take it in her stride.

'I'm not surprised you were distant during supper,' she said, and narrowed her eyes in a questioning manner. 'So, what are your plans? I am guessing you're hoping to get back and sort things out.'

Rebecca then explained to her mum about the evening when Meredith visited her for the last time.

Clearly picking up on Rebecca's emotions, she said, 'oh that must be difficult for you. I am so sorry. Do you think that will affect your time with her if you see her again, which I suspect you will.'

'I've thought about this a lot, Mum. On occasions, more so recently, I have been seemingly invisible. Meredith explained to me that only those people who need to see me actually will.' She then thought for a moment. 'So, if I get back to Meredith, and she can't see me, there will be good reason. Besides, if I am invisible to her, there is something that I can leave for her that will prevent her daughter from signing everything away.'

'Hmm, sounds a little risky. What happens if it doesn't work?'

'Well the only way I will know, is by finding my way to a period after events and seeing what happened. If my plan is unsuccessful, there will be no paintings in the hallway. If I discover it hasn't worked, I am sure I will find a way to make it happen. It always works out and that is why, I guess, that I am able to take it all in my stride.'

After her chat with her mum, Rebecca decided to have another go at the excel spreadsheet. With her eyes on stalks and weary, she decided on an early night. Just as she was nodding off, there was a gentle knock on the door. It was her mum and dad wanting to have a chat. They sat down and explained that they were fully supportive of what Rebecca was going through, and if at any stage, she needed to talk about anything, they were there. They both said that they would never truly understand what was going on, but neither of them doubted any of her experiences.

Her parent's empathy and comments helped Rebecca to an extent that surprised her. Over the last couple of weeks, in particular, although she'd taken everything in her stride, something in the back of her mind wasn't sitting quite right with her. She'd questioned the whole concept and had occasionally found difficultly accepting she could now control her destiny. Seeing Meredith for potentially the last time had left a huge void. She'd always felt that this woman would show her the way if anything went awry and had learnt to rely on her being there, even if she was only in her subconscious thoughts. The idea that she was now seemingly alone on her journeys had left her feeling a little vulnerable. Her lack of emotions towards her time with Etienne, Judith and the boys had just compounded her emotions further.

The following morning, she was awake early. Sitting on the balcony, she watched as autumn showed early signs of taking hold. With a gentle easterly breeze, fluttering across the lake, bronze and yellow leaves salsaed their way along the shore line. As she sat, watching, distant memories of fairies, pixies, and elves filled her thoughts.

She'd had a restless night, and feeling a little groggy, mooched her way down stairs. With no sign of her mum, dad, or Tommy, she made herself some toast and coffee, and went and sat outside. With a crystal blue autumnal sky and sheltered from the cool breeze, she was surprised how warm in was. Sipping her coffee and with her head full of fairies, she was in another world when her mum came out and sat next to her.

'Morning Rebecca. Any plans today?'

'Actually, I was just thinking about my fairies, and I may wander down to the woods today, and have a mooch around.'

'That'll be nice for you. You haven't mentioned the fairies for ages, and I was thinking you'd left them behind. Maybe help you think about Meredith clearly.'

'Never leave them behind, Mum. They are always there and I hope I never lose sight of them. In fact, I won't ever lose sight of them.'

'In a way, it was those guys who kind of led you to Meredith. Not directly, but you having an open mind to such things, eased your way.'

'Well they did lead me to Meredith, directly. Hiding my pencil, so I would find the key, ultimately took me to Meredith. You know I never asked her if she believes in such things. Maybe...' The thought of not being to ask her, upset Rebecca a little.

'Oh bless you, Rebecca. I am sure you will have a chance to ask her again. Besides, what I know of her, I am certain she is just like you and...' She then cuddled Rebecca. 'I think a walk in the woods will do you good. Dad, Tommy, and I are going to Liverpool today. Evidently, Liverpool Football Club has made an offer for Tommy, so we are meeting up with some officials, and so on. It's a lovely day, and I am sure you will have more fun with your fairies,' she said, raised her eyes, and chuckled.

'How brilliant, the twit playing for Liverpool. Wow, who'd have thought all those years ago when he was kicking his ball at my legs,' she said, and laughed. 'That has proper cheered me up.'

Her mum and Rebecca sat around chatting about the fairies, when Tommy's voice boomed, 'What ya on about, fairies?'

'Tommy, don't be so rude, we are talking here, and I don't appreciate you just barging in like that.'

Appearing unusually sheepish, he lowered his head, and mumbled, 'Sorry.' He then grinned and said, 'Bex, did Mum tell ya what's happening today?'

'Yes Mum did tell me. I am so excited for you, and it cheered me up no end. To think all that time ago when I used to let the twit kick his ball at me, and now the same twit will soon be playing in front of the cop. I might just tell them your real name. Seriously though, I am so proud of you, well done.'

'Thanks, I think,' he said, and sniggered, 'you better not tell anyone, as if they'll listen to my silly sister.'

'Ooh, get you silly sister. Coming from someone who chases a ball around for a living is rich.'

A little later, James joined them and after chatting about Tommy's football, the family headed off.

It had turned a slightly cloudy, but was still very pleasant, although a tad cooler, so Rebecca grabbed a yellow cardigan and headed outside. As she closed the front door, memories of her old yellow cardigan left in Meredith's time flooded her thoughts. She stood there for a moment, and decided to go back and grab the French police notes, just in case. On her way down to the woods, she thought about Rebecca Jane wearing it in the photo. As she entered the woods, crunching her way across a carpet of bronzing leaves, she felt altogether free. The thoughts of fairies had opened a part of her brain long since closed. Coming into the area where the fallen oak lay, she whispered, 'hello spry wood, hello pixies.'

Perched on the trunk of the fallen oak, she sat staring aimlessly. As thoughts of her first time here took hold of her senses, she considered all she'd been through and everyone she'd met along the way. Placing her notepad and Police papers carefully on the tree, her mind returned to the day when she found the key. There was a mysterious air around today, and she could feel something was about to happen. She hadn't felt like this for a long time, and considering her mood, turned to read again through the police paperwork.

She knew she'd put it down with her notepad, but it wasn't there. Feeling a tad uneasy, she scrambled around on the floor, but there was no sign of it anywhere. Even though she was sure she had it when she sat down, she retraced her steps kicking up the leaves as she went.

Half way back to the entrance to the woods, she stopped dead in her tracks. *This is daft* she thought, knowing she had it when she sat down. She turned and headed back to the oak, but when she got there, the oak was standing. Sitting on the bench was a frail elderly Meredith and Rebecca Jane reading the police notes. With a chill dancing up and down her spine, she headed towards them.

As she approached, it was immediately clear neither of them could see her. Having only ever come across Rebecca Jane at the wedding and seeing Meredith again compounded her already strained emotions. Wishing she could intervene, but unable to, she just stood there motionless, and listened to them talking.

'Rebecca, I am not altogether sure how these papers came to be here. Nevertheless, they are here, and we now have sufficient information to make us reconsider our involvement with Mr Renaulds.'

'My goodness, the information pertained within these documents is damming, Mother. Considering this, it is most certain that we should resolve our association with the Renaulds family.'

'I believe we should make this information available to the constabulary. They will without doubt, deal in an appropriate manner, which will conclude any further transactions. Importantly, we will then avoid any altercation.'

Rebecca stood and watched as the two headed towards the main house. Her emotions were a little tangled, disappointed that she was unable to speak with Meredith, but delighted her plan had seemingly worked. She sat on the bench for a while wondering what had actually happened. One moment the papers were there, then they'd vanished, and the next they were being read by Meredith. She made her way down towards the summerhouse feeling a little confused. On her last trip, she'd felt she had controlled the event. On this occasion though, it would seem everything had happened around her. Briefly, she wondered if again, the pixies had a part to play. She had always thought they were capable of hiding her pencil, but this seemed a step too far. 'Or is it,' she mumbled.

As she arrived at the summerhouse, it was clear she was still in Meredith's time. Unsure what to think or do, she sat on the veranda. No sooner she'd sat down she heard raised voices coming from the direction of the main house. Deciding to go and investigate, she headed in that direction. Approaching the main house, she could see a group of policemen man-handling two male individuals. As she grew closer, she recognised them as being two of them men she'd seen stacking the fire. As she stood back watching, she suddenly realised that Meredith and Rebecca Jane were wearing different clothes to those they had on only moments before. Now she'd known for some time that she was capable of jumping from one time to another, but this took the biscuit. Either way, none of that mattered now because all she'd hoped for had been accomplished.

She took one more look at Meredith, drawing comfort, knowing that once again she'd helped this woman, and in so doing had perhaps helped herself. She then headed towards the summerhouse, wondering what would be next for her.

CHAPTER 22 – PAINTINGS

As Rebecca arrived by the summerhouse, she could just feel she was home in her own time. Still struggling to get her head around this jumping from one era to another, she made her way up to the main house. Having glanced at the paintings on the way out, she reckoned if they were there when she got back, it would indicate her mission had been successful.

As she opened the front door, she breathed a little easier spotting both paintings exactly where they should be. Something was different though, but no matter how long she stared at either of the paintings, just couldn't put her finger on anything untoward. She scanned the paintings over and again, hoping, and to some degree, expecting to see something different or new. She stood there for a moment and then decided to go upstairs to get her phone. Because the paintings had changed so often in the past, she'd taken a number of photographs as a reference.

Comparing the photos on her phone, she suddenly noticed a change in Meredith's face. Instead of expressionless, she was clearly looking pleased with herself. 'She looked pleased with herself,' she muttered.

'Who looks pleased with herself?' her mother called out from the kitchen. 'I thought you were still down in the woods with your fairies.'

'I thought you, Dad, and Tommy were still in Liverpool.'

'We were,' her mum said, meeting her in the hallway. 'Your brother is now a Liverpool player.'

'Oh wow, well, he might have to pay me some money for all the training I gave him at school,' she said, causing them both to laugh aloud.

'So, what were you saying to Meredith? I suspect you were talking to her, as usual. She gets more attention than me,' she said, and chuckled.

'Mum, look at her, can you see anything different?'

Shaking her head, she responded, 'not unless she's changed her dress,' and laughed.

Rebecca then showed her mother the photo on her phone.

'Oh wow, she is almost smiling now, how can that be? Mind you, with you, I have learnt that anything is possible.' She then narrowed her eyes. 'I can't begin to understand any of this. How can a painting change, and importantly, what have you done to make this change?'

As if he'd heard them speaking, James appeared from the study. 'It took me a few seconds, but I noticed a change in her expression when I came in. I would suggest that rather than smiling, she actually looks content.' He then looked directly at Rebecca. 'Having thought about it at the time, I guessed you might have sorted the business surrounding the French crooks.' He then seemed to think for a moment. 'I suppose what with finding the suicide note from Millicent, perhaps Meredith's spirit can finally be at rest. Although,' he said, shaking his head, 'how does that make the painting change?'

Beaming a smile, Rebecca said, 'ya, that'll do it. Her soul is finally at peace, once and for all.' Considering this thought caused her a twinge of sadness, reckoning if her spirit was at rest, then it was unlikely their paths would cross again. 'I think, Dad, that because we changed events before this painting was done, perhaps she was actually content at the time. Whereas, before my intervention, she was still sad and tormented,' she said, and shook her head, 'I don't know what to think, but change it has.'

As if she'd noticed Rebecca's emotions, her mother said, 'Maybe that is why she came to bid you farewell. Perhaps she knew you were going to fix the last piece of the puzzle.' She then shook her head, 'hmm, although when she came to say good-bye, you didn't know about the situation with the French men.'

Rebecca nodded. 'I did actually know about the French invasion, for want of a better expression. There was something about it in the fourth box. Because Meredith left the boxes for me, she would have known that I would find out about the situation. And, perhaps she trusted me to fix it, which I have, maybe.' She then shook her head, 'there's no maybe about it. If I hadn't fixed it, the French men would have burnt the paintings, which I saw them doing before I went back further in time and stopped them from ever being there,' she said, and nodded confidently.

Seconds later, Tommy came bounding down the stairs in his new kit, complete with bright pink football boots.

'Take those boots off now,' Elizabeth hollered.

'But they're new, no mud, Mum,' he said, standing on one leg, waving the other foot towards his Elizabeth's face

She pushed his foot away, glared at him, and said in an unusually harsh tone, 'No buts, off now, or else. And don't you ever wave you foot at me again like that, joking or not.'

James, appearing angry, looked at Tommy, and pointed to his study.

A few minutes later, Tommy appeared in the kitchen. 'Mother, I am so very sorry. I was just so excited, and I now understand that is no excuse. I am sorry.'

'It is okay, Tommy, and I too am sorry for barking at you.'

As he turned to head back up the hallway, he paused and said to Rebecca, 'I am sorry sis.'

'It is okay: I have always known you are a... it's alright bro.' She was going to say that she'd known he was a twit since he was born, but thought this was neither the time nor the place.

During supper, the conversation focussed understandably on Tommy having signed for Liverpool. Occasionally, Rebecca managed to get a word in edge ways, but she was nonetheless, happy to sit and listen about all he'd done and all he was going to do, which included him standing every now and then illustrating a move. This made her smile, although she had heard him apologise to her mum about the boot waving so many times it was borderline annoying. Content with her day, she said her good-nights, and headed up for an early night. She knew she would have the day to herself tomorrow, and was determined to get back and spend some time with her fairies, which was her original plan, before she got side tracked once again. Laying there thinking about the way her jaunts manifested themselves now, she reckoned that the fairies could easily end up playing second fiddle again.

The following morning, she was up and getting her stuff ready to head down to the woods, something though was nagging at her inner thoughts. Ever since she'd woken, there was this notion hanging around, telling her to check the fourth box. She'd been through it and umpteen times, both on her own and with her dad. Still though, she had one of those hunches that wouldn't let go. First off, she decided to go and have breakfast with her mum, dad, and Tommy before they went to Anfield for a press event, involving Tommy.

After breakfast, and with the sound of the car still rumbling its way across the gravel, she headed back upstairs. All through breakfast, she was getting this almost tangible message going around in her head to check not only the fourth box, but also the other boxes too. As she sat on the floor, her inclination was to check through box four, primarily because that contained all the important stuff. Just as during breakfast, something was telling her to look in the first box.

As she opened the lid, there was a very slight whiff of almonds, which just not only intrigued her, but also added to her already intensified her mood. *That's odd*, she thought, wondering if Meredith was paying her another visit. She shook her head, suddenly realising the smell of almonds was there whomever she was going to meet. Thinking about it though, she had always felt sure Meredith had been with her through ever journey, so maybe. 'Oh, well, best look inside and find out,' she muttered.

She had looked through these boxes so many times and could remember the exact sequence. However, because of this, she knew there was a danger this would result in her missing something. With this in mind, she deliberately employed a methodical approach. Even with this mindset, going through each piece of paper individually and not finding anything new was becoming monotonous. Then just as she was looking at the last item in the first box, a notion came to her to turn it over and check the bottom. Several times, her dad previously checked the boxes for hidden or false bottoms, but he'd always looked from the top. She realised it was merely a hunch, and wasn't really expecting to find anything. Indifferently, she turned the box over and kind of as expected, it just looked like the bottom of a wooden box. Then just as she was about to move on to the next box, she noticed what appeared to be half of the letter M right in the corner. Grabbing her magnifier from her dressing table, she examined the box, and could see it was definitely half an M.

She leant back against her bed, and stared at the box. Rarely had her intuition let her down. However, as much as she wanted this to be a message from Meredith, it just looked like a letter on the bottom of a box. *That's it,* she thought, jumping up and searching for her pen-knife.

After a few unsuccessful attempts, she finally managed to prize the blade between the base and the side. Just as she was trying to get the box into a position where she could lean against it, she felt something cold against her hand. Turning the box over, and seeing a tiny keyhole, she sat there, wondering how she managed to miss it previously. She leant forward, and peering at the keyhole, nodded, reckoning she had the exact key downstairs, in her dad's tall-boy. 'Where else,' she muttered, flicking her eyes, knowing for sure that this was Meredith's handy work.

She hurried downstairs, grabbed the key, and was back in her room in a flash. Inserting the key into the lock, she mumbled, 'bingo,' as she heard the lock click. With one turn of the key, the side of the box came away, and a fawn-coloured envelope fell into her lap.

Feeling both apprehensive and curious, she carefully opened the envelope, and removed a frayed edged parchment that was folded in four. She sat for a moment staring at the scribbled writing. Although she recognised this as Meredith's handwriting, the scribbled appearance left her feeling a little concerned. Frowning, she took a deep breath, and started reading.

My dear future girl,

You find this, my last note to you, as I knew you would. By now, you will be aware that on the 25th February 1888, I embarked upon a new journey to be with my beloved Aunt. My daughter Rebecca Jane was at my side, when I took my last mortal breath.

The information you imparted recounting the French vagabonds, was judicious, astute, and perfectly timed. It facilitated Rebecca Jane remaining in our home. We christened our house and to reflect your intervention, re named as Chère à votre maison. I am certain that this is a familiar name.

One year later, my daughter had a horrific accident falling from her horse Nadine. Although this was indeed a sad passing, Rebecca Jane had been suffering with an incurable stomach condition, and as such, it was a blessing. Therefore, please do not attempt to intercede upon this situation on this occasion.

Fortunately, a distant relative, Veronica Moore acquired the house and with her family was happy throughout many years. I have no doubt yours, and Veronica's path would have crossed. You would have found her a strong advocate for women's votes, and a campaigner for the suffragist movement.

You must find your own way now, my beloved future girl. Find strength in your principles, and thereby acknowledge, and comprehend your mission. Step forward with character, there is much that awaits you. Know that your vision and openness to that around you changed my life from that of a lost soul, to one at peace.

My love, always, your Meredith.

With her emotions knotted, Rebecca sat there reading the letter over and again. Trying to understand how she felt, she decided to go for a walk in the woods. Still intent of giving herself some fairy time, she grabbed the art box her grandfather had given her, and headed off outside. On her way to the woods, and reflecting on Meredith's letter, knowing it was her last left her feeling quite emotional. However, there was an odd strength in the way the letter was written, and the more she thought about it, the better she felt. By the time, she entered the woods, her emotions had lifted, and she was feeling somewhat positive.

She took a slightly different route to normal, but without realising it, found herself back by the fallen oak. With the mid-day sun streaming through the young willows, she perched herself on the tree, and embraced of the mood that surrounded this place. As she sat there, she started thinking about Sam's goblins and wondered how she'd react if one of her fairies, pixies, or even elves spoke to her. This idea preoccupied her thoughts for the next few minutes. She couldn't help wondering if it might actually happen now she'd thought of it, especially the way things were working out of late. Just as quick, she dismissed the idea, reckoning it was one thing these critters hiding her pencil, but something else having a conversation with a fairy, pixie, or elf. *Well, maybe not an elf*, she thought, and shivered.

She leaned back against a branch, propped her foot up, and started doodling. With the fairies now at the forefront of her thoughts, she decided to conjure up one of their dwellings, not that she'd ever seen one. After an hour or so, and a lot of mind changing, she sat back and muttered, 'looks more like a pixie house.'

'What looks like a pixie house?' a pleasant agreeable voice said from behind her.

Frozen to the spot, she sat there unable to move, as a thousand ideas ran riot in her head. *This is just plain daft* she thought.

'Has the cat gotten your tongue Rebecca? Unusual for you, you normally have so much to say, especially to all the trees, shrubs and indeed anything else that listens.'

Still unable to move her body, let alone her lips, and reckoning who ever this was seemed to know her pretty well, she mumbled through closed lips, 'err, who is speaking to me?' Unless her hearing was on the blink, like her mouth, it sounded like the voice was right behind her and actually coming from somewhere near the tree roots.

'Speak up dear girl, I am sure you mother told you not to mumble.' Whoever it was sighed. 'Well, it isn't Meredith is it, that you know for sure. You ask who I am even though you thought of speaking with me only a few moments ago. Rebecca, please think with an open mind, something you tell others often. I will give you a clue,' the voice said and chuckled oh so quietly. 'Are you ready for a clue?'

'Err, umm, yes I think so,' she said excitedly, having just allowed her brain to let a youthful penny drop.

'I think you know only too well who I am. You spend your every day, saying, "Keep your eyes open and see that which is in front of you." Yet here you are, allowing adult blinkers to stop you seeing that which you desire. Your clue - not that you need one – would you like to swap your pencil for a key.'

Grinning, she said, 'So, you did hide my pencil. She then chuckled quietly, and started to turn around.

'You always say, "oh no, you never see them, you just know they are there." Today is no different, and because of that, you must trust yourself and know I am here, even though you are unable to see me.'

Rebecca sat there, with her leg dangling and her body half turned, not knowing what to think or do.

'Do not fight it Rebecca, just allow your mind to see me, as you have with the drawing of my home.' He then chuckled. 'I have an important message for you, although I anticipate you dismissing today's meeting, along with my message as a daydream.'

She shook her head, 'I will not, I hate it whenever the dream notion is suggested for my journeys.'

'Rebecca, I must tell you of my message. I am here in the absence of Meredith. Her aunt, also Rebecca, who you know, asked that I visited you. When the time is exact, you will feel an irresistible need to visit the servant's quarters, which you know as the summerhouse. Instead of entering the summerhouse and climbing the stairs, you must take your father's boat and be alone when you do so. Row it around the nearest island once and return to shore. Are you clear so far?'

Rebecca nodded several times, wondering where this was going and importantly who this was talking to her.'

'No need to wonder, you could have asked. I am a pixie, and my name is Ethernal. So, once you are back on land, you will find yourself in the year 1123. By the brook, you will come across and lady who has been injured with sword cuts. Her name is Matilda, and she has just been overthrown as the queen of England. You need not concern yourself with the policies of this event that resulted in many years of civil unrest. I see you are scribbling notes, please say if I am going too quickly for you.'

Rebecca shook her head, and said, 'no I am fine. May I ask, can you read my thoughts?'

'I could not possibly tell you; however, I suspect you know the answer.' He then chuckled again. 'Matilda's injuries will be severe, and you must take her to the bear lodge in the woods of the other side of the lake. Once there, you must nurse her back to health. Be aware, there are many who want her dead, and that will alone pose a relentless challenge. It is important that you gather these medicines; turmeric, honey, and clear ethyl alcohol. Do not be tempted to take medicines from your own time, although I suspect you may consider this option. In addition, you will need a healthy supply of fruits and vegetables that are high in iron. Alongside these, you will require sufficient food for two people to last twenty days. Be mindful, there are no fridges, so create a natural larder with the cool water from the stream running adjacent to the lodge. Are you clear so far?'

'I am, and my curiosity is at bursting point, you said she was queen of England. Can you tell me more?'

'She was, until the day you find her, Matilda, queen of England. She is of your kind, and was one of the first to speak out using her foresights. The peasants of this land loved her, as did we pixies, the elves, and the fairies. The gentry, however, saw her as a threat to their disdainful, wealth laden existence, and thereby challenged their combatants to rid this land of her monarchy.'

'So, what happens when I have nursed her back to health?'

'She will head to Scotland, where she will find refuge in a priory in Perthshire. She will, all being well, live out the remainder of her life there. She will write scriptures proclaiming you and your type as future redeemers of mankind. In years beyond yours, these scriptures with be held in high esteem. I must lastly add that she will speak a mixture of Saxon English and French.'

Rebecca, still scribbling notes, asked, 'you said a mixture of French and which other languages?' There was no answer, so she asked again. Her repeated question was met with silence. Slowly, she turned, and couldn't see a sign of anyone or anything. Indeed, the autumn leaves seemed undisturbed. Unsure what to think, she sat back reading over her notes. With the warmth of the afternoon sun shimmering through the trees, she leaned against the branch, and closed her eyes.

CHAPTER 23 – DREAMING OR TURMERIC

Rebecca stirred, and rubbing her eyes, shivered. It was dark, and she knew she must have fallen asleep, but how long for she wondered. Not having her watch or phone, she decided to head back up the main house.

With her head full of everything Ethernal had said, she started to look through her notes. 'Where are my notes?' she muttered. Now half way back to the main house, she stopped and went through her art box, and although she had her drawing pad, there was no sign of any notes. She knew she hadn't left them behind because she had written them on the next page after her drawing of a pixie house. That page was blank, and she definitely hadn't ripped any pages out. 'What is going on?' she mumbled.

Even though, she knew it was a waste of time, and it was probably too dark to see, she headed back to the oak tree. As she suspected, there was nothing there. Now feeling decidedly chilly, she hurried along the path back towards home. Just as she was coming to the edge of the woods, she tripped and hit the ground with an almighty bang.

Instantly, memories of her first time with Meredith filled her head. She sat there for a moment nursing her saw ankle. With her thoughts now jumping between, Meredith and Matilda, she limped back home. As she entered the house, she could hear Tommy laughing in the kitchen.

'Where have you been, Rebecca?' her mum asked. 'And what has happened to your white jeans, lying in the grass again,' she said and narrowed her eyes in that familiar way.

'Oh, I was in the woods sketching, fell asleep, and tripped in the darkness coming back. What's the time?'

'Supper time, so go and get cleaned up. Roxy will be here shortly, and we wouldn't want her to think you've been playing football with Tommy.'

'As if that is going to happen. Where is Dad?'

'In his study, but get yourself sorted before you go and disturb him.'

She was desperate to tell her dad all about today, but with Roxy coming over, she decided to wait and tell them both together. She went upstairs and after cleaning herself up and bandaging her ankle, she again checked her pad and art box for her notes. There was nothing, and she even tried rubbed over some of her pad with the side of a pencil to see if there was anything embossed of the page. Again, there was nothing at all, not a trace of evidence.

Through dinner, the conversation was all about the Tommy's day with the press at Liverpool. Although Rebecca was happy to listen and celebrate her brother's achievement, her mind kept going back to the events of the day. A couple of times, Roxy kicked her under the table, right on her sore ankle too, and mouthed for her to pay attention. As soon as supper was over the girls offered to tidy up.

'No, it is okay girls; Tommy and I are going to do it. It is payback for him waving his foot in my face,' she said and chuckled. 'Thanks anyways Roxy, Rebecca.'

'Roxy, Rebecca, do you two fancy a chat?' her dad asked, looking directly at Rebecca.

Over the next hour, she told her father and Roxy all about her experience today.

'It is weird, because it does actually feel like a dream. What's annoying is Ethernal said I would think it was a dream. What is that all about? I hate it whenever the word dream is mentioned in relation to anything that's happened to me, and here I am saying it myself.'

'Well, it is a bit odd; especially with your notes have vanishing. Maybe we can go back and check in the morning,' Roxy said, appearing curious.

'Already checked, and that's how I hurt my ankle. And, thanks for kicking it under the table about twenty-five times.'

'I am sorry, but even I was paying attention to Tommy today.'

'I know, sorry.'

'So, you say you recall her name as Queen Matilda and that it was 1123. I am sure we can look it up on the internet.'

Her father then opened up his laptop and immediately found something relating to Queen Matilda, which indicated she was overthrown in 1123. 'Well you couldn't have dreamt that all up.'

'I did know all about her as I did something for my history exam at school, so it is in there somewhere.'

'So you have spent the last however many years telling us to wash our mouths out if we dare to suggest a dream, and here you are now trying to convince us it was,' he said and laughed.

'I know, Dad, but I can't come up with anything else. I am going back to check again tomorrow.'

After continuing chatting to Roxy late into the night, she eventually fell asleep. First thing, when she woke was to try to recall the remnants of a dream quickly fading from her consciousness. Seeing Roxy sitting outside on the balcony, she called out. 'I was blinking dreaming about pixies, but for the life of me can't remember what it was about.'

'So, twice in two days,' Roxy called back, and laughed.

After breakfast, the girls headed back down to the woods for a look around. On the way into the woods, Roxy said, 'You know this is the first time I have been in this forest.'

'It's a wood, not a forest,' Rebecca answered in an ironic tone, and then laughed.

'Don't actually care, just looking forward to seeing the famous oak tree, the one you've never bovvered' to show me before.'

As they arrived by the tree, Rebecca immediately started looking around. After a few minutes, she decided to look under the tree. 'Move your legs,' she said to Roxy, who was now sun bathing, in the exact spot Rebecca sits in. 'This is odd.'

'What's odd, that you're scrabbling around on the floor and I'm topping up my tan?'

'No, when I looked the other day, I couldn't get my hand under the tree. Now though, there is loads of room.' She then shrieked as her hand touched something cold.

'What happened, been bitten by a crocodile, babe?'

After a few seconds, Rebecca produced three small coins. 'They are covered in mud,' she said and handed them to Roxy, 'These are interesting and they look very old. Need to give them a clean.'

'Very heavy, might be silver, and worth a few bob. Come on lets go give a clean up.'

'We can clean them down by the stream,' Rebecca said, and stood up.

The two headed over the stream and as she had so many times in the past, Rebecca clambered down the bank, holding the same branch, she always holds. After a few moments scrubbing with her hanky and flaking away some mud with her finger nails, she handed one of the coins back to Roxy. 'No blinking dream. Look at this coin.'

Shaking her head, Roxy said, 'I alt to be used to this by now, but even so. This coin is 1123, and is embossed with a woman's face. I even think I can make out a letter M, and an L and D. Might as well say Matilda.'

'Yeah, look at this one though, same year, man's head. What is that all about?'

The two decided to head back to the main house and give the coins a proper clean up. As they were standing in the kitchen, Elizabeth appeared.

'You two bunking a day of work today?'

'Ohh, bleep, bleep,' said Roxy.

'Ditto, we best go get cleaned up. I will ring Dad on the way to say sorry.'

They eventually arrived in work at eleven, and snuck in via the back door. Her dad, called out from his office, 'What happened girls, get stuck waiting for a train in the 12th century.' He then laughed so loud, the whole office turned around.

'Not supposed to laugh at your own jokes Dad. But it was a gooden.' Rebecca said as she entered her father's office. She then placed the three coins on his table. 'See Father, I told you it wasn't a dream.'

The three say around for the next few minutes, while her father trawled the internet for something similar. After a few moments, he found an exact match for the two coins with Matilda's head on. However, there was nothing even remotely similar to the coin with the man's head on it. Then he expanded the year from 1123 to include 1124 and 1125. He then came across a number of coins from 1125 that were a perfect match. 'Interesting, there are no coins for 1124 at all.'

Rebecca nodded several times. 'Ethernal said there was major conflict and civil unrest after Matilda was overthrown. Maybe they were too busy dealing with this to print coins. I don't know, just a wild guess.'

CHAPTER 24 – PROVISIONS

The girls spent the next two days again working on an excel spreadsheet. By Friday evening, they'd had enough and just as they were heading out the door, James called them.

'I've been doing some digging on your girl Matilda. Although, I would suggest that as a former head of the English monarchy, I should address her as Ma'am.' He then chuckled, 'so, it seems she was of great character, someone whom everybody loved. That was unless you were rich. She was the queen of the people and a great literalist by all accounts. The thing is, after she was overthrown, she was presumed murdered, and sadly it would appear that history forgot all about her.'

'Dad, that is so interesting. Thank you for finding that out. Ethernal said she was one for the people too.' She then laughed, and said, 'he also said the fairies, pixies, and elves liked her too. Hey, maybe that is what she wrote about.'

After chatting a little longer with James, the girls decided to go to one of the local bars for one drink before heading home. One turned into more and before they knew it, they were once again stopping over in their now favourite hotel.

'We should have a season ticket here,' Roxy laughed.

The following day, the girls decided to go and watch Tommy play for Liverpool reserves, only to turn up at the training ground to find they were playing away. So instead, they headed into town to a new department store that had just opened. While they were looking around, although Rebecca's thoughts kept going back to Matilda, she wasn't feeling any urgency in that direction. That feeling, or lack of it, made her think about what Ethernal had suggested that when the time was right, she'd know. Realising she was being a little distant when she heard Roxy make some sarcastic comment Rebecca decided to put Matilda to the back of her thoughts.

It had become a regular thing with the girls making a weekend of it and with little persuasion, decided to stay for another night. After heading back to the hotel to change into their newly purchased outfits, they decided to go to a Jazz bar that had just opened up. Both woke up the following morning, unusually without a hangover. After a big breakfast, and because it was a delightfully warm autumnal morning, they headed along to the quay side to watch an open-air theatre. Bizarrely the theatre group were performing a mid-summers night dream. Every time the subject of fairies came up, Rebecca's thoughts instantly turned to Ethernal. On the way home in the car, she was finding it difficult to think about anything else. Once home, Roxy stayed for around an hour before heading back to London.

It was now mid-afternoon, and she had just said farewell to Roxy. At a loss what to do, she decided to go back to the woods for another look around. Although, she'd checked twice already, was adamant she'd written up some notes. She made her way back to where she was sitting with renewed energy, determined to find some answers. She spent a few minutes looking around, and found nothing to suggest either her or Ethernal had been anywhere near the place. Even though she had the three coins, she was finding it hard not to think it may have all been a daydream of sorts. This annoyed her, even though Ethernal had said she might consider this option.

Reckoning there was nothing here for her, she headed back towards the lake. As she made her way down to the shore, something was telling her to have a look around inside the summerhouse. Heading along the water's edge, her thoughts suddenly changed direction, and her focus was on the boat. Previous times, when the boat came to mind, so did the fun she'd had with her mother. Today though, she was getting the most peculiar feeling. Recalling what Ethernal had said about creating a natural larder, she sat on the jetty, wondering how she was ever going to store enough food for two people, for twenty days. Just then, she heard the sound of a car and turning could see Roxy pulling into the drive. Reckoning she must have forgotten something, she hurried up to meet her.

'I got about thirty minutes away, and was thinking about your impending meeting with Matilda. You don't need a fridge, tinned meats, vegetables, and so on, is all you'll need. If the pixie is right, dear Matilda will be flat on her back recovering and won't give a jot where the food come from. So, me being me, I jumped the gun, stopped off at the supermarket, and well, have a look in my boot.'

Opening the boot, Rebecca exclaimed, 'I am only going potentially for twenty days, not twenty months.' She shook her head, 'that's if I go at all. Bless you, thank you so much. But I don't have a clue how we will get it all over there. Especially if I go on a hunch, which means I can't then go to the house, load up with all this, because the door might be closed by the time I get back.'

'Thought of it, and I got a local walking map from the little sweet shop. It shows a route through the pine forest. Now I don't think it goes anywhere near your lodge, but it does go close.'

The two girls had a look at the map, and after Rebecca pointed out where she thought the lodge was, they decided it would be too far to walk, certainly with all their provisions. After a bit of debate, they reckoned their only option was to load up the boat and row there. They then went to fetch an old wheel-barrow, loaded it up and headed down towards the lake. With it being so heavy, they took it in turns.

'I just hope this lot doesn't sink the boat,' Roxy laughed.

'I cannot believe you got everything, including the turmeric, honey, and where on earth did you get this alcohol from?'

'Chemist and I looked up on the net what they used in that time to treat wounds. Got it all covered even the matches, and bandages. I just hope Matilda doesn't start asking questions.'

'Questions, what does that even mean?'

'As in where did this and that come from? Mind you, I don't 'spose she'll be too bovvered' if ya tell 'er Waitrose or Aldi's,' she said, making them both scream with laughter.

Rebecca made her way along the jetty to untie the boat, and blurted, 'Flip me; Dad's only gone and fitted a little out-board motor.'

They loaded the boat, and evenly distributed the food, so as not to cap-size. They then set about trying to start the motor. After several attempts, Roxy picked up a manual from under one of the seats. On the front, written in James's handwriting was, *"in case you need this for Matilda, I got a motor. Obviously, you'll only use this to take any provisions over, just in case."*

'Seems you're not the only one that has thought of this,' Rebecca said. 'I mean, there's Dad buying an engine for the boat. You with enough supplies to feed a small country and well...'

'Yeah, but you're the one with the unique gift babe.'

Once over the other side, they again loaded up the wheel-barrow. Partially following instinct and recalling her memories, the girls eventually found the lodge.

As they were unloading the barrow, Rebecca asked, 'what's in the heavy box?'

'There's a small portable cooker, with plenty of gas, just don't let Matilda see or, or she'll be like, what the hell. There's an airbed, for you, obviously, and some blankets for queenie.'

'Flip, you've thought of everything, thanks Roxy.'

They then spent the next couple of hours tidying up, and talked about what they were going to use as a bed area for Matilda.

'You know, it's odd and I recall thinking last time I was here that it looks bigger on the outside and you'd think there was more than one small room. Just as she said it, Roxy lent against the wall and felt it move a little.

'What was that?' Roxy asked turning around. As she pushed against the wall, it moved. After a heavy shove form both of them, the wall moved as if it were a secret door. Behind, it revealed another room.

Both girls gasped, and Roxy said, 'Now I get it, if all your trips are like this, it is no wonder you are so full of excitement when you come back.

Rebecca was dumbfounded finding a new room, but was delighted all the pieces seemed to be fitting together nicely. She drifted off, remembering how she felt entering the room at the top of the spiral stairs for the first time. Miles away, she noticed Roxy was tidying up, so shook her head, and started helping.

She made her way over to a wooden bed in the corner. Examining the mattress, it appeared surprisingly okay, although a little tattered and very grubby, but nothing that a good dusting wouldn't sort. The bed though, including the struts was in surprisingly good condition. Next to the bed, were two sturdy wooden storage boxes, which if nothing else would serve as seats. The girls pottered about for a while, and felt they'd made the place look half decent, in spite of all the dust floating about. Roxy then suggested looking in the boxes.

Rebecca had already looked while they were tidying up, hopeful she might find something inside, and although they were both empty, she knew that could change at any time.

Although both girls were sure there weren't any more hidden rooms, they gave each wall some investigation. After pushing at all the walls, unsuccessfully, they reckoned it was time to head back home. On the way, Roxy asked about the first time Rebecca visited the lodge. Rebecca explained that during her fist visit the lodge she found a photo, which offered tentative confirmation that her previous trips weren't dreams.

When they arrived back at the main house, they continued to chat about Rebecca's trips over a coffee. After Roxy had left, Rebecca decided to start supper, knowing her parents would be home soon.

'So, what have you been up to today, Rebecca?' he father asked.

Roxy and I went over to the lodge. Thanks for fixing an outboard to the boat, Dad.'

'What outboard motor?' Tommy blurted.

'Nothing for you to worry yourself about,' James said.

'But I want to have a go.'

'In good time, now be a good lad, and help your Mother tidy up from supper.'

He pulled a silly face and begrudgingly got up and started helping. His expression reminded Rebecca that he would always be a twit, which made her laugh aloud. Tommy turned and pulled another silly face. To stop herself from saying anything untoward, she decided to go up to her room and see if she could find anything on her computer relating to Queen Matilda. After searching through the Internet and unable to come up with anything new, she decided on a shower and an early night. While in the shower, she thought about being gone for twenty-odd days. Reckoning this could be her last shower for quite a while, she considered packing a few bathroom necessaries even though she knew she shouldn't. Roxy had said earlier that Matilda would be on her back and wouldn't care one way or the other. *To hell with it*, she thought, and packed some toiletries into an old cloth bag she'd found in the lodge.

CHAPTER 25 - MATILDA

Waking early, she was first down for breakfast. Moments later, her father walked in.

'Morning, Rebecca. So how did your twisted ankle stand up when you went over to the lodge yesterday? The way you were limping around, I thought it would put pay to any jaunts any time soon,' he said and laughed. 'As if that would stop you.'

'Hmm, actually it was okay, ish. Roxy stopped off and brought back enough food to feed the five-thousand. Clever girl, she thought of everything I might need for my jaunt with Matilda.' She started chatting to her dad about her impending trip, when Tommy burst in, soon flowed by a frowning Elizabeth.

'Tommy, calm down, we are only going training.'

'Yeah but Mum, it's me first time training with the reserves.'

'It's my first training session, not me first,' she said and glancing at Rebecca, raised her eyebrows.

Tommy looked at her with his mouth open, and then said, 'Mum, it is definitely...'

Before she could finish, Elizabeth said, 'Tommy, it is not about whose training session it is, it's about... Oh, forget it,' she said and ruffled his hair, which made Rebecca laugh aloud.

After her dad had left for work, her mum said she was going to meet up with Ruth and Amanda for lunch after she'd dropped Tommy off.

'That will be nice Mum. You've not seen A for an age, have you? Send my love to both. Unusual Tommy training on a Tuesday, I thought that was his day off.'

'Oh I will. It is going to be fun as I think Amanda is getting married. Well, Ruth thinks so, we shall see. Yeah, no game this Wednesday so training today.'

'Oh my, you kept that secret.'

'What, about the training,' she said and laughed. 'Well, I wasn't going to say anything until I knew for sure. However, Ruth is adamant and she is never like that, unless she is certain. Right, got to dash, Tommy is waiting in the car. I love you sweetie. I will call you when I know about Amanda.'

Bye Mum, love you too.'

Other than wondering what she was going to wear to Amanda's wedding, Rebecca was at a loss what to do. She went upstairs and sat on her balcony, editing her water-fairy tale. Every now and then, between wondering about the possible wedding and editing her story, her mind occasionally drifted to Matilda. She reckoned, as always, when the time was right, she would know. However, somewhere in her deepest thoughts, she wondered if she could force the issue. Thinking about what Ethernal had said, she was now considering getting in the boat and heading around the island, just to see what happens. She then sat there staring at her laptop, and again become immersed with her fairy tale. Now deeply engrossed, her phone rang, breaking her focus.

'Hello Mum,' she said, and chatted to her for a few minutes. 'All a bit vague if you ask me. So, she said it is only a maybe, but if it does happen, then she wants me as a bridesmaid. Well, at least now, I don't have to sort out a dress.'

As she sat there thinking about Amanda's possible wedding, her thoughts gradually turned to her own wedding to Etienne. Annoyingly, it seemed like a distant memory, and although she could recall some details, it was again felt like one of those dreams you just can't recall. Her stomach rumbled, and glancing at her watch, was shocked to see it was two in the afternoon. Feeling unusually hungry, she headed downstairs to make a sandwich. Stopping at the bottom of the stairs, she paused by the paintings.

'Meredith, I so wish I could speak with you once more,' she whispered, then turned toward the kitchen. Halfway along the corridor, she felt something touch her shoulder, and again it felt like someone's hand. She stopped dead in her tracks. Unlike the previous times when she'd felt a hand on her shoulder, this time she wondered if it was Meredith, reassuring her. As quick, she dismissed the idea, reckoning it was just wishful thinking.

She shook her head, and went to make her sandwich. As she sat there eating, her thoughts drifted between Meredith, Amanda's wedding, and her impending meeting with Matilda. Feeling like she was in some kind her of limbo, she knew she had to focus her thoughts if she was going to make anything happen. She finished her lunch and decided the only way to find out, was to go down the lake and see what happens.

On her way down the hallway, she hesitated for a moment. She had never had to plan for any of her jaunts in the past because they just happened. This though, was a completely different scenario and one that required a little planning.

Right, she thought, and headed upstairs to pack a bag of clothes, and anything else that came to mind. In the past, she'd always found comfort and reassurance, reckoning Meredith would look over her. Although she'd felt something in the hallway earlier, she knew that was probably just a sign of her hopeful imagination. With Meredith now seemingly gone, she felt a little uneasy, knowing she'd be on her own this time. Zipping up her small back pack of clothes, she made her way downstairs. Standing by the door, she briefly considered leaving her mother a note. Again, she felt a sensation suggesting Meredith was there, even though she knew she wasn't. Oddly, something was telling her she didn't need to leave a note, and everything would be okay.

Although she was eager to get going, she was still a little unsure. She took a deep breath, and closed the front door. She then put her door keys under a flower pot, and made her way down towards that lake.

When she arrived there, her thoughts were all over the place. It was one thing helping someone with potentially life-threatening injuries, but the fact that this person was once the queen of England left her feeling anxious. She'd done a lot of research on the Internet regarding the potential wounds she'd be nursing, and most of what she'd found had related to modern medicine techniques, There was very little regarding methods used in the twelfth century and this just added to her turmoil.

As she stood there on the jetty, although anxious, something at the back of head was telling her the time was right. She quickly checked her bag for the six boxes of matches and a flint just in case. She then climbed in the boat and before staring the engine, sat there considering what might lie ahead. She started the engine, and glanced towards the island, again wondering what today would bring.

As the boat started moving slowly, her emotions went up a notch, reminding her how she felt the first time she entered the room at the top of the spiral stairs. With a shiver of anticipation going the length of her body, she headed out across the lake. Although she still felt more than a little apprehensive, she sped towards the island.

Arriving by the island, and feeling a little hesitant, she slowed down. Ethernal told her that once she had passed around the island, she would find herself in 1123. With this thought resonating in her head, she was finding it difficult to focus, not knowing what to expect, or if she'd see or feel a difference. She didn't have to wait too long, to find out. Passing around the island, she could hear raucous shouting and see armoured men on horseback clambering along the lake side.

She put the engine in reverse and backed slowly hiding herself behind the island, positioning herself, so she could watch the ensuing proceedings. Once she was certain the horsemen had gone, and keeping her eyes peeled, she made her way towards the shore. She moored the boat on the beach, climbed out and looked around. She was fairly sure the men on horseback had gone, although she was still feeling a little uneasy. She stood there for a moment, watching and listening, and once she was confident the coast was clear, headed towards the wood.

As she arrived at the edge of the woods, although unrecognisable, she still oddly felt at home. Unlike in her time, the woods were dominated by silver-birch, oaks, yews, and a myriad of elm. With most of the trees showing signs of new growth, she reckoned it was probably spring time. With the sun behind her, heading towards the lake edge, she guessed she had a couple of hours before darkness.

As she made her way into the woods, she could hear the sound of a man's voice moaning. Following the voice, she stopped dead in her tracks as her eyes settled upon a man lying on the ground. Unsure what to think, she approached him slowly. His cream hessian clothing was sodden in blood, leaving her feeling troubled and a positively uneasy. As she got close, he stopped groaning, and looked directly at Rebecca. Although still anxious, she felt oddly calm, and with her empathy kicking in, knelt beside him. He moved his hand, touching the back of Rebecca's hand. He lifted his hand a little, beckoning her towards him, and whispered, "Save my Queen." He then, with a tiny movement of his face, indicated behind him, breathed deeply, and closed his eyes.

She knelt there for a moment or two and realised he had taken his last breath. Feeling a pang of sadness for this unknown soul, she closed her eyes, and said a short prayer. She slowly got to her feet, and headed in the direction he'd indicated. After a few steps, she turned and looked back, again anguished for this man's soul.

Recalling what Ethernal had said to her, and refocusing her thoughts, she continued in the direction of the stream. Going on gut feel and intuition, she made her way through the wood, hoping she was going the right way. Coming into a clearing, and looking back in the direction of the setting sun, she was sure she knew where she was. With conviction, she continued. After just a few steps, she heard a faint female voice whimpering, which immediately intensified her mood. Heading in that direction, the voice, although quiet, was getting closer.

Passing a cluster of young elm, she arrived by the stream. She stood there for a moment, listening carefully. She could no longer hear the voice, but was sure she was close. Just as she was considering she might have taken a wrong turn, she heard the voice again. Although it was still quiet, it sounded as if it was coming from some dense, yellow flowed shrubs, right in front her. Making her way over, she now knew the voice was coming from the other side. She stood there for a moment trying to find a way around the head high bushes. Realising she had no choice, lowered herself down into the stream and waded through the shallow water. As soon as she was on the other side, she could see a woman lying close to the water's edge.

The woman turned towards her and said softly, 'Aidez-moi, please.'

Remembering what Ethernal had said, she wasn't too surprised to hear this woman speak with a mixture of French and English. The woman's expression was torn with grief, which had an immediate impact on Rebecca's senses. Climbing from the stream, she sat close to the woman.

As if this woman sensed her good intentions, she held out her blood covered hand, and again whispered, 'Aidez-moi, please.'

Responding to this woman's powerful, yet peaceful persona, she held her hand, and whispered, 'I will help you, je t'aiderai.'

The woman's eyes softened, and although clearly in pain, forced a smile. 'I knew you would come. I know not why I knew, however, I did.' The woman then grimaced, and whimpering, held her side.

Carefully, Rebecca lifted the woman's torn cloth blouse, revealing an awful wound. Trying to hide her frayed emotions, she breathed deeply through her nose. She took the woman's hand, and said, 'I will make you well, Matilda.'

Although clearly stricken with grief and pain, the woman forced a shallow smile. 'I knew you would come to me.'

Rebecca was now regretting not bringing any medicine from her time. Then she remembered in the bottom of her backpack, some ibuprofen she'd brought for her ankle. She knew Ethernal had told her not to use medicines from her time, but she felt there was no choice. Besides, this woman needed was pain relief. What she didn't need was an explanation where it came from. As she rummaged around in the bottom of her bag, not only did she find the tablets, she also came across a package with a note attached to it.

Wrapped up in the note was a suture kit and an anaesthetic set. She narrowed her eyes and started reading the note.

Bex, I know your pixie mate told you not to bring anything like this. If your Matilda bird has a knife or sword wound, you going to need more than spit and polish. Just use it and worry about it after. Love Roxy.

Rebecca looked at the woman lying there and was at a loss what to think. She knew Ethernal had told her not to use anything like this. However, the grief on this woman's face was telling her she had no choice.

Pouring some water into a metal cup, she added two tablets, crushing them between her fingers. She then read the packet and looking at the woman's six-inch gaping wound, added two more. She knew this wouldn't stop the pain, but if it alleviated her trauma a little, then it was the right thing to do. Aware the horsemen may still be close, was making her anxious, and she knew she had to get this woman into the boat and across the lake to safety. She offered her the cup, and smiling, said, 'this will help your pain.'

Slowly, the woman sipped the water, nodding often.

Just as she had with Meredith, Rebecca felt an instant connection with this woman. Over the next few minutes, she gradually nursed her injuries, using a swab that she had prepared yesterday.

She glanced at the suture kit, and then back at the woman's wound. She took a deep breath, and started reading the directions. Although, she'd never done anything like this before, reckoned it seemed reasonably straight forward, and besides, it wouldn't make things any worse. She then turned her attention to the anaesthetic, and as with the suture kit, this seemed uncomplicated and relatively simple. With the woman drifting a little, she leant over and whispered, 'you may feel a little pain, but this will help you.' Holding the woman's hand, she took a deep breath, and carefully inserted the needle close to the wound and pressed the syringe. Reading the instructions, trying to work out how long this would take to work, she looked up and noticed for Matilda's face seemed a whole lot more relaxed. Carefully, she touched close to the wound, which caused no reaction. Again, she breathed deeply and started cleaning the area thoroughly with some antiseptic that Roxy had also put with the kit. Without this causing any reaction from Matilda, she started stitching the wound. Although the woman moaned a little, she managed to close the wound completely. Breathing deeply, she sat back, pleased with her efforts.

Matilda's wounds were now bandaged, and her pain had clearly. Slowly, Rebecca helped her to her feet, assuring her continually. Keeping her ears peeled for the horsemen, Rebecca led Matilda back

245

to the lake's edge. As she lowered her into the boat, she could see the woman's exhaustion etched into her every breath. Rebecca had already laid out some blankets and as soon as Matilda settled down, she closed her eyes. Alarmed by this, Rebecca gently shook her, causing the woman to stir, and realised she was just resting.

Again, thinking about what Ethernal had said, Rebecca planned to discard the engine and row across the lake. Now though, with Matilda seemingly oblivious, she decided to go with it, especially as the horsemen were probably still nearby. She was aware she needed to get across the lake as quick as possible, avoiding any conflict, and importantly, not be seen. After scanning for the horsemen, she started the engine, which caused Matilda to stir briefly. She checked on her and seeing she was once more asleep, headed out. Passing by the island, she again looked back. With no sign of any onlookers, she sped across the lake.

As she beached the boat, the sound of gravel grating along the keel caused Matilda to wake.

'Where am I?' she asked, sitting up in the boat.

The anguish this woman showed sitting up made Rebecca realise how difficult her task would be getting her to the lodge. She assured Matilda, and helping her out carefully, set about hiding the boat. After struggling for a few moments, she remembered she'd hidden the wheelbarrow in the trees. She went to fetch it, and fortunately, the twin wheels detached from the bottom and fitted nicely under the boat. Although with the weight of the boat, combined with her twisted ankle, moving it still took a great effort. Eventually, after turning her ankle a few times, she hid the boat as best she could. She then helped Matilda to the lodge via a track she'd trodden down when she was with Roxy. Clearly still distressed with pain, Matilda showed a strength and character befitting of her queen status. With every tormented step taken by this woman, the greater Rebecca's admiration, and respect increased.

Resting often, they eventually arrived by the lodge. With Matilda clearly exhausted, Rebecca helped her to the bed and within minutes, she was sleeping. She then set about organising the lodge, keeping a vigilante eye on her sleeping queen. Once she'd sorted everything, she set up camp next to the bed, watching over Matilda while she slept. Wearily, she leant back against the bed, and thinking about her day, closed her eyes.

Matilda groaned, and woke Rebecca from a deep sleep. She opened her eyes to an icy pitch black room and wondered how long she'd been sleeping. Fumbling in her pocket, she lit a match, and made her way over to the fire. Again, Matilda groaned, and checking on her the best she could, set about starting the fire. Opportunely, Roxy had shown foresight and had prepared the fire, making it easy to get it going. With the room warming nicely, and the fire giving off some light, she set a couple of candle's burning. Mindful that the horsemen may still be lurking, she pulled the wooden shutters to, blocking out any external light. She then went outside to check there was no light filtering through. With no sound or sight of any onlookers, she returned inside.

She then turned her attention to Matilda, checking her wound, assuring her continually. Rebecca sat there considering her options, aware this woman was weak and suffering. Although Ethernal had told her not to use medicines from her time, she had brought some iron tablets just in case, reckoning she wasn't breaking too many rules in doing so. Besides, it was a bit late to worry about using anything like that. She then warmed some water, added a spoonful of honey, a spoonful of turmeric. Even though she knew she shouldn't, she decided to hell with it, and crushed up two iron tablets and two more ibuprofen. Her view being the last thing this woman needed was to be force fed cold fruit and vegetables to increase her iron levels. She eased Matilda up, and made sure she drank every drop.

Smiling continually in an attempt to offer some reassurance, she again checked the dressing on her wound. Although blood soaked, the bandages were now dry, suggesting her wound had stopped bleeding.

When she looked at Matilda, the woman offered up a painful smile, again showing remarkable courage.

From her first interaction with this woman, Rebecca felt an instant bond. The way Matilda was now responding to her, it seemed that feeling was mutual. She was initially apprehensive, wondering how twenty days and nights nursing a stranger would pan out. Those concerns were now long gone, and she was actually energized by the prospect of helping this woman back to health.

With Matilda sitting up, she reckoned it might be an idea to try this woman with some food. When she was here with Roxy, they'd hidden away a fresh vegetable, and some tinned beef broth, which they reckoned would be good for a couple of days. She collected it from the other room, and hiding the plastic container from Matilda, emptied the contents into a brass saucepan she got from her mother's kitchen. She then warmed it gradually over the fire, checking on Matilda continually. Over the next hour, she fed Matilda, also eating herself, aware she needed to be strong. Once they'd finished, she sat there holding her hand, comforting her often with words of kindness.

'Je vous remercie, thank you, Rebecca,' she uttered quietly.

Having barely heard a word from this woman since she'd found her in the woods on the other side of the lake, Rebecca was taken aback. She squeezed her hand gently, and whispered, 'I am here only for you.' Suddenly, she realised this woman had referred to her by name. Unsure what to think, she was now wondering how she could possibly know her name, certain she hadn't told her.

Over the next three days, with barely a word exchanged between them, Rebecca continued to nurse this woman. On the fourth morning, Rebecca entered the room to see Matilda sitting up in bed. Although she was clearly still in pain, there were real signs of improvement. Again wondering why she had used her name, she recalled Ethernal saying, "She is of your kind, and was one of the first to speak out using her foresights." That resonated with her, and she'd assumed he

248

was suggesting Matilda was like her. If so, that would mean she could also see beyond her years, just as Meredith's aunt could. Although, she was desperate to find out more, she was mindful that this woman had barely spoken, and decided to wait until the time was right.

As it was now around midday, and having checked Matilda's wounds, she decided to warm up the last of the beef broth. The outside night temperatures had remained decidedly cold, and this had helped to keep the food relatively fresh. It was autumn at home, but she had quickly realised it was early spring here, possibly March or April. In the past, whenever she had travelled back, it was always to a similar month to home. She now found herself wondering if this change of the season was part of a bigger plan purely to help her store the food. Then just as she was serving up the broth, realised it was nothing to do with the food. It was so Matilda, once well, could travel and be in Scotland during the summer months.

After lunch, she decided it was time to change Matilda's dressings. She started removing the old bandages carefully, and although this was proving a little difficult due to the dry blood, Matilda didn't make a sound. Admiring this woman's strength of character, Rebecca removed the last of the dressing. Glancing back and forth between the wound and this woman, she couldn't believe what she was looking at. The stitches had dissolved, and the scar now had the appearance of one that was months old. Unable to understand how this could be she looked at the woman, wondering how she could have healed so quickly.

She held out her hand, and touched Rebecca's face gently. 'You are not of my time, are you Rebecca?' I foretold of your coming, to my closest associates, and those I believed allies. I am now in a position to conclude they were not friends. I now understand that I was their Queen and as such, they demonstrated an acceptance towards my visionary words. Their receipt was shallow, and that born from a duty to my position. Their efforts to bring down my thrown have shown me this.' She then touched Rebecca's face again. 'You have come to me, as I knew you would. You have shown a neutral and unprejudiced kindness, of which I have not seen since my Mother's passing.'

Trying to remain unaffected by this woman's words, she said, 'You seem to know of me and where I am from.'

'I know only that you have journeyed here from years beyond my own. I suspect, by your appearance, and the medicines you have used that you have travelled back many centuries. Again, I foretold of this.'

She hadn't planned to tell this woman that she had travelled back a thousand years, not yet anyway. It would now seem she knew, and importantly was of a similar make up to her and Meredith's aunt. 'I have travelled back ten centuries, to help you alone. I suggest those that attacked you, were frightened by your vision. I know a story that relates to a woman seven centuries henceforth. She was like us, and told of her views. She was treated with contempt, ridiculed for her words, and subsequently banished from her home. In my time, although my foresight is occasionally met with apathy, mostly it accepted. In generations after mine, our kind will be seen as the way forward.' She then held her hand out and gently touched Matilda's arm. 'Our job now is to get you well. Then we can plan your escape.'

Seemingly taking everything Rebecca had said in her stride, she said, 'You showed surprise when dressing my wounds. I heal quickly, another thing that has been met in my time with disdain, and disbelief.'

Rebecca's thoughts immediately went back to a conversation she had with the university doctor. She had visited him to pick up an asthma pump for Roxy, and he had asked her to pop in for a chat. He said he would like to do body mass index check, along with a couple of other minor tests. He then explained that he and a fellow doctor had read her file and realised she had never visited the doctor other than for a fall and subsequent cut to her head. The results had shown that Rebecca was a perfect example of health, the likes of which they never seen before. At the time, she had shrugged her shoulders. Now though, she was wondering if this ability to stay well or heal quickly was also part of her genetic make-up. 'I am never ill myself, and when I did cut my forehead once, that too healed so quickly. Perhaps we are similar in many ways.'

Over the next couple of days, Matilda continued to heal at an unbelievable rate. On the seventh morning, Rebecca, having been outside to fetch some food, came in, and found her up and washing in a bowl of water, using one of Rebecca's soaps.

'I like this washing block from you time, Rebecca,' she said, smiled and started drying her hands on Rebecca's hand towel.

When she earlier left the soap on the side, she did it without thinking. However, as with using medicines from her time, Matilda seemingly took the soap in her stride. Unsure what to say, Rebecca stared at the woman with her mouth open.

Matilda came over to her, and gently pushed her mouth closed. She then smiled and said, 'it is fine. I expected this. I knew you would have the wisdom to use medicines from your time in spite of Ethernal advising you otherwise. However, this cleansing block is a joy to behold, and something I never expected.'

Unable to believe what this woman had just said, again she was lost for words.

'Please close your mouth. Moreover, I am certain your Mother told you that it was rude to stare.' She smiled. 'There is, however, no need to curtsy when you greet a queen.' She then chuckled in the most delightful way that instantly reminded Rebecca of her mother.

'You know so much,' she, said, and narrowed her eyes.

Seemingly responding to this, Matilda narrowed her eyes back at her in the most delightful way.

251

Rebecca thought *I love this woman*, which helped her focus a little better. *Right, one thing question at a time,* she thought. 'You know of Ethernal, how so?'

'Have you not worked it out yet, my dear friend?' Ethernal, with the letter H removed is...?'

Rebecca thought for a moment and then as the penny dropped. 'Eternal, as in forever, is that right?'

You know it is right. He has been here always and visits our kind when he needs to, although we only hear him. With us, we are seen by those who need to see us, when they need to see us. Ethernal watches over our kind.' She smiled, and said, 'We must ready ourselves now, and be prepared to travel. Those who want my death will soon be close,' she said with an obvious and deliberate air of urgency.

'How do you know they will be here soon?' she asked, with her head going in circles. She then grabbed her back-pack and started pacing some food.

'I suspect you are always aware that something is about to happen. It is the same for me in that I get a sensation, which I have learnt to respond to accordingly.' She then touched Rebecca gently on the shoulder. 'Do not concern yourself with food. I have long trusted allies along our path. They will feed us, and offer us shelter. I know the land here about, and know a safe route. We have six hours until nightfall, so we must make haste.'

'Please, let me check your wound before we go.'

'I am fine,' she said, and lifted her blouse.

CHAPTER 26 – THE JOURNEY

She quickly checked Matilda's wound again, still unable to believe how well it had healed. Now confident this woman was capable of travelling she gathered a few things together that she deemed essential. She then loaded them into her backpack. 'Shall we hit the road?' she said, holding Matilda's hand.

'Hit the road indeed we shall,' she said and squeezed Rebecca's hand. 'I know this land and our route. All being well, we will come upon a farm in around four hours. There, we will find sustenance and horses to aid our travel. They are family, importantly, advocates, and I trust them.'

As Matilda seemed to know where she was going, Rebecca was happy to follow. In spite of her injuries, she walked with certainty, resting only occasionally, which magnified Rebecca's admiration for this woman. It was mid-afternoon when they came to the edge of a wooded area.

Earlier, as they were walking, Rebecca had thought she heard some shouting. However, when she had stopped to listen, she hadn't heard anything, so ignored it. Now though, not only could she hear shouting, she could see horsemen similar to those down by the lake.

Rebecca and Matilda hid in the trees, and watched as the soldiers rounded up several people. Then one by one, they cut them down with their swords. Although horrified and dismayed by the ensuing acts, Rebecca felt only a modest level of emotion, almost as if she wasn't there. She glanced towards Matilda, who was red in the face, appearing enraged with anger. Watching this woman's reaction, Rebecca couldn't understand why she wasn't feeling similar. Immediately her thoughts returned to Etienne, and how she'd suddenly felt so distant once she was heading back home. Deeply engrossed in her thoughts, wondering if again, she was perhaps seeing this world through another's eyes, she realised Matilda was speaking.

'Sorry, I didn't hear a word you said.'

Matilda acknowledged her with her eyes. 'I could sense your remoteness, and only wish I could feel the same. Those poor souls that they have slaughtered are my outlying family. It would seem they have paid with their lives, guilty only by association.'

Unsure what to say, and compassionate towards this woman's feelings, she uttered, 'I am so sorry for your loss. You must feel horrid.'

'In my time, we become insular and detach ourselves from reality. However, when it is family members, it takes on a new light. Sadly, in these dark ages, these despicable deeds are commonplace.' She then seemed to think for a moment. 'New monarchs live in constant fear. Our crown is hollow, and we live safe while we hold authority, always aware there are suitors in the wings.' She bowed her head a little. 'I have hardened my soul to expect such acts as these today, and indeed was prepared for my dethroning. I followed my father to become queen. He followed his father. We have had three peaceful generations, which is rare in these times. Those now in command have travelled from afar, carrying the flag of death from lands beyond our shores.'

'These people, your family, were they the ones who were going to help us?'

'They were indeed,' she said and again bowed her head. 'We must now hide until we know it is safe. It is too far to travel to our next secure point. We must remain here and hope we can gather sufficient for our onward journey. When I became aware of my impending situation, I sent a message for horses and food to aid our travels. Without those resources, our passage will be too far to travel on foot.'

The two hid quietly in the woods. At darkness, Matilda whispered, 'I believe all is clear. We should make haste. The land to the north is open grassland, and we can travel by night. If we make ground after sun fall, we will know of any ensuing danger. The horsemen will not travel by night without torches. Once we are over Hadrian's Wall, we will be safe. I have friends in the lowlands of Scotland who will see our way clear. My families are decedents of Alexander the first. His priory at Scone, in Perth stands as a testament to his and my family. With good wind, and heart, we will be in Scone by twelve days.'

The idea of being so far from home had an instant impact on Rebecca. She started to wonder how she would get back home, having only ever expected to nurse Matilda in the lodge.

As if Matilda had read her mind again, she said, 'worry not my love. I too have travelled afar while in a time not of my own. You will find your way home. You always do and forever will. I have journeyed these fourteen years past, and I am still a child in this world we share. Ethernal will see your guiding light and will pilot you, in the same way that your dear Meredith has led in the past.'

She couldn't believe this woman had just referred to Meredith by name, and asked, 'you know of Meredith?'

'I know of her through Ethernal, although I am yet to meet with her. She does not possess our ability to travel. She is, however, a guardian, a muse, a light for all that share our vision. She left your side, assuring you it was her time to rest. This was a guise so you would learn to find your own way, as you have done. She will be there for you always, perhaps not in a physical sense, however, you will know she is there. She too will be there for your granddaughter.'

Once again, Rebecca was taken aback by this woman's words, and with her imagination going in circles, asked, 'you spoke of my granddaughter, can you tell me more?'

'Do not concern yourself, your line is strong and will carry forward. One day soon, your daughter's daughter will visit you.' She smiled and continued, 'let us go fetch the horses now, and make speed.'

Keeping vigilance, the two headed down towards the ransacked farm. Matilda then knelt beside each fallen body and said a prayer. After praying for a child of perhaps five, and appearing tearful, she stood and said, 'Fetch some food from the barn. To the right, behind a cart, you should find a package. It was put there only a day since in readiness for our arrival. I will fetch two strong horses.'

On her way to the barn, Rebecca was trying to recall the last time she rode a horse, mixed in with this was the idea that her granddaughter will visit her soon. She entered the barn, and immediately heard a child's voice. She walked towards the voice and could see a young girl cowering behind some hay bales. As she approached, the girl curled away. Stricken with trauma resonating from her eyes, the girl pushed herself further into the corner. Holding her hand out to this beleaguered child, she whispered, 'je t'aiderai, I will help you.' She reckoned using both languages might help, having often heard Matilda slip into a variation of Anglo-French.

The young girl continued to cower away, so Rebecca knelt down, and holding her hand out, again whispered, 'je t'aiderai.'

Seconds later, Matilda came in and knelt beside Rebecca. The young girl seemed to recognise her instantly and crawled forward with her arms open. Matilda then spoke to her in what Rebecca considered again a mixture of French and English.

Matilda then turned to Rebecca and said, 'this is my beloved Goddaughter. Her name is Maria. We must take her with us. I have gathered two strong horses, and Maria can ride with me. Gather the food parcel,' she said pointing to a cloth sack. 'I will ready the horses. We have at best six hours of darkness. Our next safe haven is beyond our capabilities.' With good wind, we can find solace in the Forest of Arden. There we can shelter during light.' She then held her hand out to Rebecca. 'Thank you dear Rebecca. Once in the lowlands, two days forth we will be safe to continue our journey unopposed.'

Just before daylight, they arrived in a dense ancient pine forest, where Matilda suggested they set up camp near a shallow brook.

The tall conifers instantly reminded Rebecca of home. Although she hadn't seen her mother for eight days now, she was feeling strangely comfortable about the situation. Matilda's words of assurance relating to her journey home and settled any anxiety, reassured she would ultimately find her way home. As she sat there watching Matilda and Maria bathe in the sparkling brook, she thought of Meredith. Considering her current situation, she realised how far she'd come from the first time she uncovered the spiral staircase. For her though, the key aspect of Meredith's help was the understanding imparted, and the subsequent confidence she now had. Thanks to Meredith's guiding light, she felt able to face any challenge this bizarre world through at her. Long gone were any dream notions, and with them any attempts to apply rational thinking to her circumstances. Overriding all of this, she now had an inner self-belief that she would always find her way home.

That evening having eaten well and importantly not seen or heard a sign of any impending danger, they again set off across the open grasslands. Some five hours later, under the light of a full moon, they arrived by an old estate, nestling in a valley.

As they approached, Rebecca could see light coming from a window. With caution, she followed Matilda along a hedge row. Just then, Rebecca noticed a distinct white horse, with a red marking on its flank. It was tethered to one side of a barn. Immediately she recognised this beast and was certain it belonged to one of the horsemen. She whispered this information to Matilda.

Matilda nodded and indicated back in the direction they come from.

With their rations gone, just a few mouthfuls of water remaining, and sunup only moments away, they decided to hide in some heavy scrubland a good distance from the beaten track. They sat there quietly, maintaining a vigilant eye on proceedings. Young Maria was becoming restless, and in an effort to comfort her, Matilda started singing a delightful French rhyme. Moments later, Maria was sleeping peacefully.

Just as Rebecca and Matilda had started talking, they heard male voices billowing from the direction of estate. Moments later, they watched as a dozen heavily armoured horsemen, gallop across the heath.

'I assumed we would be safe here about. The Norman soldiers rarely journey this far north and I believed they were unaware of my association with these people. It would seem the danger has passed for now at least.'

It was early afternoon, on a particularly warm spring day, and both exhausted, Matilda suggested they took it in turns sleeping.

Rebecca was adamant that Matilda needed the rest more than her, and had insisted on staying awake first. With both Matilda and Maria sleeping, Rebecca was finding it difficult to keep her eyes open, having not slept properly for days. To keep herself awake, she started thinking about the first time she'd met Meredith. Feeling quite alert, but unable to keep her eyes open, she decided a few minutes resting her eyes wouldn't hurt.

She opened her eyes, shivering from the cold, and with the moon high in the sky, realised she'd been asleep for hours. Looking around, she could see Matilda and Maria both sleeping. Knowing they needed as much rest as possible, she decided to leave them undisturbed. Quietly, she got her feet and went to spy on the estate. With no sound or sign of anyone, she again made her way along the hedge row. The house was in total darkness, and the only sound was that of two hooting owls. Knowing that owls were particularly shy, she reckoned that if any soldiers were nearby, the owls wouldn't be here. Now reasonably confident the coast was clear she decided to head down towards the building.

With caution, she approached the door, while listening carefully for any sound at all. The tethered horses were gone, and although she was feeling edgy, she was nonetheless, intent on finding some food for the other two. She turned the handle of a huge oak door, and pushed carefully. It creaked a little and then yawned open. 'Hello door,' she whispered, 'am I safe?'

There wasn't an answer, there never was, not even when she was 15-years-old, but it was just part of who she was. As she stood silently in the hallway, she grinned at herself. She stood in the hallway for a while, listening. She lit a candle, now certain the house was empty and made her way towards a door at the end of the hallway. She opened the door into a kitchen and grinned, reckoning she had struck lucky. There was bread and cheese laying on the table and enough fruit to feed an army. She gathered as much food as she could carry using an old heavy cloth sack she'd found in one of the cupboards. She then filled her water container from a pump of sorts, and headed towards the front door. On her way, she briefly considered looking in the other rooms. For once though, she overruled her curiosity, knowing she had to get back to the others before they woke.

Making her way back towards Matilda, she could see twilight was only moments away. When she arrived back, the two were still sleeping like babies. Confident that the coast was now clear, and they were all well hidden, she lay down to get some rest. She woke feeling as if she was being pushed. She sat bolt upright, and was instantly aware Matilda was nudging her gently.

'I am sorry that I startled you.'

Rubbing her eyes, feeling as if she'd only just shut them, Rebecca said, 'it is alright, I think that I must have been dreaming.'

'That is interesting, I though you detested any dream notions. Anyways, you did a good job getting the food and water.'

Rebecca's head immediately started going in circles, wondering just how much this woman actually knew about her. Before she had a chance to respond, Matilda squeezed her hand gently.

'I know all, and in time, you will too. Rebecca you will learn that our ability is greater than simply moving between eras. We can see the world through other's eyes. Additionally, when it is pertinent, we can sense the thoughts of those who are close to us and especially those who share our form.'

'I wondered how you knew so much. You even said a word that only my mother and Meredith use.'

'Meredith used the word anyways as a hidden comfort to you. I too use this word as a form of comfort for you. I too, was ill at ease when I first ventured down the paths we follow. I was also offered a heartening reflection by my guiding light.'

'I thought it was too much of a coincidence whenever Meredith used that word. Your explanation makes complete sense.'

'I am unable to understand much of what you say. However, I do comprehend your meaning.' She then smiled and said, 'we are rested and with nightfall two hours away, I propose we eat in readiness for the journey ahead.'

The next four days and nights went without any problems, and on the fifth morning, they arrived by a vast loch. With food once again running short, and one of the horses now lame, they set up camp in a wooded area near the water's edge.

'We are safe now. This is the land of my grandparent Alexander. No Sassenach would dare journey to these hills. My family's priory is on the far side of this loch. It is known hereabouts as Loch Rannoch and nestles protected in the foothills of Càrn Gorm. The loch is vast and our only way of passing over will be with boat now that the mare is lame.'

'Where will we get a boat from?' Rebecca asked, knowing for many miles, the land had been devoid of people and or buildings.

'Many would have watched our journey from higher ground. We are safe and soon my brethren will be near.'

Moments later, a giant of a man, came towards them, his feet thudding on the ground with every step. He was a handsome man, with defined features, dressed in red and green tartan. He presented himself to Matilda, offering an enormous bow befitting of his powerful status. 'My Queen,' he said with a broad Scottish accent, and his head still lowered. 'We have awaited your return. This land is yours, and we are your humble servants' Ma'am. There will be no compromise here. My men will be with us afore midday with vessels to carry you home.' He then bowed again, 'I am your servant my beloved Queen.'

Unable to digest all that was unfolding in front of her, Rebecca sat quietly with Maria. When the man left, she turned to Matilda and the only thing she could think to say was, 'My word he is handsome,' which made her laugh aloud.

Matilda covered her mouth, but could not hide her giggle. 'Handsome, he is indeed,' she said, and again giggled.

This in turn made Rebecca laugh, as it was the first time she had heard someone laugh with a noticeably distinct French accent. This made her wonder what Matilda would sound like once she added a Scottish accent in the mix. This then made her laugh aloud, which in turn made Maria chuckle, and within seconds, all three were giggling uncontrollably.

His name is Duncan Fergusson. He is the lord of this burgh. He is not married,' she said and again chuckled.

With the three of them still laughing, a boat, having the appearance of a small Viking longboat came into the bay from the right. With the sound of a man bellowing rowing instructions, the boat then passed them and disappeared to the right.

'That will be our vessel, we will soon be home,' Matilda said, squeezing Rebecca hand gently.

Before Rebecca had time to answer, a man, dressed in the same red and green tartan approached them. This man was somewhat older, smaller in stature, but still had a similar appearance of strength. Again, he bowed before Matilda. 'Ma'am, your vessel awaits you. We have moored by the jetée,' he said, gesturing over his shoulder.

Rebecca stood first, helping Matilda to her feet. As she did, she was aware this woman had taken on a completely different character, and almost every aspect of her demeanour had changed. She had noticed it earlier when the other man had been nearby. As they walked along the shore, with her head full of unasked questions, she wondered if her chances of a one to one with Matilda were now gone.

Once again, Matilda, as if she had read her thoughts, which was now becoming a regular occurrence, said, 'I hope we can find some time alone. I have much to ask and say before you venture back to you world.'

Nodding, Rebecca replied, 'I was just thinking exactly that. I suspect you know this already,' she said and smiled.

Matilda nodded, and gently touched the back of Rebecca's hand. 'With your unusual vocabulary and accent, many questions will be asked. We must be aware that our tactile relationship will cause unease, even if they believe we are related, which I will propose. In my time, a Queen is accepted to be isolated, untouchable and is expected to disengage from any physical contact.' She smiled at Rebecca. 'Even a smile from me, will cause disquiet. When alone, we can be as we wish. I will answer all questions aimed at us. I know this may seem bizarre to you. However, it is how it is in my world.'

Looking around to make sure no one was watching, she touched the back of Matilda's hand, and acknowledged her with a gentle nod.

As they arrived at the boat, Matilda was the centre of attention. Rebecca was ready for this, and so turned her attention to Maria.

The men then climbed aboard, seemingly oblivious to Rebecca and Maria. With a dignified, yet unyielding tone, and waving her arm with a remarkable degree of authority, Matilda said, 'my beloved niece and her sister are to come with us.' She then shook her head in such a way, that even Rebecca wouldn't question her.

As Duncan helped Maria, and then Rebecca into the boat, she was finding it impossible to avoid eye contact. At one point, she turned away and was sure he moved to maintain eye contact. All the time, she was thinking *I am so not spending thirty years here.* This made her laugh, which in turn seemed to get her more attention from this man. She climbed aboard the boat and sat with Maria. Purposefully, she picked an area some distance from Matilda, considering what she'd said to her earlier. She was also trying to avoid Duncan's contagious eyes, not that she really minded.

The boat set off again to the sound of a man bellowing rowing orders. As they headed across the loch, a building that Rebecca considered half church, half castle, complete with ramparts and circular spires came into view. Nestling in the foot hills of a snow capped-mountain, it was surrounded by huge spruce trees, facing out across the lake. To Rebecca, it seemed a perfect place for elves and such like, but importantly, looked like the ideal place for a queen such as Matilda.

The boat soon docked at a jetty, and again the focus was on Matilda. As Matilda set foot on the jetty, she waved a woman towards her. Rebecca watched as Matilda spoke to the woman, often pointing in the direction of her and Maria. Moments later, the woman climbed back aboard and made her way towards her.

'I am Morag; Queen Matilda's assigned Court-Lady. My Queen has designated me to attend all of your needs. Please come with me.'

Rebecca, took Maria by the hand, and followed Morag along a grassy walk way leading up a gentle slope towards the priory. From the boat, this building had a formidable appearance, but as they approached it, she was a little taken aback by its vast, somewhat menacing exterior. She watched as a number of men and woman, all dressed in the same red and green tartan, gathered around Matilda, showering attention on her.

This gave her a feeling of accomplishment, knowing the last few days of disorder had been worth the effort, now certain Matilda was among friends.

Morag led them through a huge wooden arch. At this point, another woman took Maria in a different direction, which caused Maria some concern. Rebecca spoke to her assuring her she was safe and that she would see her soon. Once Maria had settled and headed off with the other woman, Morag led Rebecca up to a room at the top of one of the turrets. Having had a much needed soak in a marble bath of sorts, she then had some food. Afterwards, she stood there staring through a tall, narrow window, looking across the loch. As she did, memories of home came to her, and she wondered what might lie ahead. She remembered Ethernal had suggested she would be with Matilda for twenty days, and that meant she could be here for another two or three days yet. Just as she was considering this, Morag entered the room.

'Would you please come with me? Queen Matilda has requested an audience with you.'

She followed Morag, down a narrow concrete stairwell, and across a court yard where a number of men and woman were back and forth, going about their business, all seemingly on a mission. She led her up another flight of stairs, which were palatial by comparison to where she'd just come from. Morag led her towards a large arched wooden door, and then knocked on the door.

'Enter.'

Instantly Rebecca recognised Matilda voice, glanced at the woman, who responded by nodding towards the door. Rebecca entered the room, followed by Morag.

'Morag, will you bring us some fruit. After, please be sure we are left alone.'

Morag curtsied, and without speaking, left the room.

Matilda beckoned Rebecca towards her. 'Please sit beside me. I have much to thank you for and am forever indebted to you my dear Rebecca. When my physician tended my wound, he was astounded. I suspect the medicines from your time are strong. I broached the subject of your medicines before and drew modest reaction from you. I am able to know what you are thinking, however, on this occasion, there was little forthcoming. Did you use a medicine from your time?'

Rebecca raised her eyebrows sheepishly, and lowering her head slightly, said, 'I might have. However, I couldn't possible divulge that information.' She then chuckled.

'I suspect you did, and it is okay because I believe my wound may have been complex without your intervention.'

Rebecca had so many questions and was unsure where to start.

Again, as if she had read Rebecca's thoughts, Matilda said, 'I suspect you would like to know more about my ability to seemingly read your thoughts. Although on the medicine subject you disguised your thoughts from me.'

'That is exactly what I was thinking, and I need to know how you knew that.'

'I have made an association with many that share our capability. I met with a woman who lived some three hundred years ahead of my time. Sadly, she was perceived as a witch and like many of our kind during that era, was burnt alive.' She then looked down appearing reflective. 'She taught me much before I returned to my time. She informed me that all who have our capacity think alike. That is why I know your thoughts. They are exactly what I would think. In time, you will know also, although I suspect you have already seen another's view. Once those thoughts are shared, I suspect you may have considered them coincidental. I did, until I learnt from that woman. You are able to keep your mind open, or else you would not be here. Maintain this unlocked view and you too will see another's opinion and viewpoint.'

The two of them sat talking about their kind, how they have been perceived and treated through the ages. Rebecca asked about Ethernal and Matilda's answer was brief, explaining that he was similar to Meredith, a guardian over their kind. Like Rebecca, she had never seen him, only ever being aware of his presence, and hearing his voice. The two then sat there chatting about their journey, and just as the subject of Maria came up, there was a knock at the door.

Matilda asked, 'who is there.'

'My Queen, it is I, Morag and with me is your niece, Maria.'

Matilda whispered, 'She is of our making, and I will see her way forward. She is strong and I suspect you will see her again.' She then looked up and called, 'Enter.'

Morag and Maria entered. Maria immediately ran over, cuddled Rebecca and then Matilda. Morag seemed alarmed by this, and presumably noticing this, Matilda said, 'It is fine for her to cuddle me, she is a child and knows no different. I will call you when I need you, thank you Morag.'

The three sat around chatting for ages, and feeling heavy eyed, Rebecca suggested she needed some sleep. Matilda stood and cuddled Rebecca and again thanked her for all she had done. She then stood back and with a hand on each of Rebecca's shoulders, looked at her, almost as if she was peering into her soul.

On her way back to her room, Rebecca questioned Matilda's behaviour. To her, it felt like she was saying good-bye. This got her thinking about what she'd said to her about knowing what others were thinking. She sat on the side of her bed feeling a little confused. She knew what Ethernal had said, and that would mean she was here for a few days yet, but Matilda's reaction made her wonder if her time was up. Struggling to keep her eyes open, she laid back and closed her eyes.

CHAPTER 27 – THE BOOK

Stirring, Rebecca opened her eyes and immediately knew she was lying in her own bed. She lay there for ages thinking about Matilda. For some reason, her memories seemed distant and felt distinctly vague. Even though she was certain it had all happened, annoyingly, it all felt like a dream. As she got out of bed, she noticed her ankle was still bandaged. This just compounded her judgment even further, as she knew for sure that she'd discarded this some days ago.

After a shower, she headed downstairs, joining her mum in the kitchen. Moments later, her father walked in.

'Morning, Rebecca. So how did your twisted ankle stand up when you went over to the lodge yesterday? The way you were limping around, I thought it would put pay to any jaunts any time soon,' he said and laughed. 'As if that would stop you.'

Instantly, Rebecca's thoughts started going in circles. She was certain her father had said these exact words the morning before she met Matilda. She smiled at her father unsure what to say or think, and remembered her mum had said she was taking Tommy football training and meeting up with Amanda and Ruth. 'Mum, do you have any plans today?'

'I am taking Tommy to football training and then meeting up with Ruth and Amanda for lunch.'

At a complete loss what to think, or say, she forced a smile. She was feeling quite unsettled, and again found herself wondering if she had dreamt the whole episode with Matilda.

'Are you okay, honey? You look rather distant and somewhat uneasy.'

'I am fine Mum, just had the weirdest dream last night and it has thrown me completely. Can I ask, although it might sound silly? Is it Tuesday today? And if so, how comes Tommy has training today?'

'My word, your dream has thrown you. It is Tuesday and as there is no game tomorrow, he indeed has training today.'

That was it, she was sure she hadn't been anywhere. Feeling quite put out that she hadn't actually met up with Matilda, left her wondering what had actually happened. Then an idea came to her that she may have actually come back to a time before she met Matilda. 'Mum, send my love to the girls.'

'Okay, I will. You can tell me all about your dream over supper tonight. Right, I am going to get Tommy. Do you have plans today?'

'Not really Mum, I'm just going to potter about.' She had decided a couple of minutes ago that the only way she was going to find out the truth was to go across the lake and check on the provisions her, and Roxy had hidden. If everything were in place, then she would at least know for sure.

Moments later, her mum popped her head in the kitchen and said her good-byes. Rebecca finished her coffee and headed down the hallway. As she passed Meredith's painting, she muttered, 'what is going on this time.' She stood there for a few seconds, and there was nothing coming back. There was no vibe, no sensation, nothing at all. For the first time ever, it was if it was just a painting. Feeling quite put out by this, she headed down to the lake.

She climbed aboard the boat, and she started the engine. With a gentle unusual north easterly breeze, it oddly felt so similar to day she left to circumnavigate the island, which ultimately led her to Matilda. With this thought in her head, she sped across the lake. A few minutes later, she beached the boat, and headed into the woods. The path trodden down with Roxy was exactly as she had left it, complete with

Roxy's footmarks in a damp area. She knew there and then that she hadn't dreamt that part of the episode.

As she approached the lodge, memories of Matilda seemed closer than they had since she'd woken. She checked inside the lodge, and it appeared exactly as she'd left it, with the bed still unmade. There was no sign of her or Matilda's presence. Feeling confused, she knew she had been here with Roxy, so decided to check on the ration's that they'd hidden. As she walked around the back, she spotted the shrub that she used to hide everything still in place. One of the first things she'd done when she was here with Matilda was to bring most of the resources inside. With nothing touched, this just served to disorientate her further.

She went back to the front and sat on the porch going over everything in her head. Through all of her adventures, although often bizarre, had never left her feeling this confused. All of a sudden, as if someone was scribing into the soil in front of her, words started to appear.

Evidence of your time

with Matilda will soon

be at your door.

Unable to believe what she was watching, Rebecca took a deep breath. She sat there staring at the words reading them over and again. Thinking about what Matilda had said about Ethernal, and not seeing him, just being aware of his presence, she wondered if this was a message from him, and if so, what did it actually mean? Part of her though, wanted it to be from Meredith, although she knew that was wishful thinking and unlikely.

Making her way back to the boat, she was now positive she had actually been with Matilda, even though it all seemed like a distant memory. As she headed across the lake and approached the island,

270

even though she could remember how she felt when she'd first circumnavigated it, it still had the sensation of a dream-like emotion. Confused by this, she slowed the boat by the island, but there was nothing, no sensation, no vibe of any description, just a far-away memory. Oddly, it reminded her of how she'd felt when she returned from her time with Etienne. When she considered this sensation, she reckoned that although the two events were miles apart, there were definitive similarities, and her mood was unsurprising.

She tied the boat up alongside the jetty and slowly made her back to the house. With her emotions settled a little, she was still at a loss what to think. Over the last couple of years, many bizarre events had come her way. Mostly though, she'd found a way of dealing with them. All that had happened with Ethernal, Matilda, and somehow finding her way home before she'd left, had created an uneasiness that she was struggling to comprehend. This mood was now compounded even further, having watched an invisible hand scribing a message into the soil right in front of her eyes.

She sat in the kitchen trying to get her head around the events of the last few days. Although she thought about creating a time-line of proceedings, she felt there was no point. Considering the message in the soil, she wondered what it had meant. Part of her was thinking that message alone had been a clear indication she had been with Matilda, but it had said that evidence would soon be at her door. In the end, she headed up to her room to do some sketching to try to take her mind off things, reckoning she would find out in good time.

Later in the afternoon, while she was sitting on her balcony, she heard a car pull across the drive. As she headed downstairs, she was met by her father carrying a huge old book. He headed towards the kitchen, beckoning Rebecca to follow him.

'This arrived at my office today, delivered by hand, and addressed to you,' he said and placed the book on the table.

Rebecca took a few moments to admire this old tan leather-bound book, complete with huge brass clasps. Wondering if this was the evidence that would arrive at her door, she glanced at her father.

'Best we have a look inside, because I have had this sitting on my desk all day, and in the end, well, this is why I am home early. Curiosity and the cat as you would say.' He then pointed to the book, clearly intrigued.

She carefully undid the brass clasp, and opened the book. On the first page was an amazingly colourful picture that reminded her of a leaded church window. It appeared to have been illustrated by hand, and was dated 1124. That was all she needed to see to know this was the evidence she'd been awaiting. Assured by this, she closed the book and turned to her father.

Unable to hide his curiosity, he asked, 'is that all you are going to look at, the first page?'

'That can wait. Right now, I need to tell you my story.' She then went on to explain every last detail of her time with Matilda. Just as she was coming to the end, Tommy's face appeared at the back window.

'Let us in, been ringing the bell for ages,' he bellowed.

Frowning, he unlocked the back door, and went to let Elizabeth in the front. 'We didn't hear the door bell Liz.'

'Take no notice of Tommy, I rang once, and he headed off around the back.'

'Rebecca and I were so engrossed with a book that turned up at my office. Sorry we didn't hear you.'

'Honestly James, we have been here less than a minute.'

After supper, Elizabeth, James, and Rebecca sat around chatting about her adventure with Matilda. With his intrigue seemingly at its limit, James suggested looking at the book.

Elizabeth had started tidying up the kitchen and Rebecca recognised this trait. Reckoning her mum had heard enough for now, knowing she could only take so much on board at one time, she turned to her dad and suggested they looked at the book in his study.

Standing up and starting to help her mum tidy up, she said, 'Mum, Dad and I are going to his study to have a look at the book. Would you like to join us?'

'I will join you shortly. Don't worry about helping me; it is nearly done now, honey.'

'Dad, I must say, I am more than a little curious about this book. How did it end up in your office?'

'I am curious too, and I am not at all sure. Evidently, an elderly man dropped it off. He didn't leave a name or anything. I quizzed the girl on reception, and from her description, it sounded like he could have been the man from the book shop.' He then raised his eyebrows. 'Which, I know is bizarre, but his shop appearing and then seemingly vanishing is at best bizarre.'

'Every time, I think I have gotten a grip on what is going on, the ice cracks, and I am back to not having a clue. My time with Matilda feels authentic but is so distant in my head, but at the same time... I don't know what to think. I felt the same after my time with Etienne, all thirty-years of it. It all seemed like a dream-like distant memory.'

'It must be very difficult for you, and can only imagine how you must feel. Maybe this book might have some answers.'

'Hmm, well as soon I saw the book, I wondered if it had anything to do with the invisible hand writing in the soil.'

273

'What was the message again?'

'Evidence of your time with Matilda will soon be at your door. That was it, and to be honest, I was so shocked watching this message appear magically in front of me, it took me a few moments to digest it all.'

'I am not surprised really. As you said, magically appeared.'

As they started thumbing through the pages, although very interesting, it just seemed like a time trial of events in the 12th century. Rebecca then noticed a slip of paper pocking out from one of the pages. She opened the book on that page and was a little surprised to see a blank page. 'This is a bit odd, Dad,' she said, pointing to the blank page.

'Look back and see if there is anything on the previous pages.'

She turned back a few pages and started reading. Like the inside page at the beginning of the book, this page was adorned with beautiful hand painted images. As she started reading, she took a sharp intake of breath.

'Have you seen something?' her father asked.

'This section relates directly to Queen Matilda.' She frowned, 'hmm. It seems I was meant to find this section.' She then carried on reading. 'It is all about her being overthrown and her time in Scotland.' She thought for a moment. 'There is no mention of her injuries, or anything to do with that. I was hoping there would be something that might relate to my time with her, especially with the book turning up mysteriously at your office. And this piece of paper inserted exactly in this section,' she said, waving the piece of paper.

'Let me have a look. Just had the idea.' He then lifted the blank page up to the light. I can't quite make it out, although I can see there might be something written.'

'I remember doing something at school. We need to mix iodine and water, and that should make it show up, if there is anything that is. Although, that said, I am hesitant about damaging the paper.'

'I agree there must be another way. I guess we could ask James Bond.' He laughed, and turned to his laptop. 'I'm sure we'll find an answer on here.' He then typed in invisible ink. 'First thing that has come up is iodine, just as you suggested. I agree with you, it might damage the paper. Here is something that might work. This one suggests an ultraviolet light. I think I have one in the office at work.'

'Not a lot of good at work, Dad.'

'Yeah, I just thought that. It will have to be tomorrow, if you can wait that long,' he said and laughed. 'Hang on; this bit says the use of iodine antiseptic wipes shouldn't damage the paper. We have some of those in the medicine box, in the kitchen.' He then jumped up and headed towards the door. 'Two tics.' Moment later, he returned with a packet of wipes, and carefully rubbed over the blank page. He then held it up to the light, and said, 'still nothing.'

'Here, let me have a go, Dad. It might need a little bit of pressure.' Rebecca then took a fresh wipe and tried rubbing with a little more vigour. After using a wipe she'd pulled from the bottom of the packet, and failing to reveal anything, she turned to her dad, and asked, 'how long have these been in the medicine box.'

'Since last week, they are for Tommy's football grazes. Incidentally, I don't think it requires more pressure. Reading this,' he said, glancing at his computer, 'it is the liquid, which makes the message appear.

They spent the next few minutes trying a couple more wipes, and after holding the page up to the light, without any success, they agreed they were probably wasting their time. James turned to Rebecca and suggested they'd have to wait for tomorrow to try the light.

Over the next hour, Rebecca and her father, sat there reading extracts that related to Matilda's time in Scotland. Towards the end of this section, she came across an illustration of Queen Matilda, standing next to a man. She glanced at her father and took a deep breath. Although the illustration was slightly faded, she instantly recognised Queen Matilda, just as she remembered her, and the dishy guard, Duncan, the person who had helped them in and out of the boat. 'I remember this man, Dad. He was the person who helped us from the boat.'

'Well, I suspect if he is in this illustration, he was more than just a man helping you from the boat.'

'Yeah, exactly, Dad. Matilda seemed to know him rather well. She told me he wasn't married, which I thought was a bit odd at the time. It would now seem that she had more than a passing interest.'

'History is littered with Queens and Kings who have had men and women who to the outside world were just commoners, but turned out to be a little more than a...' he seemed to think for a moment, 'I think the official term is equerry.'

Rebecca nodded, 'hmm, so it would seem this may have been the case with Matilda.' Although this illustration had offered her something tangible, she carried on thumbing through the pages. She still felt rather disappointed, convinced there would be something that would shed a little light on her time with Matilda. Although the book seemed to chronicle Matilda's period as Queen and her time in Scotland, there was nothing to suggest she'd ever been wounded, let alone nursed by Rebecca.

Around ten, she headed off to bed. As she lay there, she kept going over everything in her head. Although she now had this illustration of Matilda and Duncan, both of whom she recognised, there was nothing else to suggest she'd been there. To compound her frustration further, the blank page looked exactly that, a blank page, and she wasn't convinced that an ultraviolet light was going to show anything up.

After all, she thought *they didn't have ultraviolet lights in the twelfth century.*

The following morning, although tired from a restless night, she was up early, having decided to go into work with her father, reckoning she couldn't wait for him to get home. Moments later, her father joined her for breakfast.

'I thought I would find you up and ready,' he said and smiled. 'Actually glad you're coming in today, as I have a meeting with a fellow businessman who is very keen to use yours and Roxy's spreadsheet.'

'Okay, works for me, as long as I can use your light thing first.'

He grinned. 'No problem, Mr. Fergusson is coming down from Edinburgh, would you believe,' he said, and raised his eyebrows, 'and won't be here until lunchtime.'

'Fergusson,' she blurted, 'did you say Mr. Fergusson? Do you know his first name?'

Her dad, shook his head, and said, 'not of the top of my head I don't, why?'

'Well, as absurdly coincidental as this may seem, the man in the illustration, Matilda's boyfriend, was named Fergusson, Duncan Fergusson, to be precise. What are the chances of that?'

After breakfast, they headed into the office. With her coat barely off, Rebecca turned to her father who was chatting to the girl on reception. He said to the receptionist, 'excuse me a moment.' He then turned, seemingly aware of Rebecca's eagerness, and said, 'In my back room. The cupboard next to the window.'

'She mouthed, 'Thanks Dad, and headed up stairs. Finding something she thought was the ultraviolet light, decided to wait for her

277

father. With the book on the table, open, and the light placed next to it, she sat there twiddling her thumbs. 'Right,' she mumbled, deciding to go and get a coffee. She headed for the door and almost crashed into her father, coming in, carrying two coffees.

'Ooops, nearly. I was just going to get coffee, while I was waiting for you.'

'Nearly,' he said, placing the coffee's down on the table. 'I am glad you waited.'

As Rebecca watched her father plug the light in, and lift the book up, she said, 'Hang on a minute Dad.'

'Are you okay? I thought you were so eager.'

'I am eager, Dad. I am just, oh I don't know really. This whole episode has been so unlike my previous trips. I think the thing that has spooked me mostly, was waking up in bed and coming down to breakfast as if it had never happened. At breakfast, I even knew what was coming next. It was like déjà vu.'

'I am not surprised you feel uneasy. I have always admired the way you have seemingly taken everything in your stride. I sit there thinking about everything you've been through and wonder in amazement, at not only your tales, but also how you've handled it all.' He then seemed to think for a moment. 'I don't suppose this will change the way you feel, but it might offer you some tangible evidence that you were actually there.'

She nodded and indicated for her father to hold the paper up to the light.

Lifting up the page, and squinting, he said, 'not a lot, but there is something.'

'Read it, Dad.'

'Okay, it is very faded, but it says;'

To the Third Millennium Rebekha.   He read and glanced at Rebecca.

Find the Yew tree by the lodge

Thereby find your answers.

Matilda

'That's it, no more. Do you know of this Yew tree?'

'Yeah, on the other side of the lake behind the lodge is a huge yew tree. Roxy suggested it could well be a couple of thousand years old. To be honest, I was more surprised by her knowing, never having her down as a tree hugger. Also, as much as I do love trees, yews, and elms spook me a little. I can't say why they do; I just find them a bit too spooky and witch like for my taste.' She then thought for a moment. 'Although, that said, my view on witches has changed. Especially as I found out recently that those women who expressed any kind of vision around the fourteenth-century were burnt, believed to be a witch. Anyway, I am waffling. I didn't take much notice of the tree at the time, but I do know where it is.' Suddenly something occurred to her. 'Third Millennium is now, right, Dad? And, she spelled my name the way it's spelled in the Old-Testament. It is all very intriguing.'

'Intriguing it is, I must say. Yes, this is the third Millennium, and we were so close to naming you Rebekha spelled that way. Your Mother insisted it was too dated, although... Either way, she got her way, as she so often did,' he said and laughed.

'I like both ways actually.' She then lifted her eyebrows. Looks like it will be tomorrow then for the yew tree investigation. So, this Mr. Fergusson, what time is he arriving?'

Her father chuckled, and said, 'you don't need to wait around. You can go home now and check your tree Miss Eager Beaver.'

Shaking her head, she said. I am in no rush, especially now I know that I wasn't blinking dreaming. That was the most important part for me. Besides, I am intrigued to meet this Mr. Fergusson.' She considered telling her father that she had fancied him, but as quick, dismissed the idea, reckoning it wholly inappropriate.

'Well, that is what I was talking to Lucy, the receptionist about. They rang and said they should be here around 1pm.'

'In that case, I am going for an almond croissant, and a decent coffee. Want anything, Dad?'

'No, I am fine thank you. You can go home if you want you know.'

'Dad, it is fine, trust me, I can wait.'

As she entered the coffee shop, with her head in her purse, she heard a scream, and instantly recognised the voice. 'Amanda, Ruth, what are you doing here?'

'Sorting Amanda's wedding dress.'

'Oh wow, so my mum was right. She mentioned that she thought you might be getting married a while ago. Because I hadn't heard any more, I guess I thought she had it wrong.'

'Nope, it is in two months. We are here today to have a sneak look around, mostly to check out the different shops. We were planning to invite you and Liz this Saturday for a day of looking at, and trying on dresses. And that includes a bridesmaid dress Bex,' Amanda said.

The three sat down over coffee and cake, chatting about Amanda's big day. Then Ruth asked Rebecca what she had been up to lately, and if there had been on any more jaunts. Mindful that Amanda didn't know as much about her trips and Ruth did, Rebecca reservedly explained about her time with Matilda.

'Wow,' Ruth exclaimed, 'it is one thing going to eighteen whenever to meet with Meredith. But boy oh boy, not only nigh on a thousand years ago, but the queen of England no less.'

Amanda, appearing somewhat bemused, asked, 'so you went to the twelfth-century, and helped Queen Matilda?' She then thought for a moment, 'not Queen Victoria's mother, she was Matilda too?'

'Not Victoria's mum and I actually didn't know her mother was a Matilda too. I went to the year eleven-twenty-three to be precise.' She said, and aware Amanda was looking somewhat bemused, she laughed and said, 'don't worry A, I will explain it all on another time, with more detail. And when I say another time, I don't mean twenty-three minutes past eleven.'

Both Ruth and Amanda shook their heads.

'Eleven twenty three, get it?'

The three sat around chatting, with the subject going between Amanda's upcoming wedding and Rebecca's time with Matilda. Suddenly, Rebecca jumped up and said, 'sorry girls, got to dash, got a meeting with a Scottish Viking of sorts.' Noticing the two girls had their mouths open, she said, 'Not really, just me and my imagination and a name coincidence.'

'Rebecca, you can't leave us hanging like that,' Amanda said, with her palm up.

'When I was with Matilda in Scotland, a very dishy guy called Duncan Fergusson helped us into the boat, so we could get across the loch. So, Dad tells me we are having a meeting today with a Mr. Fergusson, who is coming down from Scotland.' She then giggled, 'if it's my man, he will be nine-hundred and ninety years old.' She laughed, 'Must dash. I will see you soon ladies.'

She sat down in the office, and just as she started chatting to her father about meeting up with the ladies, Mr. Fergusson walked in with an older gentleman.

Her father leant over, and whispered, 'Close your mouth, sweetie.'

Rebecca shook her head, unable to believe what she was looking at. The younger man was a double for the man she'd met while with Matilda. 'Dad, remember me telling... I will tell you later.' She then stood up, and trying to hide her surprise, greeted Mr. Fergusson and his colleague.

'This is my father, also Mr. Fergusson. Therefore, it might be prudent if we use Christian names. My father's name is Michael, and I am Duncan.'

Again, with her mouth open, Rebecca tried to compose her emotions, unable to believe what she was looking at, or hearing. As desperate as she was to ask this man a thousand questions, she knew they were here for a business meeting. The four sat around discussing the spread sheet for the next couple of hours, occasionally pausing for a coffee. This helped Rebecca stay on track, and stop her mind drifting off to her time with Matilda. Once they'd seemingly finished, she asked, 'Duncan, Michael, may I ask you about your family history?'

'Yes of course you can. What is it you would like to know?'

'Well, as a hobby, I have been researching Scottish history around the twelfth century. In particular, I have been looking at Queen Matilda, who found refuge at Scone Priory, in Perthshire. I understand that she had a close male confident, an equerry, whose name was...' Before she could finish, Duncan started speaking.

'His name was also Duncan Fergusson. We are direct descendents,' he said and smiled. 'I now understand why you looked so surprised when we walked in.'

Nodding, Rebecca said, 'I thought so, you are identical to him. And when I say identical, I mean a carbon-copy. I am sorry if I appeared surprised. I tried to hide my surprise, but clearly I failed,' she said, and smiled.

Duncan shook his head, and said, 'I can't imagine how you could know that I look like him. We have searched endlessly, but have never been able to find anything showing what he looked like. We did come across a couple of paintings of Queen Matilda. However, the only records of our family involvement suggested that Duncan Fergusson was a senior guard. As you say, perhaps an equerry of sorts. We suspected that he may have been involved with Matilda, but most of what we found was at best sketchy. By way of our own family records, we believed he was close to her, although, as with this kind of thing, it would seem it was hushed up.'

'Dad, we need to show these two men our book. As it is so heavy, will you come and help me fetch it please?' She wanted to get her dad alone. As they entered the back room, she closed the door behind her and whispered, 'we can't tell them about my journeys.'

He shook his head. 'And there I was, thinking I might need to tell you the exact same thing.'

They returned to the office with the book. Eagerly, Rebecca opened it on the page of the illustration, and said, 'Now you can see why I was so surprised when you walked in. Clearly there is an extremely strong family resemblance.'

Both Duncan and Michael appeared equally startled. 'I can see why you were so shocked, as you said, Rebecca, a carbon copy. May I enquire how you came by this book?'

'We found it in an old book shop in a town up near the lakes.'

Over the next couple of hours, the four of them went through the book. Rebecca kept staring at Duncan, and aware both her father and the older man had noticed she smiled, trying to hide her embarrassment. Although, she kept telling herself, it was because he was so similar to the boatman, she knew this man was having the same effect on her. To compound these emotions further, every time she looked up, he was staring back at her.

At around five in the evening, Duncan and Michael headed off to their hotel, asking if they could come back the following day to go through the spreadsheet with Rebecca and Roxy. On the way home in the car, James mentioned Duncan's similarity to the illustration in the book.

'I know, Dad, it's unbelievable. You've only seen a drawing. In real life, Duncan is exactly the same as the man I met when I was with Matilda.'

'I did notice you staring at him. Am I right to assume you were just shocked by the similarities?' he said, glanced at Rebecca, and smiled.

Rebecca raised her eyebrows, and trying to hide her true feelings, she said, 'Yes, totally. I am not sure I will ever get used to seeing him.'

The following morning, Rebecca, now joined by Roxy, went through the spreadsheet with Duncan. Michael and James went off to a meeting with some other financiers. At midday, the girls went to a local cafe for lunch, while Duncan met up with his father and James for lunch.

'Girl, you are useless at hiding your feelings.'

'Was it that obvious?'

'In a word, yep, from both of you. Why don't you just ask him to go for dinner?'

'I could never do that. I would be far too embarrassed.'

'Well, if you don't, I will ask him,' she said and giggled.

When they went back to the office, Duncan was waiting in reception. He went straight over to Rebecca and asked if he could speak to her alone.

Again, trying to hide her feelings, Rebecca asked, 'is there a problem with the spreadsheet?'

'Far from it, Rebecca, in fact, it is prefect, like you. I know you don't know me, however, would you consider joining me this evening for something to eat. Perhaps you could show me a good restaurant, as the food in the hotel, is at best ordinary.'

Although she could feel her face was crimson with embarrassment, she nodded. Trying to compose herself and avoid umming and erring, she gave herself a moment to think. 'Do you like Italian food?'

'I do indeed, do you have somewhere in mind?'

'I do have the perfect place down by the quay side. Shall we say five this evening?'

'That will be just the thing. My Father is heading home this evening, so if you are okay, it will be just us two.

Before going back into James's office, Rebecca stopped her father in the corridor. Unsure how he would react, she sheepishly told him that she was going for dinner with Duncan. He just smiled, and asked if she would like him to arrange a cab home.

CHAPTER 28 – DINNER AND THE YEW TREE

Rebecca and Duncan had a lovely meal, mostly discussing the book. Occasionally, Rebecca considered telling him her story, but as quick, dismissed the idea, knowing it was way too early in proceedings. At ten, they said their good-byes, having arranged to meet up next weekend.

As soon as she was in the cab, Roxy rang.

'Well, when is the marriage?'

Although, Rebecca dismissed Roxy out of hand, and laughed it off, inside she felt quite different.

The following morning, she was up bright and early. Although, she'd had a lovely time with Duncan, her focus was now on the yew tree. With winter just around the corner, she knew her time was running out to get across the lake. When her father joined her, she suggested as it was such a lovely late autumn morning, they headed over to the lodge.

After breakfast with Elizabeth and Tommy off out to football, Rebecca and her father headed down to the lake.

'How do you feel when you come down here, Rebecca?'

'It's odd, Dad, although I no longer need to go anywhere near the summerhouse to go back in time, I still get a mixed twinge of excitement and trepidation.'

'Trepidation, how so?'

'I don't know, I guess it is because I never know what is around the corner. Even when I feel like I am in control, I'm not. I knew all about meeting Matilda, but nothing could prepare me for what was ahead. When you have things like Duncan being thrown in the mixer, it is no surprise, I am a little apprehensive.'

The two got into the boat, and as they were heading across the lake, her father asked her how her dinner with Duncan went.

'Excellent, Dad. He is a good man, and we have made arrangements to meet up next week.'

'Oh, I am pleased. Michael will be pleased too.'

Rebecca narrowed her eyes.

'It is okay; we weren't planning your future behind your back. We just both agreed, that what with you both being equally academic, from a similar mould, it could be a good thing.'

'Similar mould?' she asked.

'Michael and I discussed your views on life, what makes you tick, how you think, and the way you see life. It would seem you have quite a lot in common, although I never mentioned your time with Meredith or anything like that. It would seem though that Duncan is very receptive to, shall we say, left-field thinking.'

Moments later, they beached the boat, and clambered ashore. Rebecca then led her father towards the old lodge. They checked inside first, which left Rebecca quite bemused. There was still no sign that her or Matilda had ever been anywhere near this place. She then headed outside to check on the food stash that Roxy and her left, which was again untouched. With her lips pursed, she turned to her father. 'This is ludicrous. Other then this food that Roxy and I left, there are absolutely no signs of me being here. I just don't know what to think. I hope there is something by the yew tree.' In the back of her thoughts, although never one for conspiracy theories, she was beginning to wonder is the whole episode hadn't actually happened, and instead, somehow manifested itself into her thoughts, preparing her for the meeting with Duncan. Leading her father towards the old yew tree, she tried to recall all her previous jaunts. Although every episode that she'd ever been on was at best bizarre, she'd never experienced anything like this before.

'Right, where's this tree,' her dad said. 'Maybe some of your questions may be answered. What was it the note said, "Thereby find your answers"?'

'Hmm, well I hope so, because right now, I just don't know what to think.'

As they arrived by the tree, Rebecca immediately noticed an engraving in the tree. Although it was deep into the bark and barely visible, she could just make out the name Matilda, and under it, could see an arrow pointing down. She knelt down and started digging with her hands.

'Hang on Bex; I have a small trowel in the boat. I will back as quickly as I can. If Matilda buried something a thousand years ago, you're going to need more than fingernails. Besides, we don't want you meeting up with Duncan looking like a builder,' he said and laughed.

Moments later, her father returned with a small trowel. Rebecca immediately started digging around the base of the tree. After a few minutes, without any joy, she stood up and turned to her father. 'There doesn't seem to be anything here,' she said and lifted her palm.

'Evidently, these trees are the oldest in the UK, and this one, as we know is perhaps over a thousand years old. Maybe you need to try near the main trunk.'

Again, she started digging, this time in between the roots. 'Dad, there's nothing here.' As she sat there, she noticed an odd marking on the trunk, close to the ground. On closer examination, it looked

288

unnatural. 'This is weird, Dad,' she said, pointing. 'It is, well, I know this sounds like a daft notion, but it looks like a door of sorts.'

Her father knelt down, took the trowel, and started digging at the tree. 'It is a door of sorts, although, I don't know how we are going to open it. Mind you, if your lady wanted it to go unnoticed for all these years, it would need to be difficult to open.' He then started digging at the trunk again. 'Hang on; I have my pen-knife. That might be better.'

After a few minutes taking it in turns, eventually there was some movement. Now with renewed energy, Rebecca pushed the knife blade in as far as she could, and wriggled it about. Gradually, it started moving a little more, although she couldn't see how it would open. Then just as she was considering an alternative approach, the door opened. Inside was a recess full of cobwebs. With her usual disregard, she plunged her hand in, feeling for anything. With her arm now up to her elbow, she touched something metal.

Although she could touch it with her fingertips, frustratingly it was just out of reach. 'I can feel something, Dad, but can't get a grip.'

'Here, let me have a go,' he said. Unable to get his hand in much past his wrist, he turned to Rebecca.

She tried again, although this time, changed the angle of her hand. Seconds later, she and James were staring at a small, rusty metal box. Again, using the penknife, she prized the lid open.

Inside there was a role that looked like animal skin. Carefully, Rebecca tried to untie the twine, without any success. Frustrated, she again used the penknife to cut the twine. She glanced at her father, and slowly unrolled the skin. Wrapped inside, was a role of parchment, which she opened slowly, again glancing at her father. She took a deep breath and started reading.

"Rebekah,"

"Dans votre ère, tout ce que vous découvrirez sera déduit de la validation de notre temps ensemble. En outre, votre souvenir émergera comme un souvenir lointain, puisque vous étiez seulement dans mon monde à travers les yeux d'un autre. A mon époque, tu avais une connaissance avec mon écuyer, un homme de notre fabrication. Sa lignée est forte, traversera le temps et se manifestera dans votre vie. Soyez assurés que vos choix de vie évolueront à travers une rencontre avec un homme que vous sentez que vous connaissez."

'It is in French, Dad, and although I can make it out, I would prefer to translate it accurately.'

'I agree. Why do you think it is in French?' He thought for a moment. 'Norman invasion I guess, which was what fifty-odd years earlier.' He nodded, and said, 'Let's check the tree again, and then head back. I am curious, but not as much, I suspect you are.'

As they headed across the lake, and passed the island, Rebecca again felt a weird, almost semi-subconscious sensation. It was unlike anything she'd felt before. The more she thought about, the stranger she felt, having never experienced any kind of sensation when she had been with anyone, let alone her father. This feeling was so strong she was half expecting to see either Meredith or Matilda standing on the jetty. There wasn't anyone there, but as she climbed from the boat, something in the back of her thoughts was telling her to return here alone, and soon.

With her thoughts now jumbled, she headed up towards the house.

'You're quite, Rebecca. Are you okay?'

'I'm not sure what I am feeling, Dad. I half read Matilda's letter and am very intrigued to find out what it actually says in English. Also, for some reason, I am getting a strong sensation to go back down to the lake sometime soon, just not now.'

'Well, it's unlike you to ignore anything like that. So what are your plans?'

'Read the letter, and as I always do, go with my gut.'

As they entered the house, James suggested using his computer to translate the letter. Rebecca realised this was because he was equally keen on finding out what it says. This made her think about how far he'd come from the days of pen-tapping when she was late for dinner. 'Dad, thanks for the way you are now.'

'What do you mean, Rebecca?'

'I was just thinking about the distance you've come over the last few years. From the days when you ran everything like a military manoeuvre, to now, is almost as far as I have travelled.'

'Well my beloved daughter, it is down largely to you, along with your dear Mother, and Tommy's football antics. I suddenly woke up the day you told me about the boiler. I realised just how much my work had enveloped me and how much family life I was missing out on. Importantly, you and Meredith reminded me how I was and should still be.'

They entered the study, and James started up his computer.

'Here, Dad, let me type it in.' She then sat there, typed in Matilda's note and hit the translate button. With her father looking over her shoulder, they both read the letter.

In your era, all you will uncover will be inferred validation of our time together. In addition, your remembrance will emerge as a remote recollection, since you were only in my world through another's eyes. In my epoch, you had an acquaintance with my equerry, a man of our making. His bloodline is strong, will pass through time, and manifest into your life. Be assured, your life choices will evolve through a meeting with a man you feel you know.

Rebecca read it twice more, and then turned to her father.

'Well, that answers why you felt like it was a dream. Seeing it through another's eyes is what we believed happened with Etienne. That was his name, wasn't it?'

'Yeah, Dad, it was Etienne, and you're right. I so knew I hadn't dreamt it, but it sure felt like that. Seeing it through another's eyes, certainly explains why it felt like a remote recollection, to use Matilda's words. I am not sure what to think about the last bit.'

'Well, I understand why you are not sure. To me though, it is fairly obvious.'

'Obvious, Dad, why so, what do you mean?'

'You instantly recognised Duncan, and you were right to. He shares a bloodline with Matilda's equerry. What is it that she wrote, *"His bloodline is strong, will pass through time, and manifest into your life."* To my mind, that can only mean one thing.'

'And that is,' Rebecca asked, even though she knew exactly what her father was saying and what Matilda meant.

Turning again to the computer, he read, *"Be assured, your life choices will evolve through a meeting with a man you feel you know."* He then turned to Rebecca with a questioning look on his face.

She nodded to her father. 'I need to give this some thinking time,' she said. She now had mixed emotions. For sure, she was very comfortable in Duncan's company. However, according to Matilda's letter, it would seem he could be around for many years. *Am I going to be friends with him, or more*, she wondered.

After supper with Tommy once again dominating the conversation, something she was actually pleased with as it helped relax her mind a little, she decided on an early night. Before she headed up to bed, she went to her father's computer and printed off a translated version of Matilda's letter. She then lay in bed, reading it over and again. With Roxy's comment, "when's the marriage" in her head, she nodded off.

CHAPTER 29 – BOAT AGAIN

The following morning, with Roxy's comment still ringing in her head, she quickly dismissed the idea, reckoning the notion of marriage was miles away yet. After breakfast, and again following a hunch, she decided to head down to the lake and check out what yesterday's odd vibe was all about.

Oddly, as she arrived by the lake, she wasn't feeling any sort of sensation at all. She sat down on the summerhouse veranda, and as she enjoyed the late autumn sunshine, her mind wandered back to Matilda. None of the records she'd come across mentioned the injuries Matilda had sustained. All the way through, although distracted by her distance from the episode, this aspect confused her. She had never expected to see any mention of her time with Matilda, but surely, there should have been something pertaining to Matilda's wounds. She sat there unsure what to think.

Looking across the lake, considering her thoughts, she noticed what appeared to be a small boat heading towards the island. Oddly, it seemed to be surrounded in mist, just like her first sighting of Meredith. Narrowing her eyes, she was sure she could see someone fishing from the boat. *That's odd*, she thought as the boat disappeared behind the island. Deciding to go and investigate, she made her way down to the jetty. Clambering into the boat and nearly capsizing, reminded her of her times in the boat with her mother, which distracted her a little. Remembering why she was here, she refocused her attention. There was now no sign of the man in the boat, and reckoning he must be somewhere, started the engine, and headed out towards the island.

Within a few moments, she arrived by the island, but there was no sign of the boat, let alone a man fishing. She headed around the back of the island, at a loss what to think. As she manoeuvred the boat, the mist had all but vanished. This compounded her emotions, but not as much as seeing the trees showing signs of spring growth. In a flash, she remembered it being spring when she was first with Matilda. Not only could she could sense things had changed she knew they had.

Heading towards the shore, she was instantly aware that the summerhouse wasn't there, and to compound her emotions further, could hear men shouting. If she had any slight doubts about where she was, she was now certain she was back in Matilda's time. Slowing a little, she could see a number of men on horseback at the top of the slope. Instantly, she knew the horsemen were the ones she'd seen the day she came across Matilda. That day though, they were a lot closer to the lake. For some reason, she was getting an odd sensation telling her to hurry towards the shore.

Just a short distance from the shore, she noticed a woman crouching behind one of the tall conifers and in a flash, knew this was Matilda. Beaching along the shore, out of sight of the horsemen, she clambered from the boat and headed towards Matilda, not knowing what to expect. Approaching her, she could see Matilda hadn't recognised her. It was also blatantly obvious this woman was frightened and mindful of this, approached her with care.

Crouching, Matilda uttered, 'tenir à l'écart.'

Aware this woman had just said, "Keep away," Rebecca knelt down a couple of yards away. She then held her hand out, smiled, and said, 'I am here to help you. Je suis ici pour vous aider.'

Matilda seemed to respond to this, and beckoned Rebecca towards her. 'You are my lady from afar. I knew you would be here.'

'You need to come with me quickly. I am here to take you to safety.' She smiled, and continued, 'I am from afar, and you must accept that what happens next is for your wellbeing.'

Nodding, Matilda facial expression had softened noticeably. She climbed to her feet and seemingly undaunted, followed Rebecca towards the boat.

'I know you, although you are not of my world. You came to me in a dream, and I knew you would visit me this day.'

Rebecca nodded, and holding the woman's hand, she said, 'I am not of your time.' As they climbed aboard the boat and headed across the lake, Rebecca thought carefully about what she should say. From her previous meeting with this woman, she knew she was receptive to her and so explained all she had when she had met her just a few days ago. Again, Matilda embraced her with an apparent open mind.

Rebecca then told her of the impending danger, and again picking her words carefully explained how they had met days before. Clarifying that on that occasion, Matilda had been wounded. Aware how confusing this must be, she tried to explain in detail how these events panned out.

As if she understood completely, she said, 'I know this, and I know of our prior meeting. I do not know why I know, however, I do. In your world, our meeting was some days ago, in my world though, it was in my future.'

As they arrived on the other side of the lake, Rebecca led Matilda to the lodge, suggesting it would be a safe haven.

Matilda, stood at the front of the lodge, clasped Rebecca's hand, and said, 'Our paths will cross again. Either, I will see you through the eyes of another, or you will see me through another's eyes.'

With these words, Rebecca knew her time with Matilda was hurriedly concluding. She wished her well, certain they would meet again, one way or the other.

On her way back to the lake, she suddenly realised Matilda hadn't reacted to the engine on the boat, even though it was unlikely that she could have imagined, seen, or dreamt anything remotely similar. This helped her to understand how much this woman probably knew. To compound her thoughts further, Matilda had said of seeing her through the eyes of another, and by this, she was now wondering if this meant Duncan.

CHAPTER 30 – TIME MOVES QUICKLY AND SO DOES TOMMY

As Rebecca headed across the lake, her thoughts returned to the fisherman in the boat and then back to Meredith. Although she now knew it was unlikely that she would see this woman again, she couldn't help thinking she had something to do with the fisherman. In the same way, Meredith had appeared as a misty apparition in the boat all those years ago, one that ultimately brought her to this point, just maybe the fisherman was off a similar making.

She docked the boat, and glanced at the summerhouse, pleased to be home. She headed back to the house, wondering what may lie ahead. For some reason, she felt her journeys were a thing of the past, for now at least. There was no vibe or sensation as she passed the summerhouse. In fact, since she'd bid her farewells to Matilda, she had felt noting at all. She had learnt that in most cases, she was seeing the world through another's eyes, and therefore was left with little emotional attachment. Right now though, her mood was more distant than that.

As she entered the house, her father was just heading out with Tommy.

'We are going to football. Do you fancy coming with us? Duncan and his father, Michael are coming,' he said and smiled in a knowing way.

'Dad, how long do I have, I need to get changed.'

'No rush, we are way early.'

Rebecca made her way upstairs with her head all over the place. *What shall I wear?* She thought, knowing she was going to a football match. She opened her wardrobe, and glanced briefly at a new red dress she bought a couple of weeks ago while out with Roxy. 'Well, it's the right colour,' she mumbled.

'Trying to decide what to wear,' her mum asked from behind her.

'Mum, I didn't hear you come in.'

'You were too busy talking to yourself to hear me, I suspect,' she said and giggled in a way that reminded Rebecca why she loved her so much.

Rebecca took one dress out at a time, placing them on her bed into a no-pile and a maybe-pile. She looked at her mum, and asked, holding up her new red dress, 'this one?

'Well, as you said, it is the right colour. You can always wear a light coat over the top. That way, you'll be ready for a meal after with Duncan.'

'Mum, you know about Duncan?'

'Your father told me all about it, and derr, obviously I know about Duncan. That is why I am here helping you. Hello, as your brother would say, I am ya' muvva.'

'Mum, I do love you so much, even though Tommy gets all the twit bits from you.'

'Right, make-up. Sit,' her mum said, pointing at the chair next to the dressing table, 'Something light I think.'

On the way to the game, Rebecca was a little surprised how quite Tommy was. 'Are you okay, Tommy, you don't seem your usual self.'

'Yeah fine,' he said, with an unusually dampened tone.

Moments later, they pulled into the car-park at Anfield. 'Dad, what's going on,' Rebecca said, glancing around at the hoards of people milling about.

He pulled the car into a parking space, turned and said, 'Hardly surprising it is busy. It's the Merseyside derby, and Liverpool and playing their arch rivals, Everton.'

'So you're telling me my twit of a brother is playing for the first team,' she said and pulling at Tommy's finger, laughed. 'Wow, bro, I am proud of you.'

'Thanks sis, although don't get too excited, I am on the bench.'

'Even so, Tommy, to think where it all started with me being a moving target, and now look where I got you.' She grinned and said, 'bench or not, I am so very proud.

As they got out of the car, Duncan and his father walked towards them. Michael started talking to Tommy and James, while Duncan came over to Rebecca.

While he was talking to Rebecca about Tommy, Elizabeth pulled into the car-park, with Ruth, Amanda, and Roxy.

Unable to contain herself, Rebecca screamed, which made Tommy pull a stupid face. 'Mum, I thought you weren't coming, you are such a sneak. She then embraced the girls in turn. 'Roxy, you kept this quite, seems I was the last to know.'

'To busy off on one of your jaunts, I guess,' Roxy said and laughed.

As they entered the ground, Rebecca couldn't believe what she was looking at, unable to take her eyes from the baying crowd. To her left, all dressed in royal blue, were thousands of chanting Everton fans. To her right, she could feel a tangible energy coming from the cop end. A sea of scarves held aloft, with everyone singing, *you'll never walk alone.* Mesmerised by this, it sent chills up and down her spine. So preoccupied watching the crowd, she'd barely taken any notice of the game. At half time, Duncan asked her a question.

'Sorry, I didn't hear what you said. I was so captivated by the crowd.'

He smiled, and said, 'I was watching you, watching the crowd, more than I watched the game. I reckon from what I've heard, this game is crying out for a maverick like young Tommy. Let's hope he gets on.'

Before she knew it, again captivated by the two sets of supporters chanting at each other, it was start of the second half. Like the first half, it was a bad-tempered affair, with not a lot of football going on. With fifteen minutes to go, Rebecca could see Tommy down below running along the touch line. He had a look on his face that she had never seen before. Seconds later, with the game standing goalless, the fourth official held up a board with number thirty-seven on, Tommy's number.

'Here we go,' said Duncan, as Tommy ran onto the pitch to tremendous applause.

Hearing this, made Rebecca so proud, but it couldn't prepare for what was about to happen. With minutes left on the clock, Tommy picked the ball up just inside the Everton half. Weaving the way she had seen him do so often in the garden, he glided past one player after the next. Approaching the edge of the penalty area, with people around her shouting, pass-it, she stood up and shouted, 'moving target Tommy, do what ya do.'

He dropped his right shoulder, and unleashed a left-footed shot, that cannoned in off the underside of the bar. The ground erupted with a deafening crescendo of sound. As Tommy emerged, having been engulfed by Liverpool players, he turned towards Rebecca and wriggled his hips, the way he always did whenever the subject of moving targets came up. Rebecca knew he hadn't heard her, but even so, she loved his acknowledgment.

After the game, they waited for Tommy and then all headed into town for a celebratory dinner. Nothing could have prepared Rebecca for what was about to happen. As they entered the restaurant, one they

300

had visited many times, a crescendo of sound rang out, with people staring and muttering. Just as they approached the table, a man in the corner, stood up and started clapping, instantly followed by everyone else. Seemingly respectful of their family event, everyone then sat back down and went about their business. Rebecca was overwhelmed with pride for her brother, but also knew that his life had just changed for good.

During dinner, she sat talking with the girls about Tommy. Often though, she found herself again staring at Duncan, who was sitting opposite. For some reason, she felt comfortable around this man. She appreciated his approach to life, seemingly with no ulterior motif or agenda. It was if she knew him, and although she had briefly made acquaintance with his ancestor, this was something more.

After dinner, he came over to her and asked if she would go to dinner with her tomorrow so they could get to know each other better. Without any reservation, Rebecca agreed.

CHAPTER 31 – THE NEXT CHAPTER

Over the coming months, Rebecca went on many dates with Duncan. The more she saw him, the more comfortable she became. She had sensed an honestly from him from the first day they'd met, and this trust had just grown stronger over time.

It was now mid-December, and again she was preparing for a winter holiday with her parents, alas without Tommy. Tommy wasn't able to come, having an increase in his football schedule. One evening at supper, her father asked Rebecca if she would like Duncan to come in Tommy's place.

'Dad that would be brilliant.' She glanced at her mum, and continued, 'as long as it is okay with you two.'

Her mum nodded and smiled in a knowing way.

Her father too smiled and said, 'best you check with Meredith as well.'

'Funny you should say that, Dad. I haven't seen or heard a peep from that direction since the Matilda incident, which was the day Tommy became a supper-star,' she said and laughed. Suddenly, she realised that was three months ago. Thinking about this, she wondered, as she had so often in the past, if her jaunts were over.

The holiday passed in the blink of an eye, as did the next year. It was now the day before her twenty-fifth birthday, and the family, as always, had arranged a grand event at home. With everyone there, her mum came in balancing a birthday cake, complete with twenty-five candles.

'Make a wish,' her mum said.

Rebecca sat staring at the cake, not knowing what to wish for, feeling she had everything she could have hoped for family wise, especially with Tommy now playing regularly for Liverpool and

England. Her mum and dad were closer than ever, and her best friend Roxy was always there beside her every step. To add to this, she now had Duncan, a wonderful individual. Just as she was about to blow out the candles, she heard a whisper. She turned around, but there was no one there. She took a deep breath to blow, and again she heard, 'say yes.' This time, she knew it was Meredith's voice, but also knew she wasn't there. She blew hard, wondering what this message could mean. She didn't have to wait long to find out. As the last candle faded, Duncan stood up, then came around the table, and knelt down on one knee.

'My dear, Rebecca, will you continue to bring your light into my world? Be my wife and thereby, make my life complete.'

Rebecca glanced at her mother, father, across the table to Roxy and the girls, and then turned to Duncan. 'I would be honoured to accept your proposal.'

They set a date for December the fifteenth this year, and the next two months were a frantic period of arranging everything. This included Amanda's wedding in mid-November.

Rebecca woke early and now just one week away from her wedding, she decided to give herself a little time away from the frantic non-stop arrangements. She headed downstairs and after breakfast, said that she was going for a walk down by the lake.

'Going to check in with Meredith,' her mum asked.

'Just need a little time on my own, Mum. Although it would be nice if I did see her.'

As she made her way down the now well trodden path, she could feel an odd sensation. Although she knew this emotion, she hadn't felt anything like this for months. Wondering what it could be, she sat on the summerhouse veranda, looking out across the lake as she'd done so many times. Over the next few minutes, every episode she'd been through cascaded through her thoughts. Just as she was thinking about Matilda, she heard a voice from behind her. Expecting it to be her mother, she turned. It wasn't her mum as all. Instead, it was a young blonde girl, dressed in a grey all in one cat suit affair.

Oddly, the girl was like a mix of her and her mum. A little taken aback, but oddly calm, she said, 'hello.'

'Hello, Rebecca. Please do not be alarmed, although I sense you are not. I am also Rebekha, although I spell my name the old way with a K. I am Rebekah Fergusson, as you will soon be. I am from four generations into your future, and am here to assure you. Your vision, and receptive directness, opened the door for our kind. As your dear, Meredith told you, you are indeed the beginning of society accepting our beings as the way forward. In my time, there are many like us, their eyes opened by you and your writings.'

Unsure what to say, Rebecca paused for a moment. 'You say four generations. By that, do you mean you are my great-granddaughter?'

She smiled, and holding Rebecca's hand in a way that was oddly familiar, said, 'I am indeed your great-granddaughter. I am here for such a moment. As your beloved, Meredith said to you, *"Be safe, be well, be happy, and continue to remain true to your farsightedness."* I must add that there is more for you, as there will be for your daughter.' She then turned and in a breath, was gone.

The End, or is it?

Printed in Poland
by Amazon Fulfillment
Poland Sp. z o.o., Wrocław